THE FEAR

D1166977

ALSO BY NATASHA PRESTON

The Cellar

Awake

The Cabin

You Will Be Mine

The Lost

The Twin

The Lake

THE FEAR

NATASHA PRESTON

DELACORTE PRESS

This is a work of fiction. Names, characters, places, and incidents either are the product of the author's imagination or are used fictitiously. Any resemblance to actual persons, living or dead, events, or locales is entirely coincidental.

Text copyright © 2022 by Natasha Preston
Cover art by Chekalin Nikolai/Shutterstock

All rights reserved. Published in the United States by Delacorte Press, an imprint of Random House Children's Books, a division of Penguin Random House LLC, New York.

Delacorte Press is a registered trademark and the colophon is a trademark of Penguin Random House LLC.

GetUnderlined.com

Educators and librarians, for a variety of teaching tools, visit us at RHTeachersLibrarians.com

Library of Congress Cataloging-in-Publication Data is available upon request.
ISBN 978-0-593-12501-4 (pbk.)—ISBN 978-0-593-12503-8 (ebook)

The text of this book is set in 11-point Janson MT Pro.
Interior design by Jen Valero

Printed in the United States of America
10 9 8 7 6 5 4 3 2 1
First Edition

Random House Children's Books supports the First Amendment and celebrates the right to read.

Penguin Random House LLC supports copyright. Copyright fuels creativity, encourages diverse voices, promotes free speech, and creates a vibrant culture. Thank you for buying an authorized edition of this book and for complying with copyright laws by not reproducing, scanning, or distributing any part in any form without permission. You are supporting writers and allowing Penguin Random House to publish books for every reader.

This one is for my niece, Daisy,
who has just started writing her first book.

prologue

FEAR

I watch the pathetic buzz of excitement from my car. The heavy snowstorm creates a kaleidoscope of color as students sprint into Rock Bay High wearing brightly colored parkas and the hockey team's letterman jackets. This school is all about hockey; if you don't like it, you can pretty much rule out succeeding in athletics here.

They all stare at their phone screens as they run. With my window cracked open, I can hear some of them over the howling wind as they pass me without a second glance—the way I like it. They debate the topic of the day: Who has the worst death fear?

My mouth twitches as I realize that it's working.

January through March is dead in this town, more so than usual, so I knew it would be the right time to begin my plan. My meme is spreading like wildfire. I never had any doubt that it would. Morbid curiosity, boredom, and a stream of serial killer documentaries on Netflix have made death and murder cool.

Now I have everyone talking about the most painful and gory deaths. They're sharing *their* most feared end.

I used a fake account to post the meme, some random girl's pretty face as the hook. I used it to friend-request Kason Risby. I knew he'd go for it; he's the type. As soon as he reposted the meme, I logged out of that account, and I haven't looked at it since.

The cops can trace the IP address, but it will go to a greasy truckers' café off the interstate. Far enough from our cruddy fishing town.

I watch everyone run up the steps, the jocks in a pack, the band geeks carrying instruments, the popular girls cackling. They disappear into the building quickly because of the weather, but I know what they'll be talking about.

High school is always the same. The thrill of a new challenge or dare lingers for weeks, and everyone gets involved, desperate to be a part of something.

Snow whips my face as it flies sideways through the gap in my window. My car is damp, my hair wet. I've been locked out in bad weather so many times over the years that it doesn't bother me anymore.

I think I could survive for days out in the snow.

That's one positive from my childhood, I suppose.

With a sigh, I close the window, get out of my car, and walk a few steps closer to the building. My heavy boots crunch in the snow.

They're all excited about sharing their biggest fear. Excited by something I barely made it through. It's a game to them, all laughing and debating whose death fear is actually the worst. Strangling, drowning, falling, hanging—the list goes on.

My hands curl into fists. This town must have known what I was going through, but no one dared look closer. Not one adult asked if everything was okay at home. My life was a game to the people who should have taken care of me.

Soon they will all know that *I'm* not playing.

This *isn't* just some stupid meme.

This is revenge.

Death *is* coming.

one

IZZY

Snow coats the ground like a fluffy blanket. It looks beautiful, like thousands of tiny crystals that glisten in the sun. But it also conceals what could be underneath.

Last winter it took two months—until the snow finally melted—to find my neighbor's dead dog. Two full months that little terrier had been lying there, just yards from their front door.

Anything could be lurking under the snow.

We have a couple of months left of freezing conditions, but the air has been warming. Not quite enough to make the snow melt or stop it from falling, but just enough so that I don't feel like I'm being punched in the lungs *every* time I step outside.

I walk to my car and immediately blast the heat. The roads are clear, as they're plowed regularly, giving the impression that they've been carved out of the ten inches of snow that frames them.

More storms are in the forecast.

The sun is up, but gray clouds stop it from making an appearance. January is perpetual nighttime in our little fishing town. When my car is warm, I flick the lights on and back out of the driveway. Luckily, my dad shoveled yesterday, or I'd be late to school.

I better get accepted into Florida State. No more freezing air, no more winter coats and woolly hats, and no more wondering if there's anything dead under the snow.

My sister, Lia, escaped to college in North Carolina last year, and she's enjoying the warmer climate—and the food— immensely.

It's senior year, and I still haven't gotten Justin Rae to notice that I exist or told my best friend, Sydney—Syd—that I don't really like going to parties, the mall, or any other place she drags me to.

We're supposed to be going to Mariella Whitmore's party tonight. Rich girl, wants to marry a billionaire, says "like" a lot— you know the type.

Lia calls me a shadow person because I follow silently and never stick up for myself.

I'd be offended if it weren't completely true.

My car rumbles as I pull into the parking lot. I park in the same spot as always, Lia's old one.

I check myself out in the visor mirror. My complexion is fair, clear skin and rosy cheeks that I'm so grateful for, because I'm terrible at applying makeup. My hair is naturally wavy, which suits me just fine, because I prefer to sleep in rather than waking early to style it. I have the same hazel eyes as my sister, though my left eye has a ton of green specks. Syd says it's cool, and I've grown to like it.

I close the mirror and grab my backpack.

Rock Bay High has been my home for the last three and a half years. The town used to be named Rock Bass Bay, but they dropped the "Bass" years ago in an attempt to sound less fishy. Now we sound much cooler than we are.

It didn't help, though. Thanks to bigger ports in the state, this still isn't a town you come to unless you live here.

"Izzy!" Syd says, pulling my car door open as if it's on fire. Frozen air hits me instantly. "What took you so long?"

Startled, I look at the time on my dash. "I'm actually earlier than—"

"Forget it. Have you heard? Justin dumped Gemma. He's back on the market!"

That would be awesome news if I had even a hint of a shot with him.

"I don't care," I tell her.

"Sure you don't." She rolls her incredible sage eyes and scrolls her phone.

Syd's tall, has smooth, dark skin, full lips, stunning shoulder-length curls, and the biggest smile. We've been inseparable since freshman year.

"You should go for it, Iz."

Justin has never given me a second glance with his pretty green eyes.

She gasps as if she's just remembered something. "Hey, have you seen this? It's everywhere right now."

She shoves her screen in my face as I get out of the car. I blink and rear my head back. "Well, I can't see it from three inches in front of my face, can I?" I push the phone back.

"See."

"A new meme? A game? Fear what? What am I looking at, Syd?"

There's a picture of a frozen red rose on a snowy dock. Some of the petals have broken off and are scattered around it. Text sits over the image:

REPOST WITH YOUR DEATH FEAR!
If death came for you today,
what would be the worst way to go?
#thefear

"That's not at all creepy—wait, is this a picture of *our* dock?" I look over my shoulder in the direction of the port, though school is nowhere near it. Then I look back at the picture. Yeah, it definitely is. The wooden post behind the flower looks just like the one at Puck's, the local diner. It even has the initials of the owner, Matthew, and a hockey puck carved into it.

No wonder everyone around here is going extra crazy for this challenge. They think someone we know created it.

"That's totally what I thought! Must be someone around here trying to go viral. How lame," she replies.

"They didn't leave their name. Looks like the original post comes from Janie Dow. Nice play on Jane Doe there. How long before this is flagged?"

She shakes her head and takes her phone back as we walk into school. "Who do you think it is? It screams high school, right?"

I shrug. "Probably someone who goes here."

Inside, it stinks like cleaning products and the repressed scent of feet. Our hockey team trains daily, and the smell proves it. So do all the shiny trophies from the glory days in the trophy cabinet.

Rock Bay High is *big* on hockey. RBH Blade Rockies banners hang above almost every door, with the sharkiest-looking Rock Bay logo I have *ever* seen.

Justin is captain of the team and insists on working harder so we have a shot at winning . . . *anything* this year. We actually might with him and Kason Risby leading.

I glance down the hall and notice that almost everyone is staring at their phones and muttering to each other. That's not about this meme, right?

"What's your fear? Wait, I know this. It's suffocating, right?" Syd asks, tapping on her phone as we weave between crowds of students.

"Yep," I reply. "And yours is being stabbed to death, a *million* times, like in a horror movie."

"I don't like pain, and that has to be such a painful way to go, right? I heard drowning is peaceful."

I bark a laugh.

Peaceful. The only peaceful way to go is in your sleep. That's what I'm hoping for—when I'm old and gray.

I can't believe I'm even thinking about this.

"Fire would be an awful way to go, too," Syd adds.

"I thought social media was where people went to brag about their perfect lives."

Syd links her arm with mine as we walk to homeroom. "That's so yesterday, Izzy. Keep up. Now it's all about challenges and se-rial killers."

"I'm not eating Tide Pods."

"That should be your death fear, Iz."

"Stupid people on TikTok or ingesting chemicals?"

She laughs as we enter the classroom.

"No way is being shot in the head worse than drowning," Kason says loudly, as if he wants the entire school's attention, and flicks his dark hair. He laughs and thumps Justin playfully on his muscular arm.

They're a good duo. Every guy wants to be them, and every girl wants to date them. Isn't that what they say? I'm sure that's what Kason thinks. He's a cocky asshole who's relying solely on hockey to get him into college.

Syd and I take seats at our usual desks.

Justin is . . . different. All right, he's super sure of himself and popular, but I've never heard of him treating anyone badly. He *is* a serial dater like Kason, though.

Another reason why I wouldn't go there even if I had a chance: I think he averages about three months with a girl and then moves on. Still, it's longer than Kason's three hours.

I'm in agreement with Kason on this one, though: drowning would be worse than getting shot.

Mrs. Grady takes attendance, and the bell for first period rings.

I overhear about a dozen horrible ways to die as we walk to AP English.

Mariella strolls past with her stand-in friend Jessie, as her real friends, Tayley and Debbie, aren't in her first period. "As if I'm going to die any way other than spectacularly. It needs to be, like, newsworthy, you know?"

I swear I lose a brain cell every time I hear her say "like."

In AP English, I take a seat near the back, next to Axel, a kid who could probably have his master's degree already and rarely talks to anyone. He always wears leather and a bored expression.

It wouldn't surprise me if someone said their biggest fear was "Axel staring at me to death with his threatening glare."

There's a rumor that he's older but got held back. Only that doesn't make sense, because he's a genius. There's another rumor that he intentionally failed exams to stay behind. But who would want to make high school last longer? No one.

I take a look around the room. I've never seen everyone so cheerful in the middle of winter before—especially halfway through January. And all it took was discussing the one way they'd never want to die . . .

Justin is in the last row with Tayley and Debbie. Tayley is hanging on his every word. It looks like she's begun her campaign to be his next girlfriend now that he's single again.

Mr. Morrison bursts into the room and clears his throat—he does that to start the lesson.

I try not to switch off at the constant drone of his monotone voice.

"How was your weekend?" I ask Axel.

His head twists toward me slowly. His eyes are such a light blue they're almost the color of the ice outside. They don't look real, but I can see that he's not wearing lenses. "Fine. Yours?"

I flip open my textbook. "Shopping and a movie night with Syd."

We have a very similar conversation almost every morning. I try to talk to him so that the period doesn't drag. He grunts one- or two-word replies. There is something new I can add today.

"Did you see that meme being reposted on Insta?" I ask.

"Yep."

I wait for him to expand, but seconds tick by and now I'm just looking at him like a weirdo.

"Okay," I mutter, my shoulders hunching. This period would go a lot faster if he weren't so hostile.

He gives me a half-hearted smile that's more irritated grimace and turns away.

Everyone else in the room talks, having quiet conversations and laughing under their breath. My table with Axel is always quiet.

Behind me, I can hear Tayley telling Justin that her biggest fear is being crushed.

Not a great way to go, but I think it would be over quickly. There wouldn't be a lot of time to think. Not like suffocating, where you'd know for minutes that you were fading. You'd fight and eventually realize that you're losing—dying.

I look up and see Axel turn his nose up. No, he definitely

doesn't seem like the person to take part in TikTok challenges or anything else that involves being a sheep. I know him about as well as I know a perfect stranger, but I don't imagine he does anything that he doesn't want to.

Not like me.

I wonder what his death fear is. It would probably be something like being shot with a huge military-style gun. One of those guns that goes on firing forever in movies.

Asking him wouldn't hurt. He could always tell me to go away or ignore me. He'll probably ignore me.

He picks up his heavy textbook and flips it open, the muscles in his forearms flexing. He's not on the hockey team, but I guess he works out. I avert my eyes, unsure if it's me making him uncomfortable.

"Izzy?"

I jolt at the authoritative tone in Mr. Morrison's voice.

"Sorry?"

"The partner project on Poe. You're working with Axel."

My stomach sinks in alarm, and I hope that I don't look as scared as I feel. "A group project?"

"*Partner* project," Axel replies.

Well, that's just great. How unfair is it to partner us with the person we're sitting with rather than letting us choose? I thought it was bad enough working independently beside him. We might have to meet up outside of school and say more than seven words to each other. How will he cope with that?

I peek to my side, and he's glaring at his textbook as if it's just flipped him off.

Well, it's safe to say that he's not loving the idea of working together either.

"Should we meet up after school this week?" I ask.

"Why?" he asks, as if it's not actually obvious.

"Um, to work on the project . . ."

Surely he doesn't think I want to spend time hanging out with him. I don't think I'd want to be alone with him.

"We can do it in class."

"Sure, but what if we don't finish?"

"We will."

I bite my lip hard so I won't tell him to get lost. It's not like this was my idea, yet he's making it seem like I'm forcing him into it.

"Fine. You're going to have to talk to me, though. You get that, right?"

"I don't mind talking to you, Izzy."

That's the first time in the three and a half years at this school that he's used my name. In fact, I don't think I've ever heard him use anyone's name. Also, he's lying. He obviously does mind talking to me.

We start work, or rather, I start work. I decide what we should focus on in our presentation, opting for how Poe's rather depressing life influenced his writing. Axel replies with his usual grunt to everything I suggest. I get the impression that he doesn't care what we do for this project; he just wants to get it over with.

So, I scribble lots of notes while he stares at the table like a serial killer.

When that wonderful ding of the bell rings, I sigh in pure relief.

"Axel," I say as he grabs his unopened notebook and stands.

He looks down and grunts, "What?"

Damn, he really is tall. A mountain of a seventeen-year-old, he could easily get away with being twenty-one. His square jaw, ruffled blond hair, and almond-shaped eyes make girls melt . . . until they meet him.

Just say the words, Izzy.

"What's your death fear?"

He turns his nose up in the exact way I thought he would. Yeah, he's definitely above all this meme stuff.

Still, I hold my ground, tilting my chin up and waiting.

Finally, he replies, "All of them."

"I'm sorry, what? All of them?"

He walks around the desk but keeps his eyes on me. "Falling, burning, illness, being buried alive, crushed, strangled, suffocated, stabbed, shot, beaten. They're all bad. Everyone is running around arguing over whose fear is the scariest, as if they have everything figured out." He shakes his head. "The truth is, when death comes, no matter how it comes, it's always scary."

two

IZZY

Axel's words rattle around in my head as Syd and I make our way along the busy corridor to gym.

The truth is, when death comes, no matter how it comes, it's always scary.

I mean, how insanely creepy is that?

"What did the resident freak talk to you about?" Syd asks, scowling at someone who didn't give her enough room to pass.

"Axel isn't a freak, Syd."

At least, I don't think so. Maybe he's just a bit strange. Who's afraid of *every* death?

Though, who isn't? Maybe *we're* the freaks and he has everything figured out. I'm sure if your fear is drowning but you're set on fire, it's not much better.

She laughs. "Oh sure, he's just misunderstood. Did you know that he lives alone? Like, no parents at all."

"And how do you know that?"

"I overheard Tayley talking to Debbie. She lives a couple

blocks away from him and said she's never seen his parents or any other adult going in or out of his tiny apartment."

"I question how long she's spent watching his apartment in order to reach that conclusion." I'm unsure how much I trust Tayley and Debbie's word, considering they behave as if they're constantly auditioning for *Euphoria*.

Syd scrolls through her phone, almost walking into more people. "Look at this! Justin reposted that meme with his fear. Do you want to know?"

I push open the locker room door. "I could just look myself. Besides, Kason said his fear is worse than being shot, so it must be that."

"Don't be a party pooper, Iz. That's not what he's put on his post anyway. He's scared of suffocation, too. You guys are meant to be."

"I think I might be scared of every death now," I say as a shiver ripples down my torso.

"Okay, I have *got* to know what Axel said to you!"

"Nothing much. He's not thrilled to be partnered with me."

"I can't believe we have assigned seats in Mr. Morrison's class. He's evil. I bet it's the only fun he has. You are coming to Mariella's party tonight, right? Her mom's away until Wednesday, apparently. You can't say no. We're seniors this year. It's time to attend every party and every event. We have to make this a year to remember."

"Where do you hear all this?"

We head to our lockers to change. "Mariella."

Mariella and Syd go to the same dance school three times

a week. They're not friends exactly, but at dance class, they get along. Mariella, Tayley, and Debbie are a pyramid of popularity, and Mariella is on top.

"I'll skip this party."

"You skipped the last one."

"So did you," I tell her.

"Because you did, idiot. Come on, *please*, Iz. I can't go alone. You'll have fun, I promise. Besides, don't you want to snoop around Mariella's massive house again?"

"We don't even like anyone going."

"We don't actively dislike them, either. Iz, please. I don't want to spend every evening sitting at home, waiting to get a life."

She might not dislike them, but I think they're all self-centered mean girls who will speak to you only if they need something. The guys aren't any better.

"All right, but this is the last time you can drag me along this month."

"Deal." She beams at me, her dark eyes happy for now. "February is only two weeks away."

I change quickly and follow Syd into the gym. It smells of dirty socks, sweat, and despair. No one likes being in here, but the weather is too bad to do much outside.

"Sydney and Izzy, you will be our goalkeepers," Miss White says. She, too, is evil.

"Soccer," I groan, trudging to the goal as if my life is over. For the next thirty minutes, it's going to feel like it.

Can this be my fear? Death by soccer ball? I'm about to get

hit—a lot. Soccer isn't my sport. The boys take soccer very seriously and shout if we don't win. To be fair, so does Mariella.

I personally couldn't care less. Basketball and hockey, I like.

Standing in my goal, I bend my knees, ready to spring either way, hopefully to catch the ball before it slams into my face or the back of the net.

Miss White tells the boys not to kick the ball too hard as they're playing with the girls. I grind my teeth, but I don't actually want to be bruised, so I let it go.

Kason kicks the ball to Justin. Mariella runs at Justin, and I really hope she manages to tackle him so I don't need to try to save this.

I take a breath, bouncing from foot to foot.

Whatever happens, I'm going to go for this.

Justin runs around Mariella and kicks.

My eyes bulge and I leap to the left as the ball hurtles toward me.

I actually do it. I block the ball from going into the net . . . with my face.

The damn thing ricochets off my forehead, and I land on the floor in a heap.

I push myself up, rubbing my forehead, as Justin jogs over. "Izzy, I'm so sorry," he says. "Are you okay?"

"Yeah. I'll survive."

"I didn't mean to kick it that hard."

"It's not your fault I'm a terrible goalie."

"Not really. That was an excellent save. A lot of people would've backed down so they don't get hurt."

Smart people. That's what I should have done.

"Well, that's good, but now I have a concussion."

He winces. "Do you need to go to the nurse's office?"

"That was a joke." I drop my arms, my cheeks catching on fire. I guess I can add "not funny" to the list of things I am. Why am I such a dork around him?

"Right." He nods, turns around, and walks back to his side of the indoor pitch.

Syd gives me two thumbs up, as if that encounter with Justin was something positive. He kicked a ball into my face, and then I behaved like an idiot.

"Okay?" Miss White asks.

"Fine."

Kason kicks the ball to the other team, and we get ready to start again.

I'm going to have bruises everywhere by the time we're done.

We play for another twenty minutes. I let in three and save four.

"Let's wrap it up," Miss White calls.

Oh, thank you, Lord.

I might not be the fastest out there, but I am the fastest when it comes to getting back into the changing room. No one wants out of gym class more than I do. The others trail after me as I run for the door.

Syd and I change and then go our separate ways for the third period.

I do have to get through AP math with Axel again. At least I don't have to sit next to him, though. He sits alone near the back of the class.

I like math. The answer is the answer and that's that.

I walk into the classroom and take my seat. While everyone is filtering in, I listen to the fizz of excitement the death fear meme has caused. It's incredible how happy this creepily morbid thing has made people.

Axel is already sitting down when I look over my shoulder. He's glancing at his phone, scrolling and occasionally shaking his head with a clenched jaw. Is he looking at people's fears? He thinks every way to die is the worst. But he can't *really* believe that, right? I mean, being burned alive has to be worse than falling down some stairs.

I might be giving this meme more thought than I should.

Mr. Heston turns our attention from gossip to math.

But no one is into it, and it's the same for the rest of the day. Everyone half-heartedly listens to the teacher while scrolling to see all the awful ways we could be murdered.

three

IZZY

By the time I leave school, I'm ready to watch or read something light and fluffy. If it was still December, it would be something cheesy from Hallmark. That's the level of happy I need right now.

Hearing about death all day has been kinda depressing, and I could use something upbeat after constantly reading about gory murder.

As if that weren't distressing enough, I have a red circle on my forehead from the soccer ball in gym. It's almost gone now, but I did spend all day looking like . . . well, like I was hit in the head with a ball.

Syd and I walk to our cars with our chins tucked, trying to keep the bitter wind from biting our cheeks.

"I need summer," she mutters.

"Me too. Are we going to the diner before this stupid party?" I ask. The only thing that will make this bearable is one of Matthew's hot dogs.

"The party isn't stupid, and of course we are!"

"I'll meet you at Puck's."

We go our separate ways for the five minutes it takes to drive from school to the town square. It takes two minutes in better weather. I pass the first dock at the port. Boats are out as usual, because fishing doesn't stop for snow or ice, apparently. The water would probably freeze over if there weren't a constant ring of fishing boats coming and going.

The only time they stop is if there's a blizzard. Which has happened five times so far this winter.

I park in the lot, wave at Syd's dad out on a boat, and dash along the shoveled sidewalk to Puck's Diner—owned by Matthew Grayson. Ex–minor league professional hockey player and the person closest to reaching fame that Rock Bay has ever had.

He's Kason and Justin's hero, though I'm sure they're hoping to get to the majors.

Syd and I take a seat in an ice-blue booth. The tabletops are painted with the layout of an ice hockey pitch, and framed game photos hang all over the walls. Most important, Puck's has the best burgers, hot dogs, and slushies in the world.

"Tell me you two aren't getting in on all this nonsense," Matthew's wife, Lenora, says, stopping by our table with her notepad and pen. She's a glamorous woman with shiny hair and a new dip manicure every two weeks. Half the town thought she would leave Matthew when his injury stopped him from playing.

"The fear thing, you mean?" Syd says. "We haven't reposted anything yet, but I think half the school has by now. More, probably."

"We're not going to," I add.

"Good. You guys want your usual dogs and cherry slushies?"

"Please," Syd and I reply in unison.

"All right. Amiyah's already here. She's in the bathroom," Lenora says as she walks toward the kitchen.

Amiyah is my cousin, and she makes up our trio. Uncle Samar is a surgeon at the local hospital. He's loaded, so Amiyah attends St. Mary's, an all-girls private school just outside town.

She bursts through the bathroom door and runs to our table, her curled black hair bouncing behind her. Sliding into the booth beside me, she shoves her phone in my face.

I wish people would stop doing that.

"Have you seen this?" she asks.

"You're so yesterday, Miyah," Syd says.

"It's all over your school, too?" I ask.

"It's all anyone can talk about. It's from here! I'd recognize that dock with Matthew's carving of a puck and initials etched into it anywhere."

"That's what we said." I push her phone away, and she drops it on the table. "You haven't done it, have you?"

"Everyone has, Iz. I thought you hadn't seen it, because there was nothing on your profile. Not that I don't know your biggest death fear. Did you order? I have, but I told Lenora I'd wait for you two, and I'm starving."

"We ordered," I say. "Why did you share it? It's creepy, Miyah. Who would even think of something like that *and why?*"

"It's just a bit of fun. Lighten up, Iz."

Syd laughs. "Izzy's freaked out by it."

"No, I'm not!"

"You've been weird about it all day."

"How?"

She frowns. "You just have."

That's her argument when she has no evidence or facts to back a claim up.

"If not doing it makes me weird, then you're weird, too," I say.

Syd grabs her phone.

"Put that down!"

Miyah rolls her eyes. "Chill, will you, Iz? It's a *joke.*"

"It's about death."

"This dude just wants to go viral. Like people on TikTok with their unboxing videos or playing games."

I will never understand why someone would watch someone else playing Minecraft. However, I do love unboxing videos.

"Are you going to Mariella's party?" Syd asks.

"When have I *ever* turned down a party?" Miyah replies.

"Your parents' Christmas party," I say.

"Ugh. Stuck-up assholes from their social circle. That's my idea of hell. Anyway, I went to that."

"Only because I agreed to go with you. And because Uncle Samar gave us fifty dollars each to pretend to be happy about it."

He's my favorite uncle.

"Your fear is being dragged by a car! Miyah, what the hell!" Syd's mouth falls open as she stares at her screen, reading my cousin's repost.

Miyah laughs. "It's, hands down, the worst way to go! Could you imagine? Ooh, our food is here."

My heart races.

I wouldn't have even thought about that as a way to go. I know that, with the amount of textbooks Uncle Samar has around, Miyah has access to all things gross and gruesome, but her mind is darker than I thought.

She was once obsessed with medieval surgical methods after reading one of her dad's books.

While we eat, I try to forget about the meme. Despite the fact that the whole diner is talking about it and trying to figure out who started it.

We overhear Matthew denying any involvement and insisting that just because they took a picture here, that doesn't mean he's responsible. He seems half annoyed and half pleased that his carved post was used.

I don't know if that means someone who knows him started this or if that was the only recognizable landmark. The creator wanted the town to be identified.

Who knows?

"What are you two wearing?" Syd asks as we finish eating.

We all chuck some cash on the table to cover the bill and tip.

"I'm not dressing up," I tell her.

"Neither am I," Miyah says. "Even if Tayley, Debbie, and Mariella will be in tiny dresses. Besides, my parents would never let me leave the house with too much exposed skin."

Syd's shoulders slump. "Jeans it is."

"My friend dropped me off, Iz, so I'm coming with you," Miyah tells me.

"Okay."

I zip my coat as we walk to the door. Miyah and I go to my car, and Syd goes to hers.

After cranking up the heat, I drive home.

"Who do you think made that meme?" I ask.

Miyah scrolls through her phone, paying no attention to anything else. "No idea. They must be bored, though. What I'd like to know is *why.*"

"Miyah, not everything on the internet is exactly logical. There are quizzes that tell you what kind of sandwich you'd be."

She laughs and finally looks up as we reach my house. "That's true."

I park in the drive and let us in. We go straight up to my room to change. My dad works for a finance company, and my mom is a dental secretary. Neither of them will be home until after seven p.m., and we'll be gone by then.

Miyah opens my closet door and tilts her head to the side. "I need to borrow a shirt. I only brought jeans with me."

"Grab whatever you want." I sit on my bed and unlock my phone.

My feed is flooded with nothing but *fear.*

four

IZZY

I pull up at Mariella's house. "Mansion" is probably a better way to describe it. It's huge, with a sprawling front lawn. The driveway has been meticulously plowed down to the black asphalt, but it's packed with cars, so we park on the street. Her parents own a dance and workout clothing line, and Mariella is in most of their social media posts and ads. You can always tell when she's done a shoot, as she behaves like she's a fashion model for the rest of the week.

Syd always thought Mariella would end up going to Miyah's school, but that girl would never go anywhere without boys. Dating is her religion.

I wonder if she'll be making a play for Justin, like Tayley is.

We take off our coats and toss them in the car—we don't want someone stealing them or, worse, vomiting on them.

"Come on, it's freezing out here!" Miyah says, wrapping her arms around the skintight top she borrowed from me. There might not be much skin on show—you're welcome, Uncle Samar and Aunt Ellen—but there doesn't need to be when the top looks painted on. It's one of my favorites and looks incredible on her.

I let her take my hand and drag me up the drive.

A cold shiver rattles down my spine. Instinctively, I look over my shoulder and see Axel standing on the opposite side of the road, talking to some guy whose face is obscured in the shadows.

Is Axel coming to the party? That would be a first. The guy he's with looks older. Maybe there is some truth to the rumor about his being held back.

"Izzy, hurry up!" Miyah says, tugging on my hand to get me to walk faster.

I turn away from Axel, who never even glances in my direction. "Sorry."

He's probably just talking to a friend. Though it's strange to think of him as having a friend, since he's made no effort to get to know anyone at school.

We step inside, and we're welcomed by warm air and the smell of beer.

Mariella's house is a sea of red Solo cups, bodies making the most amazing shapes—almost like they're being electrocuted rather than dancing—and others with their face attached to someone else.

I love to dance, but I would feel too self-conscious to do it here. Not all of Mariella's friends are nice, so I can only imagine what they might say.

"Beer?" Miyah asks. "Oh, sorry. You're des."

"Yeah, thanks for reminding me that I have to stay sober. Though I do get to watch you all make fools of yourselves, so . . ."

"Whatever, don't be bitter."

Miyah, much better at blending in than I am, immediately goes for a beer and starts talking to Tayley. I wish I had her confidence. Not that I want to talk to Tayley.

I leave Miyah and walk into the kitchen to find a soda. There's only beer in the coolers.

Justin and Kason are laughing and shoving each other at the far end of the kitchen, both spilling beer onto Mariella's marble floor.

They look up as I grab a Dr Pepper, but they turn away just as fast and neither says anything to me.

But then Justin does a double take. He frowns and his forehead is almost lost to his shiny blond hair. Is he trying to work out whether I've been invited?

My heart leaps anyway.

I'd be offended if I cared. Okay, so maybe I care a *little* bit. Being invisible isn't always fun, but at least I don't have the pressure of fitting in.

At least the mark on my forehead has disappeared.

Axel spoke more than two words to me today, though, so it hasn't been a total fail.

I take my can into the living room to see whether Syd has arrived yet. She was getting a ride with Emma from her biology class, since they live close to each other.

I find Syd and Emma with Miyah on the sofa, all three of them with beers in their hands. They're giggling and looking over at a couple of guys from the hockey team.

"There you are!" Miyah says, as if I've been gone for an hour.

I hold my drink up. "Remember, some of us have to remain sober."

Shouldn't Emma? I guess I'll be taking Syd home.

Emma shrugs and sips her beer. "Right. See you guys later. I'm off to find Kason."

"You are not getting back into a car with her," I say once Emma's gone.

"Absolutely not! I'm coming with you!" Syd replies.

"Look, there's Justin and Kason," Miyah says. "Did you see their fears? Creepy!"

"Yours is way worse," Syd tells her.

I nod. "She's got you there."

"Whatever." She sighs and her dark eyes gloss over as she watches them. "I wish I went to your school."

"I couldn't do the no-boys thing," Syd says.

I zone out as I spot someone who looks like Axel walking from the kitchen out the front door. No way. It's hard to see as Danny and Beck jump up and down to "Cake by the Ocean" in front of me, but I definitely saw messy blond hair and a leather jacket.

Debbie walks into the room wearing a tiny yellow dress that would make my parents choke if they saw me in it. She looks like a model.

She raises a Solo cup to her mouth and takes a long swig. Her pale eyes are tense, and she's clenching her free hand as if she's holding in a tantrum.

I remember seeing her explode when she didn't win prom queen last year. She walked around for ten minutes looking like her veins were going to pop . . . then she screamed at poor Gemma for daring to breathe in her vicinity.

Someone must have made her mad.

Maybe Kason rejected her.

Or maybe she had an argument with Axel. They both came from the same direction, and he just stalked outside as if he was storming out after an argument. Now she looks like she wants to destroy the entire human race.

No way would she even speak to him, though. Unless it was to tell him to get out of her way or call him a freak.

Oh my God, I would die if it turns out she's been hooking up with him. She's never dated anyone other than guys on the hockey team. In fact, I've heard her say that Axel is disgusting and probably spends his time pulling the heads off small animals.

Imagine if the beauty was sleeping with the beast.

"I'm going to get another drink," I say absentmindedly, following Debbie into the kitchen.

Miyah and Syd are too preoccupied talking to Jeremy and Billy, who made their way over after noticing them staring.

I swerve around a couple of people before I bump into them and get beer spilled on my top.

Debbie is glugging her drink by the fridge. I step deeper into the room. A couple of people are around, but they're not paying attention.

"Debbie, are you okay?" I ask.

Mariella laughs beside me.

Jeez, where did she come from?

"She's fine, Izzy. Right, D?"

Debbie looks up and chucks her bottle into the recycling bin. "I'm fine." She walks toward the exit, throwing a dark look at her friend, hands clenched, shoulders tight.

Doesn't look like she's fine.

"Ignore her. She's renowned for causing drama. It's, like, her party trick."

I turn to Mariella. "What happened to her?"

"I have no idea. She's, like, always attention seeking. If you ignore her, she'll come around. Why are you so bothered anyway, wallflower?"

She walks away, giggling to herself, and I want to throw something at her. I won't, of course. I can't even stand up for myself by telling her to shut it.

This has happened before, the Drama Queen Debbie thing, I mean. I've been dragged to enough parties to know that Debbie kind of has a temper, but she's usually back dancing in no time.

There's a power play between her and Mariella that is riveting. The fight for queen bee is heating up. So far, Mariella is winning.

Taking another soda, I sit at the large table and open the Kindle app on my phone.

The party is stretching on, but Justin's wearing a tight-fitting pale blue T-shirt, so that's making it bearable. Or it was until about five minutes ago, when he vanished. I don't even want to think why he would have snuck off.

I get four chapters into my thousandth reread of Harry Potter when Tayley walks into the room with Jessie trailing behind her. They both look over, and I pretend that I haven't noticed.

"And that's why she'll never be popular," Tayley loudly whispers to Jessie. They fall into fits of laughter.

I mentally roll my eyes. I'd rather be a bookworm than an asshole.

Where did Debbie go? She's usually right beside Tayley, as if the whole of her is an extra limb.

It's now been an hour and thirty minutes since I arrived. Can I go yet?

I stand as Miyah storms into the kitchen with narrowed eyes. She sees Tayley first and then me. "There you are, Iz!"

"I said I was going to the kitchen."

She looks at my phone. "To read?"

Tayley and Jessie giggle again as they walk out and leave us to it.

"The party is boring," I tell her. "I'd rather be at Hogwarts."

"Did you really just say that?" Justin asks from the doorway.

He's back, and I die a thousand deaths.

I'm sure my face is an unflattering shade of red. Clearing my throat, I reply, "I like Harry Potter."

"More than parties." His eyes sparkle with amusement. It's a good look on him, even if it's at my expense. His blond hair is slightly different, like he's had to restyle it.

Don't think about why.

"Maybe if this party was any fun, Izzy wouldn't be bored," Miyah shoots back, walking past him.

Justin smirks at me and then retreats.

"Can we go now?" I ask, then I notice the tightness around her dark eyes again. "What's wrong?"

"The guys at your school are disgusting."

"Yeah."

"I'm not making out with a guy I've known for three minutes. Where are all the gentlemen?"

I shrug, because I don't have a clue. "So, can we go?"

"Yeah, come on. This was way more fun in my head."

I bounce over to her and push my way through a crowd of people who either don't see me or don't care. Miyah, on the other hand, sways through as they part for her.

Syd is scowling when we find her by the entrance.

"Great night for you, too?" I ask sarcastically.

"I'm swearing off flirting with the hockey team."

"Sure you are."

"I mean it, Iz. They're all animals."

As we leave, Justin smirks at me again. He probably over-heard our conversation. Whatever, I'm too over tonight to care. Mostly.

The snow starts to pick up as we get into my car, but I don't actually mind driving in the snow. It's the full-on blizzards that freak me out. We put on our cold coats and turn the heat on high.

Miyah leans forward and peers up at the sky. "Why isn't it spring already?"

"It snows in spring, too," I tell her.

"Not *this* much!"

I can practically hear Syd's eyes roll.

The car crawls along, my wipers swishing back and forth so fast they're barely visible. Snow hits the windshield like hundreds of tiny bullets.

It's getting worse.

All right, it might be close to exceeding my snow-driving comfort level now.

I squint as if the action will improve my eyesight.

"My curfew is in fifteen minutes, Iz," Miyah says.

"I'm sure you'd rather be late and alive," I quip.

"You're doing fine. The roads aren't that bad."

She wouldn't say that if she was driving. I can see just a few feet in front of me. My lights might as well be off, because all I see is a blur of white flying toward me.

"We're not going to die going twenty," Miyah says. "We'll only hit a snow pile."

"Stop talking, Miyah. You're not making this easier!"

"You two should've been sisters," Syd says, yawning.

Miyah and I have grown up together. We've spent summers and weekends sleeping over at each other's houses. My mom and hers are close.

A flash of something solid catches my eye as I slowly turn a corner. "What's that?" I ask, gently applying the brakes so we don't skid.

"What are you doing?" Syd asks, leaning between the seats. "I have a curfew, too. We can't stop!"

My heart stutters. "There," I say, putting the car in park and pointing to the blob of pale yellow, half on the sidewalk and half in the road ahead of us.

They both look up and frown. "I can't see," Miyah mutters.

"Something's poking out into the road."

"Just go around it," Syd says.

"No. Someone could have hit an animal. A deer, maybe. I'm going to look."

"Izzy, the storm is getting worse!"

"I don't want anyone else to hit it. It's dangerous and cruel."

I lean forward, trying to get a better look, but the snow really is turning into a blizzard and making it almost impossible to see. I swing the door open, ignoring Syd and Miyah shouting at me, and run out in front of my car.

Shielding my eyes, I rush to the sidewalk. My boots slip underneath me. I throw my arms out to the side to steady myself.

"Izzy!" Syd shouts.

I slow, step up onto the sidewalk, and approach.

Then I see her. Lying on the ground in her yellow dress is *Debbie*.

five

IZZY

Oh my God.

With a trembling hand, I pull out my phone and drop to my knees beside Debbie. Her eyes are wide, the snow collecting on her eyelashes. A pool of blood circles her head and drips down the curb.

Debbie. This can't be real.

Behind me, Miyah screams and Syd cusses.

When did they get out of the car?

"Call 911!" I say, thrusting my phone at Syd as my heart races. She takes it instantly and almost drops it.

What do I do?

"Debbie?" I say, reaching out and touching her neck to feel for a pulse. Thanks to Uncle Samar, I know a bit of first aid, but my mind is all over the place, whirling faster than the snow.

I check her pulse, but there is nothing fluttering behind her skin. No blood pumping through her veins, like I thought. She's too still, her chest not moving, and she's pale. Her lips are a deep shade of blue.

"She's dead, isn't she?" Miyah asks. Her voice is hollow.

She's definitely dead. There's so much blood, and the back of her head looks . . . I swallow bile that stings my throat. The back of her head looks *crushed*. Did she fall from the roof?

I glance at Ruby's café beside us and can just make out the flat roof through the snow. She must have been up there.

My stomach lurches.

I look up but all I see is those white bullets pelting at my face.

"Th-the cops and paramedics are coming," Syd says, crouching down beside me.

I hear Miyah on the phone saying "Daddy," so it won't be long until my uncle, aunt, and parents arrive, too.

"What happened?" Syd asks, more to herself than to me.

Snow seeps through my jeans, and it feels like it goes straight into my bones. My long, dark hair sticks to my face. I shiver from the temperature and the situation.

"She wouldn't jump," I say. At the party, she fell out with her friends, or at least had a fight, but surely she wouldn't have jumped. Mariella was catty when she told me Debbie was fine. Debbie seemed annoyed rather than hurt or upset.

Could she have killed herself?

Syd grabs my arm. "You don't think she would? What are you saying? You think she . . . fell?"

"Look at her."

Syd swallows audibly and shakes her head. "Not again."

"The back of her head, Syd. It's—"

"Don't. I don't want to hear it. I know what you're going to say, so let's pretend you already said it. I get it." Her voice is several octaves higher than usual. "We don't know what happened. She might have been depressed and suicidal."

If she jumped, would she have done it backward? Right now, her big eyes are staring up at the sky, not down at the ground. She wasn't facing out toward the dock when she fell; she was looking the other way.

I think that maybe . . . she could have been facing the person who pushed her.

In the distance I hear sirens, and the flash of blue light bounces off the swirling snow.

I stand as the sheriff's car pulls up.

"Sydney? Isabel?" Sheriff Rosetta says. He knows everyone in town. He looks at Miyah. "Are you okay?"

She nods, but I can tell that she's not.

None of us are.

"What happened?" he asks.

Another cop car pulls up, followed closely by the ambulance.

"We were driving home from a party and I—I noticed something on the road," I say, wrapping my arms around myself. "We stopped to see what it was and . . . it was her."

"All right, girls," Sheriff Rosetta says. "You sit in my car until we're ready to talk to you, okay?"

The EMTs run past us.

Officer Duggan follows us to the sheriff's car, and we all get in. Syd and Miyah climb in the back, so I'm left in the passenger seat next to the cop. I've known Carl Duggan for years. He went to school with my parents.

"How are you?" he asks as he turns up the heat.

I hold my hands over the vent and feel my fingers tingle at the sudden change in temperature. "I don't know," I reply.

"You're in shock. That's very normal, Izzy. I've called your parents. Can you tell me what happened tonight?"

"W-we found her. Like that. Face-*up*."

Will he find that weird, too?

"Before that."

"Oh. Uh. Yeah." That's easier to talk about. "We were all at a party at Mariella Whitmore's house. Debbie was upset at the party. She must've left without telling anyone, but she sometimes does things like that. She . . ."

"Go on," he prompts, but saying something negative about her now feels wrong. "It's okay, Izzy."

"It's not the first time she's left a party without a word," Syd says. "I think she hopes her friends will follow her."

"You specifically?" he asks.

"Well, no. We're not really friends with her. I just mean her friends at the party."

He nods. "All right. What happened next? Do you know if anyone was in contact with her?"

"No," I reply. "Not that I know of. Her friends seemed to think she just wanted attention."

"These friends are . . . ?"

"Tayley Ward and Jessie Gardner."

"What time did you leave?"

"Ten or fifteen minutes ago."

"It took you a while to get here from the Whitmores' house."

My eye twitches at the question. Behind it, the insinuation that we've done something we shouldn't in that extra time.

"I couldn't see well in the storm, so we were going slow," I tell him.

He nods. "What did you see?"

"I . . . I saw a flash of yellow on the ground when I turned the corner." I take a breath and continue. "At first, I wasn't sure, but I remembered what Debbie was wearing, and I had to stop and check."

"You did the right thing, Izzy."

"She's . . . d-dead." I curl my fingers into my palms and stare out the window at the flashing light of the ambulance. "There's nothing the EMTs will be able to do, is there?"

He ducks his head, tucking his long chin into his chest. "Let's leave that to them."

I think we all know what that means.

"Daddy!" Miyah shouts. She taps the window.

"I'll let you out," Officer Duggan says. The back doors don't open from the inside, so he gets out and opens hers for her as Uncle Samar and Aunt Ellen run toward us.

Miyah leaps into her parents' arms. I get out, too, and walk around the car.

"Izzy, come here," Aunt Ellen says, holding an arm out for me.

I don't realize how much I need a hug until I'm tucked into her.

"It's going to be okay, girls," Uncle Samar says.

"Goodness. Oh, that girl and her poor parents," Aunt Ellen says softly. "Are you two okay?"

Miyah shakes her head. I nod but it's a lie.

"Sydney, are you all right?" Uncle Samar asks. He stands taller, ready to take charge. Syd nods, too. Turning to Officer Duggan, he says, "Okay. What do you need from the girls? When can we take them home?"

"We're going to need to interview them while everything is still fresh in their minds. It looks like Sheriff got Ruby to open the café. Shall we go inside? We'll get the girls coffee or something."

"All right."

"Izzy and Sydney, we'll send your parents in when they arrive," he says. "This way."

We pass Sheriff Rosetta on our way inside. I hear another car pull up with more flashing lights just before Officer Duggan shuts the door.

Old Ruby Bricks is standing by the counter in her tiny café, tying her apron around her back. "I can't believe it," she says.

"Would you make the girls something hot to drink, please, Ruby?" Officer Duggan asks.

"Hot chocolates, girls?" she asks.

"Please," we all say together.

"Take a seat," Officer Duggan says. Miyah, Syd, and I sit at a table in the middle, and my aunt and uncle pull another table up to ours and sit with us.

No one says anything. I twist my hands, wringing my fingers together, as we sit in silence and listen to Ruby clatter around in the kitchen. She usually works quickly.

Ruby brings over a tray with three large hot chocolates. "Anything for anyone else?"

They pass.

"When all your parents arrive, I'll start the interview, okay?" Officer Duggan asks.

"Sure," I reply. Though didn't he already ask us some questions in the car? He jumped the gun. We're minors; he should have waited. Not that it really matters—everything we're about to say will be the same. After what I've just seen, I literally don't care if I've already told him about attending a party.

I take a sip of the smooth, boiling drink. My hands start to warm up around the mug despite the fact that the rest of me is still damp from the snow.

When I hear voices outside, I first think that it's my dad shouting at the officers to tell him where I am. But it's not.

It's a cop shouting, "There's another body!"

six

IZZY

Another body.

My jaw drops.

Debbie isn't the only dead person outside.

How is that possible?

Officer Duggan leaps to his feet. "All of you need to stay in here." His voice has changed from soft to hard. He's not asking us to do anything; this isn't a request. He's telling us we're not to move.

"That can't be," Aunt Ellen mumbles.

Uncle Samar stands as the door slams behind Officer Duggan.

"Someone else is *dead*!" Syd says as her eyes go scary wide. "What the hell! I didn't see anyone else out there. Did you, Iz?"

"No! Only Debbie . . . but we didn't exactly look around," I say, staring at the window Uncle Samar is peering out of.

"I can't believe it," Ruby says, sitting down at our table. "This is a quiet, friendly town."

"What happened tonight?" Uncle Samar asks. He turns

around, probably because he can't see anything but snow and the constant flashing of blue light outside.

"Izzy was driving us home, and we saw Debbie on the sidewalk," Miyah tells him.

"She'd left the party early," I add. "I think she fell off the roof."

"Fell?" he asks.

"Well, not quite," I say, hesitating. "I think she was pushed."

"Isabel, that's quite an allegation," Aunt Ellen says, patting my shoulder. "We don't know anything yet."

"We know there's a second body."

She swallows. "Let's leave the investigating to the cops, okay?"

I nod to appease my aunt, but it's obvious, right?

Okay, I could be getting ahead of myself.

Ruby utters a prayer under her breath and makes the sign of the cross over her chest.

"Izzy?" Mom and Dad cry at the same time as they burst through the door.

Syd's parents are right behind them.

"Are you okay?" Mom asks. They crouch on either side of me, Dad wrapping an arm around me.

"I found her," I whisper as tears well up in my eyes. Seeing my parents cracks the strong exterior I've been putting on.

Mom pulls me into a hug, and Dad's arm drops. I curl against my mom and close my eyes, wishing I could stop seeing Debbie's head, flat at the back.

"Did you see what's going on out there?" I hear Uncle Samar ask Dad.

"Cops everywhere. Half just outside, the other half by the river across the road."

The river.

I let go of Mom and sit up, wiping tears from my face. Miyah, Syd, and I all look at one another.

"Someone's in the water," I mutter.

"It's a suicide pact," Miyah announces.

"Amiyah, stop," Aunt Ellen says.

"It makes sense," Syd says.

I sip my hot chocolate, to have something to do, and shiver. Could that be possible? Who left with Debbie?

No way. My heart drops to my frozen toes. *Axel.* I saw him at the party, walking out of the house, and shortly after, Debbie stormed out of the kitchen. Did they go off somewhere together?

I put my drink down and jump up.

My parents shout my name as I sprint out the door.

Snow swirls wildly in circles around me.

"Izzy?" Sheriff Rosetta shouts as I jog toward him.

"Isabel—" My dad's voice is lost to the storm.

The sheriff puts his hands up and I stop, squinting so the snow doesn't go in my eyes. "You can't be out here. Go back inside."

"Is it Axel?" I ask, shouting over the whistling wind. "Oh God. The body, is it Axel Gray?"

"Izzy, I can't discuss this with you."

I shake my head, trying to look over his shoulder, but the storm is too bad to see even a few feet ahead. "You know who it is. Can't you just tell me if it's him or not?"

"What do you think you're doing?" Dad asks, pulling my hand. "I'm sorry, Sheriff."

He shakes his head. "It's okay. Go back inside, I'll be right in to talk to you."

"Please!" I say.

"Go back, Izzy." It's an order.

Dad tugs me along until we're back inside.

"What on earth do you think you were doing?" he demands, closing the door behind us.

"I—I think it might be Axel out there."

Dad frowns. "Who?"

"A kid in my year. I have classes with him."

"No way! Axel?" Syd says. "Why do you think it's him?"

"I saw him at the party, which is weird, right?" I ask, and Syd nods. Axel doesn't do parties. "Debbie left right after him."

"That doesn't mean it's him, Iz," she replies.

Mom sits and whispers, "I can't believe . . . These are children."

"It doesn't mean it's not him either," I say. "Why else was he there?"

"A murder-suicide," Miyah says.

My jaw drops for the second time.

Axel was weird today. Could he really have killed Debbie and taken his own life? I sit next to him in class. How could I have shared a table with someone like that?

I sit down again to try to make sense of everything.

The room falls silent, only the mechanical tick of the cream clock on the wall making any noise. Everyone is lost in their own thoughts and probably questioning whether this night is real.

I watch the second hand of the clock go around three times before Sheriff Rosetta walks into the café.

"What's going on?" Uncle Samar asks.

"Who's out there?" Dad adds.

Mom pats my knee, and I take a sip of my drink, which my stomach almost rejects.

The sheriff brushes snow from his hair and walks deeper into the room. "I'd like to go through the girls' story," he says, holding up his notebook. "I'll continue where Officer Duggan left off."

"Please tell me if it's Axel out there."

"We haven't identified the body," he replies.

My hands tighten around the mug. "Girl or boy? Please?"

He takes a breath. "Male. That doesn't mean it's Axel, though."

I sink into the seat. "Have you seen that meme circulating?" I ask.

Syd scoffs. "Really, Iz?"

"What are you talking about? What meme?" Sheriff asks, ignoring Syd.

"It's a post about the worst way to die," I tell him. "The picture was taken here, at the dock. You can see Matthew Grayson's carved puck and initials in it."

"The worst way to die? Can you show me?"

"Okay." I pull my phone out of my pocket. "Everyone has been reposting it and sharing their worst fears."

He scratches his head and then reaches out for it. "Lord."

"Axel said something at school today. He said that every way to go is bad, and I saw him shaking his head as he scrolled. Like he was frustrated with everyone sharing it."

Sheriff's dark, beady eyes peer at me from where he's holding my phone. "I see."

"Could this Axel have killed Debbie and then taken his own life?" Uncle Samar asks.

"We can't speculate on things like that. We need evidence," Sheriff replies, handing me back my phone.

He sits down and faces me. "Let's go through this again, Izzy."

I tell him everything that happened from the moment we arrived at Mariella's party, right up to the cops' arrival at the scene.

He scribbles everything down. Officer Duggan is in the background watching. The parents and Ruby are silent. Miyah cries softly, and Syd is as still as a statue.

Me, well, I'm pretty sure I must still be in shock. I feel nothing.

seven

IZZY

It's almost midnight by the time we're finally allowed to go. The cops have everything they need from me for now, apparently.

I have so many questions, and I don't know when I'll get any answers. On the way home, I check social media. Axel hasn't been on since earlier this evening. He's not super active anyway, but it still doesn't look good.

If the second body was him, the cops will want to tell his family before they release any information.

Tomorrow I'll have to go back to school and face a circus. I'll have to pretend that I'm okay. I'll have to look at empty seats where Debbie and Axel—maybe Axel—should be sitting.

I take a hot shower and get straight into bed.

Mom comes into my room as I'm pulling the quilt up to my chin. She sits down next to me, leaning against the headboard.

"Are you okay?" she asks.

I curl my fist around the quilt. "I found her."

"Oh, honey, I know."

"I can't believe she's dead. And Axel."

"We don't know it's him."

"Well, it's someone. Do you think we'll know tomorrow?"

"Probably. I think you should take a few days off from school. They'll understand."

I shake my head. "I'm not leaving Syd on her own. It'll be fine. The sooner I get it over with, the sooner I'll stop being the girl who found Debbie."

Well, the sooner people will stop staring at the girl who found Debbie.

"Gosh, her poor parents," my mom says. "They must be beside themselves."

I like Debbie's parents. They've always been kind. They both work at the port in the fishing tackle shop they own. I'm glad we didn't see them from inside the diner. I don't think I could have taken it.

"I'm exhausted, Mom."

"Right." She gets up and smiles at me. "Try to get some sleep. Come and get me if you need me, okay? I don't care if it's the middle of the night."

It's already the middle of the night.

"I will. Love you."

"Love you, too."

When she leaves my room and shuts the door, I curl up in my blankets and close my eyes.

Debbie's body instantly pops into my mind, as if there are photos of her on the insides of my eyelids.

When I do fall asleep, I'm restless, and I wake up feeling more tired than before.

Mom and Dad are waiting for me when I get downstairs.

"Morning. How are you feeling?" Dad asks.

"I'm okay," I reply, wringing my hands in the doorway.

"Are you sure about school?"

"Yes, Dad."

"No one would blame you if you need time. Especially not Sydney," he says.

"I want to go."

"Amiyah's staying home."

I push off of the doorframe and sit down at the table, where Mom puts my coffee. "Good for her. I feel fine to go."

"All right. I will be calling Principal Beckett, though. You leave anytime you need to."

I agree, and after I've eaten, I drive to school.

Syd isn't here yet, but I'm early. I park in my spot and walk into school. I avoid making eye contact with anyone who turns in my direction. Which is basically every person I pass. Some do double takes.

I turn a corner and gasp.

He's here. All six feet of him is right in front of me—alive.

"Axel," I whisper, and tension melts from my body.

"The cops were at my apartment in the early hours," he says.

I blink to make sure I'm not seeing things. Piercing, icy eyes and a scowl. Yep, that's definitely him. "You're here. You're okay."

"Yeah." He scowls again. I'm not sure his face will do anything else. "Kind of. I just heard that you were the one who found Debbie. So, it was *you* who told the cops I was involved."

"What? No! That's not what I told them at all. I never said I thought you were involved like you did something bad. I was scared because I thought you were the second body."

His blond eyebrows shoot up like rockets. Noted: his face does surprised, too. "You thought *I* was dead?"

"I saw you at the party, which is pretty unusual for you, you spoke to Debbie there, and you left right before she did."

His strong jaw twitches. "I was trying something new."

He was trying something new?

"Really?" I ask.

"Yeah."

"Anyway, I thought Debbie followed you. When the cops said there was a second body out there . . ."

"You assumed it was me?"

I nod. "But clearly it wasn't."

"And you obviously have no idea who it was."

"All I know is that it was a guy. The cops wouldn't say anything more."

"They asked me if I started that stupid meme."

"Do they think the deaths have something to do with that?"

"Debbie's fear was falling."

I whack his arm with the back of my hand. "God, it was! Okay." I lean against the wall so I don't faint as my head swims with this revelation. "We need to check everyone who reposted that meme and see which boys picked drowning."

"If their privacy settings are public."

"Yeah, well, we can't do anything about that."

His lips straighten. "Why do you keep saying 'we'?"

"You don't want to know?"

"It'll be on the news soon enough, Izzy."

"Do you not care at all? Two of our classmates are dead."

"Why do you assume the other person is a student?"

I open my mouth to reply but catch myself, because I don't have an answer for that.

"Just let the cops try to do their job," he says and walks off.

"Isabel Tindall to the principal's office," the loudspeaker above my head taunts.

My shoulders slump. I knew that was coming.

I spin around and head toward the office, passing yet more stares and some terrible whispering. *Yeah, I found her!*

Gritting my teeth, I pick up my pace until I get to the principal's office.

"Hello, Izzy," Principal Beckett says. "Come have a seat."

I don't want to, but sure.

"How are you?" she asks as I sit in the wrinkled leather chair.

"Wanting to get through the school day."

"I've set up a meeting with one of the guidance counselors for you this afternoon. We'll be offering the same to every student."

I nod. "I suppose it's not optional?"

"I would rather you saw someone today."

That's her nice way of saying no.

"Okay, I'll go."

"Fifth period with Lara."

I happen to like Lara. She's the only guidance counselor who doesn't smell like cheap perfume.

"Okay. Can I go?"

"You're not usually this hostile."

I blow out a breath as my cheeks heat. "I don't mean to be. I'm sorry."

"Would you like me to see if Lara will see you now? I'm sure, given the circumstances, she will."

I sit taller. "No. Thank you for the offer, but I'll wait. I want to see Syd."

"All right. If you need me, my door is always open."

"Thanks," I say again and get to my feet. I return her smile and leave her office as fast as I can.

Syd is leaning against the wall waiting for me as I leave.

"You good?" I ask, stopping in front of her.

"It's *not* Axel."

"Yeah, I ran into him. Literally."

"I barely slept," she says, rubbing her eyes.

"Same here."

"Have you seen all the posts about Debbie online?"

"I've avoided everything social media this morning."

"Well, everyone is sharing lovely things about her as if she were an angel."

"That's what people do."

We walk toward homeroom together.

"People are hypocrites," she huffs.

"I don't know, I think we all deserve kindness when we die. Anyway, Axel said something interesting."

"You've spoken to him?"

"For a second. I thought I was seeing a ghost at first. He asked why I assumed the second body is a student."

Her eyebrows rise. "He's got a point."

"I know. Who could it be, though?"

"The cops must know by now."

"Do you think that death meme is at the center of all this?" I ask.

"Careful, you'll turn into a conspiracy theorist."

"I'm serious, Syd. I know the cops are looking into it, but Debbie died by falling—or being *pushed*—off a building the same day she reposted her fear of falling. I mean, duh!"

"What are you saying?"

"That some unidentified person wanted to know how to kill her."

Her eyes slide to me slowly. "And then he drowned himself?"

She speaks the words slowly as if she doesn't think I can keep up.

I gasp and jump out of the way as Justin runs down the hall with pinched eyebrows, almost barreling into us. Mariella and Tayley are hot on his heels.

What the hell!

"No way is it true!" Tayley shouts.

"What's not true?" Syd asks.

Tayley looks over her shoulder as she follows Justin toward the office. Her cheeks are stained with tears. "Body number two is *Kason*!"

eight

IZZY

Syd and I turn to each other, wide-eyed.

Kason. Kason died with Debbie. Well, not *with* her. But they must have been together last night. They were only a road apart.

Syd grabs my arm. "I can't believe it. Were they seeing each other?"

"Maybe he wanted to and she didn't. That could be motive for pushing her."

Syd takes a step back. "You believe Miyah's murder-suicide theory?"

"I mean, it could be true."

"Did Kason share his fear? I know he said it in the halls."

I slide my phone out of my pocket and hit up his profile. There are already tons of posts from friends, saying how shocked they are and how much they'll miss him.

With trembling hands, I scroll until I find it. "Drowning," I whisper. "This isn't a murder-suicide. . . . Syd, it's just *murder*."

"Hell, no," she mutters, grabbing my phone to check for her-self. As if I would make this up. "You're crazy."

"What else could it be?" I ask.

"I don't know, but we don't have a serial killer on the loose."

"I never said that! There must be a reason why only Debbie and Kason were killed."

Although we don't know it was only them, but since we haven't heard about anyone else being dead or going missing, it's not a ridiculous assumption to make.

"Such as?"

"I'm not sure. I barely knew them, but Debbie left that party for a reason."

"That's not unusual."

"Yeah, but it's still weird. Who hated them?"

"The hippies, goths, band geeks, nerds—"

"All right, all right. Who hated them enough to kill them?"

Her teeth snap together.

We all know they were disliked by everyone "below" them, the ones the popular kids picked on or overlooked, but to kill them over dumb high school stuff? I'm not sure.

"We need to get to homeroom," Syd says.

I really don't think much work is going to get done today.

We walk past whispering cliques of students, all having the same conversation, though some are kinder about Debbie and Kason than others.

Syd and I walk through the door and take a seat. She leans closer. "Look."

I follow her line of sight. Tayley and Mariella are outside the window, huddled together, crying and wiping their tears, with two teachers and the principal surrounding them.

They've never been the nicest people, but my heart aches for them. They've lost two friends.

Syd frowns. "Tayley's overdoing it."

"Sydney!"

"What? Just look at her, doubled over. If you watch, every few seconds, she glances around to see who's watching."

"Her friends are *dead*."

"I'm not saying she's not upset, but I'm also not saying the girl wouldn't use this to her advantage. With Debbie gone, she's got a better run at queen bee."

"Dude, you have got to shut up before someone hears you!"

Besides, Mariella already has that title.

"Oh, I'm not going to say this to anyone else."

"We can hear you, though," a voice I know suddenly pipes up. Syd's eyes snap to me, and we both freeze.

I look over my shoulder, and my stomach drops.

"What are you doing over here, Axel?"

He usually sits on the other side of the room, in the far corner.

He smirks down at us and takes the seat directly behind mine. "Just thought I could use a change of scenery."

Syd waves her hand, dismissing him. "Whatever, loner. We weren't talking to you."

Axel's eyes narrow. "The cops are going to want to know if anyone had a grudge against Kason and Debbie."

"Back off," Syd hisses and turns around.

"What's wrong with you, Axel?" I ask.

"You told the cops that I uncharacteristically went to a party on the same night two students were found dead. That's what's wrong with me."

"We *just* talked about this! I thought *you* were the one found dead. Sorry that I cared."

He tilts his head.

"I never thought you were the killer," I tell him. Though I'm lying, because the thought did briefly cross my mind. It might again if he keeps glaring like he wants to reach over his desk and strangle me.

"Oh my God, Iz, ignore him! He's trying to piss you off."

I twist in my seat and face forward. Why is he trying to get to me? Surely he can't blame me for being worried that he might have died. Could he be worried that the cops might seriously think he's involved?

After a speech about Debbie and Kason in homeroom, we're all sent to first period. Some kids took today off, so it feels a bit empty, and some have gone to speak to the guidance counselors.

In AP English, Tayley is absent but Justin is sitting at the back on his own.

I take a breath for courage and walk up to his table. My heart beats faster the closer I get. I wipe my hands on my jeans.

"Justin?"

His eyes flick up but his head stays tilted down.

"I just wanted to see how you're doing. Which is dumb, I know. Obviously, you're not great. I'm sorry about Kason . . . and Debbie."

He blinks twice before he replies, "Yeah. Thanks, Izzy."

I smile and turn around, wincing.

That went great.

Not.

Axel smirks again as I sit down beside him.

"Shut up," I mutter.

"Didn't say a word."

Mr. Morrison shuffles into the classroom and pushes his thick-framed glasses up. He clears his throat. "All right, class. I understand that we're all emotional today. We're in shock and grieving the loss of two of our students. If anyone feels that they need to be excused, do let me know. If you need to speak to anyone today, guidance is open to all at any point." He makes eye contact with me.

"Are you still making us do work?" Sadie asks.

"Yeah, we shouldn't be here at all," her best friend, April, adds.

"We still have a curriculum to follow," he replies. "Do you need to speak with someone?"

They both shake their heads, slumping lower in their seats. They're both athletes. Neither of them was friends with Debbie or Kason. In fact, I've overheard them bitching about that group on more than one occasion.

"They did it," Axel whispers in my ear.

I side-glare at him. "No part of this is funny."

How can he joke about a double murder like that?

He leans back, admonished. Good.

"Did the cops say anything to you about what they think

happened?" he asks after we're instructed to work on our partner assignment.

"Of course not."

"What was the scene like?"

My jaw drops. "Are you *serious*?"

"You got me involved in this, Izzy."

My stomach twists into a knot. I really wish I could move to another table. There is something seriously wrong with him.

"But you're not involved, Axel. The cops talked to you like they talked to me and will probably talk to half the students and staff here. That doesn't make you involved; you're just being morbidly nosy."

He shrugs. "Call it what you want. You can't tell me that you wouldn't want to know if this was the other way around. You're no different."

"I might want to know, but I wouldn't ask!"

"Right, because you would never speak up about anything. You can't even tell that hockey meathead that you like him."

My face burns. "I don't like him."

"Sure you don't."

I grit my teeth and somehow make it through the entire period without punching Axel's pretty face.

nine

IZZY

I walk into the guidance office and take a seat. It smells like artificial fresh air in here from some scented sticks on a side table. Above those is a bulletin board with flyers about mental health and a number of help groups.

None for seeing a dead body.

There are eight smaller rooms inside this one so each counselor can speak confidentially to students. It looks like an ant's nest, and with the tiny windows, it feels like one, too.

On the opposite end of the bench is Tayley. She twirls her long red hair around her finger. I've not seen her in any classes today. She looks over with puffy, blotchy eyes and sits taller. She must have a lot of questions for me. Everyone knows it was me and Syd who found Debbie.

"Hello, Izzy," she says.

We're doing this. She never talks to me unless it's to be mean. "Hi."

She takes a ragged breath like she's about to cry again. "You found . . ."

I nod, my heart seizing. "I did."

"Was she . . . Did it look like it hurt? I hate to think of her suffering."

Debbie's crushed skull flashes in my mind. "I don't think she suffered," I say. "I think it must have been very quick."

She presses her lips together and nods solemnly. Hopefully knowing that is comforting. No one wanted Debbie to suffer.

Well, almost no one.

The killer didn't care.

Axel seemed to revel in the details.

"Do you know why she left the party?" I ask.

"Kason kissed Mariella. Debbie had a crush on him forever, and they dated for a while, but he called it off. This was last year, so I thought she was over it."

There is no way she would tell me all of this if I hadn't been the one who found Debbie.

"Did Kason follow her when she left?"

"I didn't see him leave, but he must have gone after her. He was at the party for a little while after she left, definitely ten minutes or so, then I can't remember. Debbie didn't live near the town square, so she must have arranged to meet him."

So did the killer just get lucky to have them in the same place alone? Though we don't actually know if they were killed at the same time. If they were together, wouldn't one of them make noise or call for help while the killer was trying to get the other?

Maybe it *was* a murder-suicide, with either Debbie or Kason the killer. I suppose she could have jumped backward off the building. It's not impossible.

"Do you know if Debbie was . . . suicidal?" I ask.

Tayley sucks in a deep breath. "The cops and Debbie's parents already asked me that. No, she wasn't. She might have been a bit emotional sometimes, but that doesn't mean she was depressed or suicidal."

No, it doesn't, but it doesn't mean she wasn't, either.

"Are you okay?"

She shakes her head. "Not at all."

"I can drive you home if you don't want to stay here."

"You don't need to be nice to me because my friends are dead."

"I don't know, seems like a good time to be nice."

Her smile is small but visible. "I guess it does. Thanks, but I don't want to be home. Mariella's here. Justin and the guys from the team, too. I want to be around friends. My mom would fuss a lot, and it's not helpful."

"Izzy, are you ready?" Lara asks.

Tayley smiles again and looks away.

I grab my bag and follow Lara into her shoebox office. A desk, three chairs, and a filing cabinet is about all that can fit in here. The tiny window lets in a little bit of natural light.

Lara closes the door and sits behind the desk. I take the seat near the window and look out at the perfect white clouds that dominate the sky. They look like they're threatening more snow.

"How are you, Izzy?"

"I'm okay."

"Anything you talk about in here is confidential, you know that."

"Fine. I'm scared and still in shock, I think. The whole thing was . . . surreal, you know? I don't think anyone expects to ever see something like that. Besides cops and FBI agents."

I take a breath and she smiles sympathetically. She's probably going to write up a report about how unstable I sound.

She tucks her short bob behind her ears. "Being in shock is completely natural in these circumstances. Is there any part of last night you would like to talk about?"

"I've had to talk about it a lot. The cops went over it more than once . . . then my parents wanted to talk on the way home. I feel like I've relived that moment a thousand times."

I would much rather forget it.

"It's fine if you don't want to discuss it right now."

"She was lying in the snow in her little yellow dress. When she was on the roof, she must have just been in that dress. No coat. She would have been freezing . . . and scared."

Lara's forehead creases. "I can't imagine the pain she must have been going through in those brief moments before."

Before she jumped? Does Lara think it was suicide?

"We don't know how she died yet," I say.

"Oh?"

"I mean, we know *how* but not whether she jumped or was pushed."

Lara keeps her pale eyes on me. They're almost as light as Axel's. "That's true, we don't know the details yet. I didn't mean to insinuate anything."

Nor do we know how Kason ended up in the water. The water is deep, and I don't know if he could swim, but surely he would float on his back while shouting for help. If he was able to.

The killer picked a rather busy part of town to kill people in. Though I guess all the businesses were closed at that hour and only a few people live in the apartments above them, so it's not like it would be impossible to kill them there. Ruby lives above the café and heard nothing until the cops were banging on her door.

Kason and Debbie would have shouted for help if someone grabbed them.

So then . . . if it was murder, they had to know their murderer.

"You look like you're holding a lot in, Izzy. It's okay to let it out, whatever it is."

I twirl my long ponytail around my fingers. "I'm just confused. I don't like not knowing what happened or why. That stupid death meme, then this . . . it's unnerving. Have you heard anything? The cops can't think they both took their own lives, surely?"

"I spoke to Officer Duggan earlier, but he couldn't share any details. I'm sure they will investigate thoroughly."

"Do you think I'm crazy for not believing the suicide thing?"

"Not at all. It's natural to question things. But what I would really like to know is how you're handling what you saw."

"I try not to think about it. I never saw a dead body before last night."

"It's a traumatic experience."

"Yeah."

That's exactly how it felt and still feels. I don't know what I'm supposed to do, what I need. I'm numb and desperate for answers. Why them?

I wish someone would wave a wand and take away the image of Debbie.

"I don't want to talk much about it. Not until it makes sense to me anyway."

"Do you think it will ever make sense?" Lara asks.

"Probably not, but the more I talk, the more muddled things become."

"It's usually the other way around," she says gently.

"Yeah, well, I don't trust myself not to be influenced by what other people say."

"What are others saying, Izzy?"

"Lots of things, murder, suicide pact, murder-suicide. I'm sure you've heard. Gossip is spreading like wildfire out there."

"Why do you think the others will change your mind?"

"Not necessarily change my mind. It's just that I start to think about their opinions and ignore my gut. Until we know more, I'd rather not obsess."

"Do you think that's going to be possible?"

I slump back in my seat and cross my feet, my pink Converse high-tops too cheery for a day like this. "Nope. But I can try, right?"

Lara tilts her head. "I'd be lying if I said I'm not concerned about you."

"What do you want me to talk about?"

"Nothing if you don't want to, but I don't want you suffering in silence either."

"I saw a dead body and I need time to figure it out. That's all. I'm not bottling anything up, and I do talk to Syd."

"Good, I'm glad you're talking to someone. Do you think you could make me a promise?"

"Depends on what it is."

"You'll come back when you feel ready? It can be one of the other counselors if you'd prefer. Or even someone outside school."

"Sure. I can make that promise."

"I'm glad to hear that. Is there anything you need from me right now?"

"Nope."

"Do you feel okay to stay at school? You will be allowed some time off if you need it. Please do accept that if being here gets too difficult."

"You mean because everyone is talking about me."

"That's not the first thing that came to mind."

"I'm sorry," I say, shaking my head. "I don't mean to be stand-offish."

"It's usually that, silent, or hysterical."

"Silent seems like the best one."

"I don't know. I would rather some emotion and interaction."

"I've not been very helpful with that."

"You've said everything you're ready to for now, right?"

I nod.

Her deep pink lips smile. "Then that's fine."

"Should I go now?"

She shrugs. "That's up to you. For the next fifty minutes, you have my full attention. Use that how you wish."

I wring my hands and then look up at her. "I wish I could stop thinking about murder."

"Since last night?" she asks.

"Yes. I don't usually think about something so awful. It's just . . . the meme thing and two students dying the same day, in the exact way they'd feared. That's no coincidence."

Lara nods but doesn't say anything.

"I think someone killed them. . . ." I take a breath and place my hands on her desk. "And I'm scared because we have no idea if that person is finished."

ten

IZZY

Lara let me go after my *the killer might not be done* bomb, because I stopped talking, but I noticed her watching me very carefully. I think she might spend the rest of our allotted time filling up a notebook or two about me.

My file at Rock Bay High is about to get a whole lot thicker.

I walk along the deserted corridor but stop when I turn the corner and see Axel talking to Officer Duggan.

Sliding behind the lockers, I peek at their interaction.

What are they doing? Axel told me the cops had paid him a visit, so what would they have to talk about now? The exchange looks tense, both standing tall and talking in hushed tones. I can't make out what they say, but Axel is frowning—not unusual, to be fair—and Officer Duggan has his arms folded strongly across his chest.

What's going on here?

The cops haven't spoken to me again. Why would they need

a second chat with Axel? Unless it was him asking to talk to Officer Duggan.

Morbid curiosity or something more?

"What are you doing?"

I startle, grip my heart, and spin around.

Justin stands in front of me, one eyebrow raised and arms folded just like the cop's. "Well?"

"Nothing," I say, my heart fluttering from being caught snooping and being so close to him.

"You're spying on the freak and that cop."

"Where did you come from?"

"Guidance. Same place as you, I'm guessing. Why are you being shady?"

"I'm not. I wanted to speak with Officer Duggan, but Axel is . . . so I'm waiting."

"It looks like you're hiding."

"I'm not hiding. I'm leaning against a wall, waiting."

His green eyes sparkle with amusement. "Sure you are. Got a crush on the freak?"

"He's not a freak, Justin."

"That's a yes."

Does he really not know that it's him I'm crushing on?

I can't expect him to be on top of his game: he's just found out his best friend is dead. I can take a bit of attitude. If it was Syd who was found dead, I'm not sure I would be the friendliest person either.

"The cops are everywhere in school now," he says. "I saw

them arrive while I was with Mykelti. She's the hot guidance counselor."

I roll my eyes. "They'll want to talk to the people who knew Kason and Debbie."

"Obviously. They're searching for their killer."

My spine prickles. "Why do you say that?"

"Because they were killed. Come on, you can't tell me you think this was accidental," he says as if I'm slow.

"Does anyone think it *was* accidental?"

"Exactly." He looks over my shoulder. "The cop is headed in this direction. Later."

I watch him walk out the main entrance. Is he leaving school? Maybe he's going home.

I turn my attention back to Officer Duggan and smile as he reaches me. Axel has disappeared. My pulse thuds with unease.

"Izzy, how are you?" he asks.

"What's going on now? Do you know what happened to Debbie and Kason?"

"We're investigating."

"Uh-huh, investigating what exactly?"

"Izzy . . ."

"Fine. I'm just wondering how worried I should be. Don't we have a right to know if someone is targeting students?" I snap my teeth together, my heart almost breaking through my rib cage.

I can't believe I just said that to a cop.

He squares his shoulders. "Izzy, I understand that you're scared after what you saw, but you need to leave the investigation to the police."

"I just want to know."

He nods. "As soon as we have any new information, you will know."

His eyes slide away as he says that. I'm not stupid. I know that the cops don't always release all the information about cases or investigations. Do they already know something they're not willing to share?

"See you later," he adds, and heads off in the direction of the principal's office.

I walk to my last period in time for the bell and sit at my desk. While the class whispers and scribbles notes on paper, I pretend to focus on my textbook, but I'm too distracted.

I glide my pen over my notebook so that it looks like I'm doing something and the teacher won't question me. If she asks to see what I've done, she'll find wiggly lines, and I'll be in trouble.

Earlier, Officer Duggan never told me someone *isn't* targeting students. Wouldn't he have done that so I wouldn't worry? I rub the ache behind my forehead.

Officer Duggan is a friend of my dad's. Maybe he was warning me as best he could.

Justin looms over me, making me jolt in my seat. He stands tall in front of my desk with his arms folded over his chest.

My brain short-circuits.

"I thought you went home?" I ask.

"I didn't," he says.

"You left. Where did you go?"

"That's none of your business."

I wince at his harsh tone. He's only just started to acknowledge that I exist and I'm annoying him.

His reaction is suspicious, though.

I shove my textbook in my bag and shrug. "Whatever. Did you want something?"

"I don't think I've ever heard you say 'whatever' to anyone."

He almost sounds impressed. I try not to cringe.

"Justin, it's been a really long day. What do you want?"

He watches me. "All right. I didn't want anything. You didn't hear the bell, and I didn't want you to spend all night here."

Oh. The room is empty; even the teacher has left. I would have realized eventually.

"How very charitable of you," I reply.

"You're angry with me. I can't imagine why."

I stand and start to walk. Much to my confusion—and delight—he follows. "I'm not angry with you, Justin. I just want to get home."

"Aren't you going to Puck's?"

It's a great miracle that I don't trip over my own feet. He's never asked me that before. *Ever.* "Um, no. . . . Why?"

"Everyone's going there to have a drink for Kason and Debbie."

I stop and he almost walks into me.

"They are?" I ask. I haven't heard anything, but I haven't seen Syd since lunch. She's the one who knows what goes on around here.

"You should be there."

"Oh, I don't know if they would want that."

"It's a respect thing, Izzy. I know you weren't friends, but this is about—"

"You're right," I say. "It doesn't matter what my relationship with them was like."

"I *am* right."

"I'll see you there," I say.

He nods and walks away. Instead of heading for the exit, he goes deeper into the school.

Okay then.

Syd is leaning against my car when I get to the parking lot. I tread carefully, as the ground is layered with ice despite the salt that's been scattered.

"Puck's," she says.

"You heard, too. Not that I'm surprised."

She smiles but it doesn't quite reach her sage eyes. "Let's roll, Iz."

We get into our respective vehicles and leave school.

The roads are treacherous. The snow from last night has compacted despite the town's efforts to clear them, so it takes longer than usual to get to Puck's. I pass Ruby's café, keeping my eyes in front of me so I don't see where Debbie died. I don't look right either, so as not to glance at the river Kason was floating in.

I assume, given how easily he was found in a storm, that the killer didn't attempt to weigh down his body. Nor did he try to hide Debbie's body.

This asshole wants us to know what he's done. Or she.

Syd is ahead and gets the final space in the parking lot closest to Puck's. I continue around the corner and park.

It's only three-thirty, but the sky is full of gray clouds, making it darker than it should be. Most of our days in winter are dark.

I pull my coat tight around myself as the bitter wind stings my skin.

"Back off!"

Jumping, I turn to peek at the voice. Axel's talking to a guy who was in my sister's year, Tristan Sykes. They look up at the same time, as if they sense I'm watching.

Axel frowns. "Izzy."

"Just going to Puck's," I say, walking up to them with jelly legs.

"See you around," Axel replies and walks across the road.

"Axel?" Tristan calls.

Axel waves his hand over his head. "Bye, Tristan."

"Everything okay?" I ask.

Tristan clears his throat. "My cousin only has one mood. How's everything? Lia doing okay?"

Tristan and Axel are cousins? I never would have guessed, but then people might not think Miyah and I are.

"Lia's great, loving college. Things with me . . ."

His dark eyes widen. "That was really stupid of me. I heard that you found Debbie. I can't imagine what that was like, Iz."

"Sucks," I say, condensing it to the simplest form.

He smiles sympathetically, running his hand over his short black hair. "Yeah, I bet."

"Now I have to go into Puck's and have a drink in her and Kason's memory."

"You don't want to do that?"

I rub my hands together to warm them up. "It's not that I

don't. I guess it just feels hypocritical, since we didn't really like each other. They'll all be in there all evening, too."

"Look, I have thirty minutes before I need to be back at work. You want to take a walk and you can talk about it, if you feel like it?"

"A walk?"

"Why not? Might clear your head."

He's only doing this because I'm Lia's little sister and he feels sorry for me. But I really don't want to go and listen to people talking about Debbie and Kason just yet. I know they're dead.

"Sure, a quick walk before Puck's would be good."

We cross the empty road and head along the sidewalk.

"I totally didn't know you and Axel were cousins."

"On our dads' sides. They weren't close."

"Really? You have different surnames, so I never put it together. No offense, but you guys don't seem close, either."

We walk past the dock, and Tristan raises his hands to a few people on a fishing boat.

"His mom never put my uncle on the birth certificate because he was never around, and no, we're not close. He's moody, thinks the whole world is against him, and keeps to himself. We grew up together, but I don't know much about him."

They grew up together? I didn't know that, either. Not that I know Tristan that well.

He waves to someone else, on another docked boat.

"Do you work here now?" I ask.

"Yeah. I left the factory last month."

"You like being on the boats?"

He nods. "Long days and hard work, but I like it."

Lia and Tristan belonged to the same circle—the popular one. Most of them are at various colleges around the country now, but Tristan's dad was a fisherman and owned a boat. Tristan sailed a lot with Lia and their group last year, before their senior year ended and they all went their separate ways.

"That's cool. I haven't seen you around in *ages*."

He twists toward me as we walk. "That's because you've always thought of me as Lia's annoying friend."

"I did not!" I say, but that's not strictly true. I've never found him annoying, but he was just Lia's friend to me. I never really thought about him much at all.

My heart beats harder as we walk past the area where Debbie died. It's still taped off, but there's no evidence that a body was there anymore.

"You okay?" he asks.

"That's where she was."

"Keep going, Iz. I'll walk you to Puck's the back way."

"You don't need to walk me there."

"I do, actually." He scratches his jaw. "I mean, after last night . . ."

The fact that someone killed two teenagers yesterday.

"Thanks," I say.

"So, tell me how senior year is going, before yesterday. What colleges have you applied to?"

"Just about every single one in Florida, and I'm crossing my fingers for Florida State. I'm ready for heat. Being a senior is okay,

I guess. Not much different, except people talk a lot more about grades and tests."

"Yes, they do."

"You aced those, Tristan."

He smiles. "They're not everything. What you need to do is work out what makes you happy."

"I like that."

"Any ideas?"

"I want to change the world. Nothing too big, really," I say.

Laughing, he starts to walk down to the dock.

"Where are you going?" I ask.

"Can I show you my boat before we go back?"

"Your boat?"

"I made that sound cooler than it is. I inherited my dad's company after he died. I'm the captain now."

I follow him down. "That's awesome. I really hope you have a hat and a parrot."

"Captain, Iz, not pirate."

I laugh and take his hand as he helps me step onto the boat. It's one of the smaller ones docked here but will probably crew about fifteen.

"I love it. I'm sure your dad would be happy knowing you've taken over the family business."

His smile falters just slightly, and he grabs hold of the side of the boat. What did I say wrong? "Nothing beats being on the water," he says.

I look out to the water and follow the route across the bay to the sea, but then something close catches my eye. "Hey, what's that?"

"What?" he asks, leaning over the side where I'm looking.

"Do you see it?" I ask, pointing. "Right there."

His eyebrows pinch together. "Yeah. Let me get something to grab it."

I hear him move away, but I'm too focused on whatever is floating in the freezing water. It looks like material, but the water is dark and the sun is blocked by thick clouds.

My breath comes out in short pants, and I can see it curl in front of me.

I gasp as something flies over my head. Spinning, I grip the edge of the boat.

"Sorry," Tristan says, dipping a hook into the water.

"I'm jumpy," I tell him.

He pulls the material close and lifts the pole up. I back away as he brings it onto the deck. "Don't touch it," he says. "Looks like it's from a shirt."

The material is red-and-black-checked with frayed edges, like it was ripped.

"Tristan . . . Do you think this is from Kason? I don't remember him wearing that, but I can't remember what shirt he had on."

Tristan meets my eyes and lays the pole down. "Him. Or whoever drowned him."

My jaw drops.

If it is, that means Kason fought hard.

eleven

IZZY

"We should call the cops," I say, staring at the ripped shirt. "There might be evidence left behind even if it's been in the water."

"Yeah. I mean, it could be nothing, but Kason was killed just over there," he replies, nodding his chin in the direction of the police tape near the end dock. He pulls his phone out of his pocket and dials.

I crouch down to get a closer look, as if there will be a name label inside it. There's only a bit of fabric here anyway. There are no buttons or holes, but there is a seam. It's probably from the bottom of the shirt.

Did Kason rip this from his killer's back as he tried to escape?

"They're on their way," Tristan says, hanging up. "I can't believe this is happening here."

"Nothing ever happens here," I mutter, standing up.

"Let's step off the boat, Iz. Do you need to get coffee or something? You must be freezing."

It's only as he says the words that I realize how cold I am. Vapors rise in front of me with each breath.

"You're out here, too."

"I'm used to being out here by now, working on the boats six days a week. The cold doesn't bother me."

There's a *Frozen* joke in there somewhere, but I've lost my sense of humor.

"I'm fine. I guess the cops will want to talk to us."

"I was going to run to the café and get you coffee, Izzy. We can't go anywhere," he says, zipping his hoodie right to the top.

"Oh. Actually, that does sound good."

My phone beeps as Tristan jogs along the dock and across the road to Ruby's. My frozen fingers are stiff as I awkwardly press the keys to reply.

Syd: *Where are you??*

Me: *Chatting with Tristan. Be there soon.*

I look over to the dock at the end, the one with Matthew's initials and puck scratched into the post. The one Kason was found by. He must have been petrified.

Turning away, I tuck my hands in my pockets and pray that Tristan comes back soon.

I step closer to the end of the dock and lean against the post. Maybe I should have gone with Tristan. The cops would just have to wait for us.

Something catches my eye at the end of the square right by Puck's diner. Or, rather, someone. A person wearing a dark hoodie turns away from me and disappears around the corner.

A shiver slides down my spine.

Was that someone watching me?

I glance back to Ruby's, willing Tristan to walk out the door. What's taking him so long?

I'm being paranoid. There are loads of people going to Puck's today to pay their respects to Debbie and Kason.

My breath quickens to the point that all I see is vapor now. If someone came for me, would I see them before it's too late? My own breath would be aiding my killer.

Calm down. You're not about to be murdered.

It's creepy when the town is so quiet. I like noise and people. Where is everyone?

The only person I've seen is Tristan. But he couldn't be the one watching me. Tristan's hoodie is a zip-up. I don't think I remember seeing a zip on whoever was watching me. Did I?

I'm about to crawl out of my skin or hide on a boat when I see Tristan jog across the road, carefully holding a takeout cup in each hand.

He beats the cops and hands me a vanilla latte.

His hair doesn't look like it's been ruffled from a hood.

"You do still like them, don't you?" he asks. "I never forgot how obsessed Lia was with them. She always brought them to you."

"Definitely. Thanks."

I wrap both hands around it and take a sip.

"Sorry I took so long. There was a line."

"That's okay," I reply, shrugging one shoulder as if it was no big deal and I didn't almost freak out.

"Ah, looks like they're here," Tristan says, nodding his chin toward the road.

Sheriff Rosetta and Officer Duggan park on the side of the road and walk along the dock toward us.

"Isabel, this is becoming a habit," the sheriff says.

"We both found it," Tristan says. "We're not sure it's anything, but since Kason was found in the water near here . . ."

Sheriff looks away from me. "You did the right thing, son."

The Rosettas and the Sykeses were longtime friends. I remember Lia saying that the sheriff would often be at Tristan's for cookouts. She said she was scared to even sip a beer in case he caught her.

"Where was it?" Officer Duggan asks as they both hop onto the boat.

"Close to the front of my boat," he replies. "We pulled it out with that hook. Neither of us touched it."

Sheriff nods. "Good. Bag this up, Carl."

He turns to us. "It's probably nothing."

"Kason wasn't wearing that," I tell him.

"I remember. It doesn't necessarily mean this is connected to the incident last night."

By "incident," he means double murder.

I sip my latte as we answer the few questions they have for us. There's not much we can tell them, really. We found the scrap of material and pulled it out of the water. You couldn't get a more boring story.

"Let me walk you to Puck's, Iz," Tristan says before turning back to the sheriff. "Do you need anything more from us?"

Sheriff shakes his head. "I know where you both live if we do."

Why does that sound like he's suspicious of us—of me, probably? I certainly didn't choose to find any of this. I would prefer to not have seen a dead body.

"Of course. Come on," Tristan says to me while holding the sheriff's gaze in a bit of a standoff.

Okay. Tristan doesn't seem a big fan. He probably doesn't see much of the sheriff since he lost his dad last year.

I grab his wrist and pull. "Let's just get out of here, Tristan."

He turns and I drop his arm.

When we're back on the sidewalk, he asks, "Why did he sound like he thinks this is your fault?"

"You picked up on that too, huh? I have no clue."

"Don't let him intimidate you, Iz."

"I won't," I reply as if I'm tough enough to stand up to a cop. But really, they haven't been unfair to me.

We walk around the corner, the long way, down the back alley. The buildings here are packed tight, backing on each other with only a small gap for industrial trash between.

"Is Lia coming back soon? I haven't spoken to her in a while."

"I'm not sure. Probably soon. I thought you'd keep in touch. You two never . . ."

He chuckles. "No, we never did anything, and we didn't fall out, either. She's a good friend, that's it. Would that have been a problem?"

What?

"Huh? No," I reply, frowning. Why would he think it might be?

Dipping his head, he nods as we stop outside Puck's. This conversation is getting a bit weird.

"Think you could do me a favor?" he asks, finally raising his eyes to mine.

"What's that?"

"Call me if you need a lift or someone to walk with."

"Well, I don't have your number, so . . ."

Smirking, he holds his hand out. I finally see the family resemblance to Axel when he smirks. Knowing what Tristan wants, I place my phone on his palm and let him punch his number in.

"See you later, Iz," he says, passing me back my phone and crossing the road without looking.

What just happened? He asked me to call him. Does he actually want me to call him? All right, I need to calm down and not get ahead of myself. He's only worried about my safety because of Lia.

Why would he ask if I'd be okay if something had happened between them? Why would that matter?

Do *not* read too much into this.

Do I like Tristan like that?

Oh, great.

Syd bursts out of the door as I reach the entrance to Puck's. "Dude, *where* have you been?"

I take another sip of my latte and follow her inside. "I was just talking to Tristan. I told you."

I'm half tempted to tell Syd about my conversation with him, but she wouldn't be logical. She would tell me that he's secretly in love with me and I should go for it.

When we're not around almost the entire senior class, I'll tell her what I found in the water.

Puck's is packed with people. I dodge a few as I follow Syd to her table. Someone has printed off pictures of Debbie and Kason and stuck them to the walls. Matthew doesn't seem to mind as he hands out baskets of fries.

At the center of each table is a small candle in a glass holder. That's new for today, too. My throat swells.

"What's going on?" Syd says as we slide into a booth. There are three milkshakes on the table, two half empty and the other full to the brim—mine.

"Who else is sitting with us?" I ask.

She points to Miyah, who's talking to a couple of guys from the team. "Your uncle dropped her off and is picking her up again in an hour, apparently."

"Cool. Thanks for this," I say, pulling the striped straw toward my mouth. "So, Tristan and I found something in the water."

Her eyes bulge. "Another body?"

"No! A scrap of ripped material. Red-and-black-checked, looked like it was from a flannel shirt. Kason wasn't wearing one."

"Hell no, Kason would never wear anything like that. He'd call it lumberjack wear. Whose do you think—oh, I get it. You think it belongs to whoever killed them."

I hold my finger up and swallow a mouthful of banana milkshake. "*Maybe*. The sheriff has taken it, but we don't know anything for sure."

"Right. We shouldn't get ahead of ourselves."

"We're going to feel really stupid if their deaths were accidental and we've spent all this time letting our imaginations run wild."

We sound like we're trying to convince ourselves. There is absolutely no conviction in our voices at all. It's like when I tell myself that I won't have dessert when I go out to eat. An hour later and I'm digging into a massive wedge of fudge cake.

Syd twiddles her neon-green striped straw in her fingers. "You thinking that we're talking bull right now, too?"

"Uh-huh," I reply.

Miyah drops down beside me in the booth. "Forty minutes and counting. I swear my dad is treating me like an infant. What're you two gossiping about?"

Syd opens her mouth to spill my gossip, but I get there first.

"We're talking about the candles being a nice touch."

Syd eyes me suspiciously but goes along with it. "Tayley said Debbie burned candles in her room a lot."

"It's so sad," Miyah says. "My school is making me have daily therapy for two weeks at least. Dad wants me to do it for a month. How about you, Iz?"

"Yeah, not daily, but I've got guidance counseling. It's awesome you could come," I say, bumping her arm with my own.

"It took a lot of convincing, but I wanted to be with you two after yesterday. I'm not allowed to leave Puck's until Dad comes in to pick me up, but at least I'm here. You freaking, Iz?"

"Yep," Syd says, answering for me.

"I'm doing fine, *considering*."

I might not be as strong or assertive as they are, but that doesn't mean I'm falling apart.

"We know. I just worry about my little cousin," says Miyah.

"I'm younger by four months."

She picks up her milkshake and shrugs.

Justin walks by and does a double take. "I wasn't sure if you'd make it when Syd arrived alone."

I meet his eyes, surprising myself by not instantly looking away embarrassed. "I said I would."

"I'm sure Tristan had something very important to tell you."

"How did you know I was with Tristan?"

Could it have been Justin outside when I was waiting for Tristan and the cops?

"I saw you walk off with him when you arrived."

I didn't see him then. Not that I was looking, I suppose.

He has never much cared what I do. Why is he now super concerned with my movements? I told him I was coming. There seems to be an issue with the fact that I didn't come straight here, and I have no clue what that could be. It makes no sense, since we barely spoke before now.

"Is everything okay, Justin?" Syd asks.

Miyah snorts.

"Fine," he replies without looking at her.

"Do you want to sit with us?" I ask, completely ignoring Miyah's proud, Cheshire Cat grin.

"Thanks, but I'm doing the rounds, thanking everyone for coming."

We didn't get a thank-you. I got attitude for arriving later than he would have liked. I hope he's been to speak to the other students who got here after me if he's mad at late arrivals.

Somehow, I doubt that.

"That's nice of you."

"He was my best friend."

I nod. "I know, and I really am sorry for your loss."

He holds my gaze for a second, then walks off.

twelve

IZZY

Syd tilts her head to the side when he's gone. "Well, that was weird."

Miyah speaks a heartbeat later. "You asked him to sit, Iz. I'm so proud of you!"

I ignore her again. "He's mad at me."

Miyah waves her hand. "He has no right to be. Ugh, I should have told him where to go."

"Stand down, Pink Ranger. Justin just lost his best friend. He's grieving and wants this part, this vigil, to be perfect."

Syd laughs. "If he does it again, Miyah, you can get him."

I smile at my best friend. "You're not helping."

"Tayley's crying on Justin's shoulder," Syd says, looking at a booth across the room. "He looks *so* uncomfortable."

"Have you seen Mariella?" I ask.

Miyah nods. "She was here earlier. Maybe she went to the bathroom."

My spine stiffens. *"Maybe?"* Someone around here is killing. "I'm going to check."

"You're going to check?" Syd asks.

I sip my milkshake. "The last time we lost someone, she turned up dead. I just want to make sure Mariella's okay."

Syd raises her hands in surrender, knowing that I'm going to go no matter what she says. I leave our table, hearing Miyah compliment my new "kickass" attitude, and push my way through the crowd.

Mariella is nowhere to be seen in the diner, and she would definitely be with Tayley. I've never seen her sit with anyone other than her clique.

On my way to the bathroom, I ignore Justin's eyes following me and push the door open. When I say "ignore," I'm not referring to the somersaults my heart is doing.

"Mariella, are you in here?" I call, stepping into the room.

A toilet flushes, and a silver cubicle door opens. Mariella steps out and flicks her long, heavily highlighted hair over her shoulder. She always looks perfect—manicured nails, neat eyebrows, rosy cheeks, expensive clothes.

She dabs a tissue below her lined eyes and turns her nose up. "Izzy Tindall. Why are *you* looking for *me*?"

My stomach twists until I feel sick. God, she can be horrible. "I . . . just couldn't find you."

Her painted lips curl into an ugly sneer. "So?"

That's surely not a surprise after last night.

"Well, I was worried."

"Because my friends are dead. What, you think I'm next?

Like, someone is out here killing off the popular kids? You're safe, then, huh. There must be a long list of dorky suspects. Are you on it, Izzy?"

Debbie's death has not made Mariella a better person.

I bite my tongue, because although I want to tell her to go to hell, I don't actually want to sink way down to her level.

Taking a breath, I push away my irritation. "I don't care about not being popular."

"Sure you don't. Everyone pretends like they're okay with not being popular, but deep down, we all want to be on top."

"It depends on what your idea of being on top is."

"I bet you liked seeing her like that."

My spine straightens of its own accord. "Excuse me?"

"Debbie. Like, I bet you really enjoyed that."

"How could you even think that? You're hateful, and I can't believe I ever worried about you."

I turn around and walk out of the bathroom. Syd and Miyah stand when they see me storming toward our table with clenched fists.

"What happened?" Syd looks over my shoulder as Mariella leaves the restroom. "She was in there. She's fine. Why do you not look fine?"

My hands shake with anger. "As soon as Miyah gets picked up, we're leaving. She's horrible."

"Oookay."

"What happened?" Miyah asks. "I'll kick her ass, no problem."

I slump down in my seat and tell them everything.

Miyah shoots daggers at Mariella with her eyes.

Syd pushes a basket of fries toward me that weren't here when I left. "Forget her, Iz. She's not worth it."

Uncle Samar picks Miyah up, but Syd and I ordered hot dogs so we stay an extra ten minutes. I seethe through every bite.

How dare Mariella say those things to me?

As soon as we're done, I leap to my feet and Syd follows me to the door.

Justin turns as we pass him, but he doesn't say anything.

The cold sinks into my skin as soon as we're outside, but I'm too livid to care.

"Are you going to calm down?" she asks as we walk to the parking lot.

"Not yet. She seriously turned up the bitch tonight."

"I thought we were looking past that today?"

"Didn't you hear me before? She accused me of liking seeing Debbie dead, so . . ."

She scowls. "I should go back in there and tell her exactly what it was like to find a dead person."

"I just want to get home. My parents won't like me being out late."

"I'll walk you to your car, Iz."

"No, it's fine. I'm not far and there are plenty of people around." A few people are out now that it's past five. A few carry flowers, probably to add to the memorial near Ruby's café.

There's still a cop car parked up near Tristan's boat.

"Text me when you get home."

I nod. "You got it."

We wave as she gets into her car, and I carry on down the street, ignoring stares from people passing by.

I get in my car and drive straight home.

My mom and dad are waiting in the kitchen for me.

Syd and I text before I'm quizzed on my day. I'm finally allowed to go to my room when I've assured them I'm fine.

But I'm not fine, and when I'm finally alone, I cry.

Wiping my tears, I flop down on my bed and open my laptop. I click on the original death fear meme. The cops will be looking at this, too, but I can't sit around and do nothing. I want to know everyone in town who has reposted this and what their fear is.

Miyah did but she's not allowed to be anywhere alone or drive by herself now.

Something else Mariella said bothers me. Debbie and Kason were both popular. What if this person *is* targeting that group?

God, I think almost the entire school must have reposted this. I recognize so many people as I scroll down.

There's one that scares the crap out of me.

My sister's fear is online for everyone to see.

thirteen

IZZY

Lia answers on the second ring. "Izzy Bee, how are you doing?"

"You shared your fear! What the hell is wrong with you?"

"Whoa. Will you slow down? Look, I'm coming home for a few days, so we can talk then. I'm at the airport."

"No!" I stand up as if I can run to her and stop her from boarding. "Lia, you have to stay there. You reposted that meme!"

And she was popular in high school.

"Iz, you have got to start making sense."

"The death post!"

"Oh, that. Yeah, I meant to delete it last night. I know it's in bad taste now."

I growl internally. She's not getting this. "Debbie and Kason died in the same way they posted."

The line goes quiet.

"Lia? Listen, leave the airport and stay at school."

"I can't. I'm already here."

My face falls. She's at the airport in Arrivals.

"All right. We can fix that. Get back on a plane and go back. I'm not being crazy here. You need to leave."

"Let's not lose our heads. I'll delete the post now. I want to be there for you. What you found . . . well, it has to be traumatic. I can't believe it. Debbie and Kason. I knew them, you know? Not well, of course, but our paths crossed."

"Lia! None of that matters. I'm fine. Go home. Please."

"I *am* home. Chill before you burst a blood vessel. I'm getting an Uber. We'll talk more soon."

"No, you don't—"

She hangs up, and I shout, "Damn it!"

Spinning around, I run from my room and fly down the stairs. "Mom, Dad, you have got to tell her to go home!"

I only stop myself from getting knocked out by slamming my hands into the kitchen wall.

"Izzy, slow down," Dad says. "What's wrong?"

"Lia is coming here. She's already landed."

"We know. I booked her ticket this morning."

"She can't be here. Don't you get it? She reposted that death meme."

Mom and Dad look at each other.

"Debbie and Kason were killed in the same way they posted that they most feared. What if the killer isn't done? Lia could be in serious danger. You need to tell her to go back to school."

"We don't know anything for sure yet, Izzy," Mom says.

"We know two people are dead. We know the post was created in town. We know Debbie was scared of falling, Kason of drowning, and that's how they died."

"The police will be looking into this," Dad says, handing me a glass of water. "But for all we know, this is some freak who had a grudge against Debbie and Kason. There's nothing to suggest that this will happen again."

"There's nothing to suggest it won't."

Why aren't they more worried?

"And we'll take precautions. I don't want you or your sister going anywhere alone. If you're out, you go together. After school, you come straight home until this person is caught."

Mom nods. "It's going to be okay, sweetheart. Nothing will happen to you."

I know, because I didn't repost the meme.

"You're really not going to tell Lia to go back?"

"She's safer with us," Dad replies.

"Seriously?"

"Dad's right, honey. She's safer here."

She's not, but it's three against one and I'm not going to be able to change their minds. I take my water and go back upstairs. They're crazy if they're not concerned.

The cops need to find something soon, because I can't cope with not knowing. How much danger are we in?

I change into pajamas, brush my teeth, and crawl into bed. As much as I'd like to stay up and see her, I'm so drained that I fall asleep in minutes.

Lia's still asleep when I leave for school the next morning, arriving with only a few minutes to spare. This morning, I don't feel much like talking, and I know there will still be only one thing being discussed.

Syd lifts her hand in a lazy wave when I get to homeroom. I sit beside her. "Lia's home."

"Why?"

"I found a dead body. She's being a big sister. Only, she re-posted that dumb meme, too. She and our parents think she's safe at home. No one will take me seriously."

"Well, she could be perfectly safe here, Iz. Maybe the killer just wanted Kason and Debbie." She lowers her voice. "They were hardly the friendliest people. In fact, and I hate to speak ill of the dead, they were kind of assholes. It's not really a surprise that someone had a grudge."

"Why just them? If popular people are being targeted, then Justin, Tayley, Mariella, and all their friends have targets on their backs."

"Kason and Debbie were the worst—closely followed by Mariella. Kason used women and threw them away like trash. Debbie was flat-out nasty to everyone who didn't agree with her or look a certain way."

I blow out a breath that seems to deflate me like a balloon. "Maybe you're right."

Mariella was hardly as sweet as sugar yesterday, but she's not usually quite that bad. She isn't—wasn't—at Debbie's level.

This might already be over. There could be no danger any-where.

One thing nags at me, though. Why bother making that meme if there were only ever two targets? The killer might have wanted to murder them in the worst way for them, but taking a picture of the dock and making a social media meme seems like a lot of effort.

They couldn't even know for sure that Debbie and Kason would share it. Though it was a safe assumption that they would. They post and repost everything "relevant" so they can stay . . . well, relevant.

The bell rings, so we get up and walk to class.

I take a seat at the table I share with Axel and wait. His seat is empty so far. He's not really one to get to class super early, but he's usually here by now.

Maybe he's using Debbie and Kason's death to take the day off. It'd be so easy to do right now.

Mr. Morrison calls on the class to work on our partner projects, then he sits down and sips his coffee.

I flick open my textbook to research Poe's early life.

The door is shoved open. Mr. Morrison startles and almost spills his coffee down his cream shirt, earning some chuckles around the class.

"Axel, what time do you call this?" he grumbles.

Axel doesn't respond or even look at him to acknowledge that he's listening. Mr. Morrison tuts and goes back to his coffee.

Axel yanks the chair and scrapes on the floor, making me wince.

"Everything okay?" I ask as he sits down.

The temperature drops as he gives me a sideways glare.

I try again while subtly moving over slightly. "Why were you late?"

"Why are you talking to me?" he grunts.

"We're partners," I say, beaming a smile his way.

"Great." He flips his book open to read. It's not even related to our project.

"I think I'll do the talking during our presentation," I mutter.

"You're a good little girl, so of course you will."

"All right, what's up your ass?"

"I'm bored."

"You've been here for twenty seconds."

He doesn't respond, but he does run his hand through his messy hair. I don't think he bothers doing anything with it, but he's one of those annoying people who don't have to. He always looks good.

I'll never tell him that.

His face and his personality are so starkly different. One look at him can give me butterflies, but as soon as he speaks, I get this hollow feeling in my gut and want to hide.

I clear my throat. "So, I didn't know you and Tristan were cousins. He's friends with my sister."

"Fascinating."

"Are you hangry?"

He does the glare again, this time looking like he wants to strangle me. I seem to get that expression regularly.

"Something's put you in a bad mood, and I don't buy the bored thing."

"Izzy." He sighs my name. "I really don't care what you *buy*."

"What happened? Did you have to talk to the cops again?"

His hand freezes midair as he goes to turn the page of the book he's pretending to read.

Bingo.

"What did they say?"

"They were just confirming where I was after I left the party. Remember telling them about that?"

If he's innocent, why is it an issue?

"Where was that?"

"At home."

Why would they need to do that again? Is there some sort of evidence that suggests otherwise? There can't be or he would surely be in an interview room right now.

"They wanted to know where everyone was, I'm sure."

"They'd already asked that night, Izzy. I don't like this. You've dropped me in it."

Axel is agitated. Why?

"I was worried you'd died! What, do you think someone is setting you up here?"

He shrugs. "How many people do you think they're inter-viewing more than once?"

They haven't been back to me yet. "Lots, probably."

"They think I did it. They're going to find out how much I hated Kason . . . then they're going to pin it on me."

My face falls. Wait . . . just how much *did* Axel hate Kason?

fourteen

IZZY

"Axel . . . why did you hate Kason so much?" I ask, clearing my throat.

His expression changes, and he looks at me like I belong in an asylum.

"All right, I mean besides his being a womanizing bully."

"Does there need to be more?" he asks.

"Yeah."

"He did something to me last year."

"What did he do?"

His eyes tighten. "Like I'm telling you that."

"You don't think they would have found out that you were at that party? They've interviewed everyone there."

"Whatever. You made me a suspect, and I'm not telling you why they haven't taken me off that list yet."

"Do you not have an alibi at all? No one saw you after you left the party?"

Debbie went missing after Axel had left.

His jaw twitches, and I feel like I'm walking on very thin ice.

"Is there no one who can vouch for you?" I ask again.

"No!" he snaps. "I was home alone, and I didn't leave."

I jolt at the acid in his voice. "Right. It's okay."

He takes a breath.

"Is it okay? There's no one, Izzy. No one to have my back. I'm on my own, and I don't exactly make a lot of friends."

Crap, he really doesn't have anyone on his side. "There must be something. Can't your phone prove where you were?"

"I guess we'll see."

"What does that mean?"

"It means, it depends on what the cops find. I didn't make any calls, and I sure as hell don't have my location turned on."

"There must be some way they can find that out."

"I don't know, Izzy."

He turns his body away slightly, not enough so it looks like he's avoiding me, but I can see more of the back of his head than the side.

Great, he's back to being mad at me.

This is ridiculous.

I turn to my own work, my stomach tightening in anger.

It's hardly my fault that no one can back him up, is it?

He did have plenty of time to kill them.

My palm curls around my pen.

Axel had the opportunity to do this, and he just admitted that he hated Kason. He wouldn't tell me that if he was the killer, surely.

For the rest of the class, he pretends that I don't exist, and my mind races.

Why would he kill both of them, though? Unless Debbie witnessed Axel drowning Kason and he had to kill her to shut her up.

I don't think I've ever seen Axel in a shirt like the one I found, or in any color other than black, but I've hardly been keeping track of his wardrobe.

At lunchtime, I meet Syd in the cafeteria and watch a new snowstorm roll in.

The principal will be watching to see if she needs to shut school down and send us all home. We've had no alerts that the storm will cause disruption.

"What gives, Iz?" Syd asks.

I pick at my sandwich. "Axel doesn't have an alibi."

"Does he need one?"

"The cops seem to think so. He also mentioned that they're going to find out how much he hated Kason."

It bothers me that he's alone, and it shouldn't. He could have friends and his cousin closer if he weren't so hostile and angry at the world.

"What does that mean?"

"That there's evidence of how much he hated Kason out there, apparently. Maybe on his phone or laptop, I don't know. He's obviously done something to him."

"Something as in told a girl he cheated on her or as in *drowned* him?"

"I really don't think Kason would have cared if Axel squealed about a girl. He openly cheated on every girl he ever dated. If you can call that dating. Anyway, I think it was something more serious than that. It's got Axel rattled."

"So, you think the drowning thing?"

"No . . . Maybe. I just can't see him doing that, you know?"

As much as Axel seems to hate everyone and everything, I just can't picture him as a murderer.

"Who can you see doing it? Because serial killers rarely look or act like killers. At least, not at first—it's how they get away with, you know, the serial part. Though as soon as you see their mug shots, they totally look like psychos."

"This killer isn't serial," I say, as if that's at all relevant. "Axel had time to kill them, he hated Kason, and he admits there's something out there that proves how much he hated him. It's not looking great for him."

"Why aren't you calling the sheriff about this right now?"

"Because I don't think all that actually makes him a killer. He's convinced they want to pin it on him. Two murdered teens, Syd—the cops will want to wrap that up pretty quickly. What if they charge Axel and he's innocent?"

She bites her lip and pushes her pasta around with her fork. "Okay. I'm with you, but we can't keep this to ourselves if we find anything more that makes him look guilty."

"Agreed. I'm going to keep a real close eye on him."

"Oh, make besties with the potential killer, Iz, fab idea."

"We're not going to start braiding each other's hair."

"You're hilarious."

I drop my half-eaten sandwich on the plate. "I'm not hungry. I'm going to head to the library for a while. I need to keep busy."

"I'll come with you. I want this day over, too."

We throw away our trash and head out, and I can feel both Justin and Axel watching us the entire time.

I'm not sure which one is making me more uneasy.

fifteen
FEAR

Sliding the large wooden door shut at my base, I toss the bag of rope onto the table and stretch my back. I flex my hands as I walk to the sink to get some water.

Since making plans in autumn, I've been building my strength. It takes a lot to overpower a person trying to get out of your grip, to carry dead weight, to strangle a person with your bare hands.

My body is a weapon that I need to master. I've proved that I can do it, but pushing one person off a building and drowning another didn't take the physical strength that I will need to squeeze the life out of a human.

I want to feel a life drain away under my fingertips.

I gulp down the entire glass of water and wipe my mouth with my hand.

Sweat drips down the back of my neck. I've only just caught my breath from the workout at the gym and the run across acres of fields to the barns. I've always kept myself in good shape, but that's not enough for what I'm doing now.

I need to be fitter. I despise every person in this town, and I need to take them down one by one.

I strip off my damp hoodie and throw it on the table. The ripped plaid shirt is draped on the chair. Growling, I knock it onto the floor and sit down.

This barn is the only one not on any map. It's hidden out of the way, at the end of the field behind the tree belt. It's not on a map because not every dwelling here was built with permission. There's a cluster of three small barns near the entrance to the farm and two more across the field from this one. I have plenty of room.

My family sold this land when I was a kid, but the new owners have done nothing with it. I heard talk about their having big money in the city, but of course I was never given any details. They will probably wait to see if the area picks up before deciding whether to build houses on the land.

It won't.

Unlike some of the locals, I don't really care what they do with it as long as they leave it for now. I'll find something better soon enough. I need a place long-term.

This isn't something I'll be able to stop doing. The urge to kill is starting to become overwhelming. It simmers under my skin, and I know it's only a matter of time before it boils over.

The other barn is a risk that I need to consider further down the line. First, I need to figure out how close the cops are to finding me, how they respond, where they search, and whether they'll look this far out of town. I'm sure they will eventually, but I'm hidden by a dense patch of trees, bushes . . . and snow.

On the table are my notes. Names and fears, all collected from every repost I was able to access. Every single one fed the darkness that's been growing inside me for the past year.

The hate and anger I feel toward everyone in this town shocked me at first. I tried to push it away and pretend that I didn't want them to pay. But I couldn't sit back and ignore it. Now I embrace it, as if I could live off this feeling alone.

They still pretend that my family was good, still speak highly of them.

There was never anything good inside their rotten souls.

I grit my teeth as fresh hatred explodes in my chest. I'm prepared and ready. I've thought of everything. I've taken care of Victim Zero and gotten over the aftermath. I'm now two, technically three, down.

No one is going to stop Fear.

sixteen

IZZY

After school, I go straight home to see my idiot sister, since she refused to go back to college.

We're watching TV now, and I stare at the screen with my jaw dropped. The news is on, reporting about Debbie and Kason, and although it's not actually news, I'm still stunned.

Lia wraps her arm around my shoulders. "It'll be okay, Iz."

"They've confirmed that they were *murdered*."

It's what I knew, what everyone already knew, but hearing the words on TV makes it so much more real. It's definite. No more hope of its being a horrible accident. Someone out there murdered them. Someone who probably lives in town.

"That's not a surprise, Izzy Bee, you know that."

"It's not but . . ."

"I get it," she replies. "Come on, I'll make you a strong coffee. I got really good at making them, now that I can't afford to hit up Starbucks twice a day."

My phone lights up with notifications. I don't even want to look. I leave it behind and follow Lia.

In the kitchen, I sit at the table and watch her. "Do you think Mom and Dad will come home early from work?"

She shrugs as she pours two large cups of coffee. "They might but they know we're safe here. The doors are locked *and* no one else has been threatened."

"We don't know whether Debbie and Kason were threatened. They were just murdered."

"Don't overthink."

"They're not the kind of people you try to intimidate. There would have been posts about it, something about how no one threatens them and they'll silence whoever tries."

"They sound delightful."

"That might be the point," I say. "They were both popular and not, er, delightful."

"You'll be fine, then, loser," Lia teases.

"Funny."

She's not wrong, though.

"You're trying to run a hundred steps ahead, Iz. You don't have all the information the cops do. They said there's no evidence that anyone else is in danger. We have to believe that."

"Do we?"

"Isabel Rose Tindall."

"Did you just go Mom on me?"

She laughs, stirring the coffees. "I did. I'm worried about you."

"You reposted that meme. It's you we should worry about."

"Iz." My name is a groan.

"When do you go back to school? You shouldn't miss too much."

"Relax. I'm only here for a couple of days."

Good.

She gives me my coffee and checks her phone. "Hey, there's a vigil being held on Sunday for Debbie and Kason."

"Where?"

"The square, outside town hall."

"Killers always go to those things."

She looks at me over the top of her screen.

"What? They do!" I say. "I bet half the force will be there in normal clothes but, duh, the killer knows them."

"You should take my place at college for a while."

"The point is that you need to get away. Miyah reposted that meme, too."

She sits down beside me. "I spoke to Aunt Ellen today, and Miyah isn't going anywhere alone. Uncle Samar is going to take her to school, and Aunt Ellen will pick her up. She's safe even if there is still danger."

"Yeah, she was allowed to go to Puck's, but he had to take her. Lia, did you know that Tristan and Axel are cousins?"

"Er, yeah, he lived with Tristan. Why?"

"You never mentioned it."

She blows out a breath that lifts her bangs. "Should I have? You've never mentioned Axel to me before in your life."

All right, fine. I'll give her that one.

"I don't want anyone else to get hurt. Who do you think would do this?" I ask.

"I have no clue. This is a town where everyone says hello and you never turn down someone who needs help. What if the killer asked for help and was turned down?"

"By Debbie and Kason?"

She shrugs. "Maybe."

What would this person need from the star of the ice hockey team and a girl with jelly for brains?

"They weren't nice people, Iz. They wanted to rule the school, even when they were juniors. We had to put a stop to that a few times."

"We?"

"Me, Jade, and Tristan."

"What did you guys do?" I ask.

"Nothing major, obviously. We just put them in their place. They don't get first pick at everything just because they want it."

"First pick at what?"

She sighs. "It's not important, just dumb stuff like organizing dances and other school events."

"I didn't know you talked to them."

She makes a face as if I smell. "I wouldn't say that. On a couple of occasions, I told them to get back in their lane. We were hardly on speaking terms."

"All right."

Of course, Lia would have known them. It's not like they blended into the background. Seems as if my sister knows more about my classmates than I do.

Is she downplaying it? There was clearly tension between her crew and Debbie and Kason's. Could it have been a bigger rivalry than she's telling me?

seventeen

IZZY

The following day, Lia meets me at Puck's for dinner. She's been out catching up with people in town, so we agreed to meet there after school. We order burgers, fries, and Cokes.

"I missed Puck's," she says. "We'd come here almost every day after school."

Lia's friends were the ones you wanted to be seen with. She's always been so effortlessly cool.

"How are you holding up today, Izzy Bee?"

"Everyone stares at me like I'm a circus freak, I can't get rid of the image of Debbie's body, and you and Miyah reposted that death fear meme."

Lia sips her Coke. "So, not great, then. Miyah and I will be fine. Didn't almost everyone share that thing?"

"That's not good, Lia."

"Did the cops confirm that it's a hit list? I haven't heard anything about the meme from them."

"No, they probably won't, at least not yet. It would cause

panic, right? Surely you don't need to be told that by the cops, though? It's *obvious*."

She rolls her big hazel eyes. "You're going to drive yourself mad. An awful thing happened here, but that doesn't mean it's going to get worse. Debbie and Kason were friends and had plenty of enemies, so it's perfectly reasonable to believe that someone had it in for them and not every teenager in town."

I wish I had Lia's confidence. There's no second-guessing for her. She plows ahead, certain that she's got it figured out.

"I might look Tristan up. Do you see him out much?" she asks.

"Sometimes. Don't you speak to him anymore?" He mentioned not speaking to her much as well.

"I try to, but I'm pretty busy now that I'm in college, Iz," she says patronizingly. "He probably doesn't have time to keep calling me, either."

Matthew arrives just before I'm about to tell her to get back on a plane.

"Sure is great to see you back," he says to Lia, putting her plate in front of her.

"Aw. I've missed you and these burgers."

"Thanks," I say as he places my food down. "Have you seen Tristan recently?"

Lia gives me a look that I know means she's calling me names in her head.

Matthew frowns. "No. He hasn't been in for a while, actually. I hope everything's okay."

"Lia was just saying that he doesn't keep in touch that often."

"He's probably busy working. High school isn't forever," Matthew says, staring off into the distance as if he's replaying memories in his head. "Well, hopefully he'll drop in soon. Enjoy the burgers."

Lia dumps a heap of ketchup onto her plate. "What's going on in your head right now? You barely spoke to Tristan for the entire four years I was hanging around with him. Now you're obsessed with his movements."

The memory of him giving me his number flashes in my mind, and my cheeks heat.

"I'm not obsessed. Don't you think it's weird that he's not around as much?"

She holds her finger up. "You and Matthew haven't seen him. That's not everyone. I know what you're thinking about him and forget it. He's the sweetest guy in the world. He was the one who took me to the emergency room when I fractured my wrist. He gives money to the homeless and volunteers at a soup kitchen. He would never hurt anyone."

"All right," I say, picking up my burger.

Though she doesn't know if he still does all those things. She hasn't spoken to him in ages.

Lia nods and dives into her fries. Almost literally.

While we eat, Justin, Tayley, and Mariella walk into the diner. Jessie trails them with her cousin Katy; I wonder if one of them will be let into the inner circle now that Debbie is dead. I haven't seen Justin hang around with any of the other guys on the hockey team since.

If he's not with Tayley and Mariella, he seems to be alone.

It's normal for people like Axel to fly solo, not Justin.

He was pretty tight with a couple of them, but he's keeping his distance now.

Justin looks from me to Lia and changes direction, going to a booth near the front of the restaurant and not his usual table.

"Ugh, I hate that guy. He thinks *way* too highly of himself," Lia says. "Did I ever tell you about the time he tried getting in a fight with Tristan because he didn't start in a game? As if juniors get picked ahead of seniors. He thought he was better and would lead the team to victory."

"No, what happened? Did they actually fight?" I only loosely followed that. Coach does use more seniors in games, and Tristan was the best last year. Now he's left and Justin has moved up the ranks.

I remember Lia telling me that they had a couple of run-ins, not a fight.

"Justin was mouthing off that if Coach wanted to win, he would need to swap him in for Tristan and let him play the whole game. Tristan bit back and Justin got one shove in before Coach broke it up."

"Justin's whole life is hockey," I say. "He's going to play in college."

"Oh, we all knew he was good. But no better than Tristan, and he had less experience. He's hotheaded and hates when things don't go his way. He threatened Tristan before storming out of the changing rooms."

"Who told you?"

"Tristan. He followed Justin to warn him to back off. The kid has no respect."

It's funny to hear Lia calling Justin a kid, as if she's not only one year older than him. They definitely spoke more than Lia led me to believe yesterday.

What else does she know about Justin and his crew?

eighteen

IZZY

Justin steps in my way as I head out of Puck's to my car.

"What's she doing back?" he asks, tipping his chin in Lia's direction, though she left a minute ago to get gas.

Tayley and Mariella watch us, openmouthed, from their table. I hear Mariella whisper, "Why does he keep talking to her? It's weird."

Jessie and Katy lean in closer, probably now wondering if they're going to have to compete with me for the spot in the inner circle.

They're *really* not. I'm far too much of a pushover, even if I wanted it.

"She wanted to come home for a few days. She's still on break." Do I need to clear it with him when my sister is allowed to visit?

"Seems strange since she hates us, that's all."

I try not to stare at him too much. "I don't think she *hates* you guys. Besides, it's not like she came back for you."

Why didn't I know about this rivalry between Lia's group and Justin's? I just assumed that, because they were in different years, they wouldn't really be on each other's radar. I barely know anyone who isn't in my year and only know some of last year's seniors because of my sister.

Justin snorts. "I think you would be surprised. She's not as sweet as she looks. Izzy, you are so unobservant." He smiles as if he's just heard an inside joke. "It's endearing and maddening at the same time."

He finds something about me endearing . . . and it's the thing I hate most about myself.

"Why is it maddening? I like to keep to myself. I couldn't be bothered with all the class politics and who you can or can't talk to. *That's* what I find insane."

"Maybe."

Tayley and Mariella straighten like meerkats. They're clearly wondering what Justin is doing talking to a big loser like me.

"I'll see you later, Justin," I say, pushing past him.

"Izzy?" he calls, but I don't stop. I'm not hanging around to hear how much he dislikes my sister and her friends.

I thought I knew quite a lot of the gossip in this town, mostly through Syd, but we've clearly missed most of it.

I zip my coat higher and walk against the flurry of snow falling. Two more months and all this white crap should be gone. I love it until January hits.

My car is parked at the end of the lot. It's dark out and the streetlights make the settled snow look orange.

"Izzy?"

I stop and look over at the voice. Officer Duggan. He's holding a takeout bag from Lin's Chinese restaurant.

"Hi," I say.

"How are you?"

"I'm doing okay. Have you guys found anything out about Debbie and Kason's killer yet?"

"I'm afraid I can't say."

That's the reply I expected. "I figured as much."

"I want you to know that we're doing everything we can to solve this case. I won't rest until this guy is behind bars."

I bet that's what he says about every case. Not that this town has ever seen anything like this before. The last big case we had here was when my neighbor's dog went missing.

"You should get home, Izzy. It's freezing."

He sounds like he wants to say more, add "and unsafe," but I presume he doesn't want to freak me out.

It's way too late to worry about that. I'm officially freaked.

"Yeah. 'Night," I say, walking away.

"Goodnight, Izzy."

I reach my car and notice something . . . off. It takes me a minute to figure out that it's not sitting straight. My front tire is flat against the road.

Shoulders slumping, I mutter, "Great."

I didn't notice it going down, and I've only been in Puck's with Lia for an hour. She'll probably be at the gas station now, so she won't pick up if I call. Not that I imagine Lia will know how to change a flat.

I've done it once before, but that was two years ago.

How hard can it be?

I'm about to find out, I guess.

Cold pinches my fingers as I pop the trunk, grab the tools I need and the spare. Lugging the new tire onto the road, I let go and stand back so it doesn't hit me.

"Need a hand?" Tristan shouts from . . . somewhere.

I look over my shoulder both ways and finally see him walking away from the port. He crosses the empty road and jogs to me.

I haven't seen him in months, and now that there's a double murder, I've seen him three times in a week.

"Got a flat," I tell him, like it's not obvious.

"Let's get it changed fast or you're going to freeze." He puts the jack under the car and pumps.

"Thanks, Tristan."

I stand the wheel up.

"How long have you been here?"

"An hour maybe. I was having dinner with Lia."

He looks up. "She's here?"

"She's home, but she's not here now. She left to get gas a few minutes ago."

If I'd just ignored Justin, I probably could have caught her. I've never been very good at ignoring him.

Tristan runs his finger over my tire. "Izzy . . . look here. You see that? I think someone did this on purpose."

"What?"

"The tire looks cut."

"Oh my God!" I crouch beside him, shining my phone flashlight at the tire.

"Can you see this slit? Like someone poked a knife in." He looks at me. "Who would do that?"

"I have no idea," I whisper.

"You didn't see anyone when you arrived?"

"Lots of people. I have no idea who would want to damage my car."

Could it be Axel? He was mad that I got him involved with the cops, despite my doing it because I was concerned.

"You should report this. Are you alone now?"

"Since Lia left, yeah."

"She should have waited with you."

I shrug. "It's fine. I was talking to Justin anyway."

Tristan and I change the tire together. When we're done, he stands and brushes off his knees. They're soaking through from kneeling in the snow.

"Do you want me to follow you home? I'll check the other tires and under the hood, but the car looks okay now."

"I'll be fine."

"All right."

I watch him look under the hood. I wouldn't have a clue if anything was wrong. He drops it back down and smiles.

"You're good to go."

"Thanks so much. Hey, do you know where Axel is?"

He tilts his head. "Why are you asking that? Do you think he did this? Because I know he can be a dick, but I don't think he would slash a tire."

He doesn't *think* he would.

"I don't know. I guess I'm just trying to think of who has a problem with me, and I can only think of Axel."

"I thought you two got along okay. As okay as he can get along with anyone. Aren't you partners on a project? He mentioned something about Poe when I called to check in with him yesterday."

He must talk to Axel more than I thought if he knows that.

"We are, but that doesn't mean he likes me."

"It's impossible for anyone to dislike you."

I'm glad it's getting dark now, because my face is on fire.

"I'll call him when I get home, okay, Iz?"

"Yeah, thanks."

"You should get going before you freeze out here."

I nod and open my door. "Thanks. See you later."

Tristan walks off toward the town square. I get into my car and start the engine. Turning up the heat, I warm my hands and put the stick into reverse. As I'm about to pull out of my space, I slam on the breaks. Across the road a figure dressed in dark colors—possibly a black hoodie—watches me from the side of a building.

My heart leaps, but when I look back, they're gone.

nineteen

IZZY

I stare at the same spot for a minute, but they don't come back. There's not even a shadow. It's not the first time I've seen that person. They were watching me the day Tristan and I found the scrap of shirt in the water.

Ice crawls up my spine.

He disappeared as soon as I caught him, as if I wasn't supposed to see him. Could it have been Justin or Tristan? Would Tristan have had enough time? He would have needed to run.

The figure was tall enough to be either of them. They both tower over almost everyone. But I obviously can't tell from a silhouette who it was standing there.

Axel is also tall . . .

Izzy, leave.

I hit the door lock button and pull out of the parking space. Taking one last look at where the dark figure was, I turn the car around and drive out of the lot. People are still walking around, some in groups and others alone. That person could have been walking idly, talking on the phone and not looking at me at all.

I try to reason with myself, with my fluttering heart, but my tire was slashed tonight. Someone had to have done that on purpose. Tristan said it looked cut, and he was right. A neat gash in the rubber.

Axel surely wouldn't hate me enough to do that. Why would a killer damage my car rather than murder me? I know I didn't share that post, but surely that wouldn't affect the killer's motives. Could they stick to their own set of rules even if it meant I caught them?

I clench my sweat-slick hands around the steering wheel.

My slashed tire feels like a warning.

Tristan put the old tire in my trunk and told me to contact the cops so they can take it. I'm not sure what good that will do.

Would he have done that if he's the one killing people?

I pull into my drive, and only Lia is home.

Cutting the engine, I get out and run to the front door.

She's watching TV when I get inside.

When she notices me, she pauses *The 100*. "Damn, girl, you were ages. I was about to call and check up on you."

"Someone slashed my tire."

She sits upright, and her eyes bulge. "Someone did *what?*"

I slump down on the sofa next to her and blow out a breath I feel like I've been holding since the parking lot. "They slashed my tire. Thankfully Tristan was around and helped me change it. The old one is in the trunk. He said I should report it and see if the cops want to take it."

"Jeez, Izzy Bee. Did you see anyone or anything suspicious?"

"Not really. There was someone watching me as I left. Well, I think they were, anyway."

"Who?"

"I couldn't see."

"Did Tristan?"

"No, he'd already left, headed in the direction of Puck's, and this person was kind of around the back of Ruby's."

"In the alleyway?"

"Yeah, they disappeared pretty fast, but I didn't see if they went down the alley or just around the square."

"I should call and report this," she says. "You okay, though?"

"I'm fine. Just weird having it happen to me."

"You haven't pissed anyone off lately, have you? Wait, what am I saying, you're too nice. No one could ever be mad at you."

Tristan said the same thing, but I still have a slashed tire.

"Someone obviously was!"

"We don't know that. It could be totally some dumb kid messing around. Where were you parked?"

"End corner of Puck's lot."

"So, the perfect place. They could have come from in front of the car and gone back across the road without being seen. You were just in the wrong place."

"And the person watching me?"

"Let's not presume. It could just be someone hanging about."

In freezing temperatures? If this was summer, I would probably reach the same conclusion. "You think I'm overreacting."

"I think you're a bit in shock. It's totally understandable."

Lia has reverted to saying "totally" a lot, like she did last year. It suddenly let up when she went off to college, where she tried to speak more properly. At one point, I thought she might start talking in a posh English accent like the royal family.

I shake my head. "I need a bath. I'm cold and just want to relax in pajamas."

"Okay. Don't worry. I'll figure it out, Iz."

Like she always does—Lia has a solution for everything. When we were kids and messed up, she would be right there to fix it or explain. About a month before she left for college, I overheard my parents having a conversation about us. They thought that when Lia moved away, I would come out of my shell a little, as they put it, and not rely so heavily on my big sister.

It doesn't look like that's happened, and she's been away for four months.

I go upstairs to take a bath and then change into fluffy pajamas with little pandas all over them. Lia is in the kitchen with a mug of hot chocolate when I get back down.

"You just missed Officer Duggan. He swung by on his way back to the station."

"Back to the station? I saw him when I was walking to my car. . . ."

"No, Izzy. Oh my God, do not accuse a cop of slashing your tires!"

"He was walking though the parking lot, and I didn't see his car."

"He was probably cutting through from the station; it's a two-minute walk. Maybe he was getting something to eat."

Doesn't make sense. "He got Chinese already, so where was he going just now?"

"Well, he didn't say. Obviously."

"Did he take the tire?"

She nods. "He told me to get you to call him. Have your drink first, though, or it'll get cold."

"Did he take it seriously?"

"He took the tire, didn't he?" she replies, pushing a mug toward me.

"But he didn't stay . . ."

"Is there anything you held back from telling me?"

"No."

"And you're going to call him now and go over it. I don't see the problem."

She might not, but I don't think that's how you're supposed to do this.

"Izzy. They're dealing with a double homicide, a potential killer on the loose, and you're stressing over his not talking to you in person about a slashed tire. He has priorities, and those are the dead bodies of your classmates."

I slump into a seat at the table. My cheeks prickle with heat. Okay, maybe I was a bit too self-involved just then.

"Drink the hot chocolate and make your call. He's expecting you. Mom and Dad will be home soon, so I'm going to make them a chicken stir-fry."

Lia works in the background to make our parents' dinner, and I relay everything that happened to Officer Duggan on my phone.

When he signs off, he says, "See you Sunday, Izzy."

It's only when I've hung up that I realize he means at the vigil for Debbie and Kason.

Maybe my tire slasher will be there, too.

twenty

FEAR

I get out of the SUV and walk into the hidden barn.

In the old, beat-up kitchen, I flick on the percolator to make coffee and scroll through social media. My lips curl at the fresh wave of fears, most from far away, some even international.

A lot of the fears bring back harrowing memories. I've lived some of these, to the brink of death and back again.

Tonight's kill won't take long. I grit my teeth, as I can almost feel the emptiness that follows after twenty-four hours. I need to plan the next one and the next. I want them all so badly I can taste the high.

I tap the screen. Julia Stone is scared of starving to death. My free hand automatically drifts to my stomach. I can still feel the unbearable ache from being a hungry kid.

I don't know Julia, but she's tagged in one picture with Izzy, Julia in the background. They were at a party, it looks like at Tayley's house. She sure looks familiar.

Maybe she attends a different school.

Julia's profile also helpfully tells me where she lives and some of her routine. Drama class at Henderson's School of Performing Arts three afternoons a week—some weeks are "super tough" on her vocal cords.

Henderson's is on the outskirts of town before heading into the city. Its name makes it sound a lot more professional than it is. No one from there has gone on to have a career on stage or screen. They get together to sing, dance, and put on mediocre performances in the town hall.

Julia has a Dalmatian called Rolo and drives a silver MINI Cooper. She has a lot of photos with grandparents and posts about missing her parents while they're overseas.

Ah, and that's why I don't recognize her. She goes to the private school, St. Mary's.

I pour my coffee and sit down as I look through more photos of her. The same preppy uniform Izzy's cousin wears, which clings to her as if she's buying a size smaller to show off her figure.

She's pretty, black skin, perfect hair, and painted nails. Clearly she takes care of herself. I wonder if she knows Izzy or if they've just attended the same party once or twice. I only ever see Izzy consistently with Sydney and Amiyah.

Julia has defended her fear in the comments, her friends claiming that starvation wouldn't hurt as much as other methods. She's written, "It's clearly the scariest one, as you'd know death is coming long before it does. You won't change my mind!"

My heart races harder. Yes.

Death would be a long time coming. Debbie and Kason's deaths were over too fast. Debbie died seconds after I pushed her.

Kason lasted only a few minutes while I held him under the ice-cold water. Tonight's will be even faster.

But I could keep Julia for days or weeks.

I could watch her, and the rush would last longer than minutes.

My mouth salivates at the thought. I take a sip of coffee.

I plot as I read more and more about Julia. She hangs out with a girl named Eve most of the time. There are countless pictures of them with pursed lips and raised eyebrows.

Was she at Mariella's and I just didn't see her?

Her fear feeds the darkness inside me. God, I wish I'd seen her post first.

But I can make up for that now. I check my watch. One hour until I have to be at Debbie and Kason's memorial—Victims One and Two.

Number three is picked.

I know that I should slow down, but I can't help planning ahead. I haven't taken number three yet, but I'm too excited about this.

I have one hour to plan number four—Julia.

Most girls in this town share their entire lives on Instagram and TikTok. It makes them easy targets. They might as well drop a trail of bread crumbs wherever they go, leading me straight to them.

It almost takes the fun out of it. I like to follow and watch. I want to know my victim when they're alone before I strike. Kason put up a strong, independent front to the world. He didn't shy away from conflict and kept his head high—so high he thought he was better than everyone.

It was a satisfying kill, holding him under while he struggled for his life. He fought hard and he was strong, but I'd been preparing for this for months. I was stronger.

I hold my arms out in front of me, stretching toward the floor the way they were that night. Thick tendons protrude through my skin as I squeeze my fists, imagining Kason thrashing in the water below me.

The strong wind was my cover that night. He made so much noise, but I don't think it would have been heard by anyone walking by the port, not that anyone was out in the cold that late.

I release my fists, sit down at the table with my dark hoodie, phone, and blade in front of me.

I want longer with my next victim. I tap the screen and open Insta to search for Julia's house.

Fear is coming for you.

twenty-one

IZZY

Sunday morning is usually my favorite time of the week. There's no school, and I spend most of my day either reading, hanging out with Syd and Miyah, or watching TV. But now I'm finding that I have too much time to think, mostly about the way Debbie looked when I found her, my tire being slashed, and someone potentially watching me.

It's a bright midmorning, the sun shining though the thin, puffy clouds. I don't think we can expect any snow to fall today.

The whole town has gathered to remember Debbie and Kason. I'm standing with Syd and Lia. My parents are behind us, talking to neighbors and Matthew from Puck's. No one can "quite believe what's happening here."

Mom and Dad were furious that someone had slashed my tire, but, as I expected, the cops have found nothing so far. It's just not the sort of crime where you leave evidence. You can get in, do it, and get out without touching anything but the knife you take away with you. Besides, Lia was right when she said it's not the cops' top priority.

They're calling it mindless vandalism, and it might be. I'm still worried that it's more.

Mayor Whitby speaks loud and clear about how Debbie and Kason will be missed and how the town needs to pull together. Occasionally, his voice wobbles and he has to clear his throat and thump his chest. Once composed, he speaks fluently about our "friends."

Syd elbows me. "Does he look scared to you?"

"Yeah, but I think everyone is."

No one seems to be looking around, wondering if the person standing next to them is a cold-blooded killer.

Even Axel is here with Tristan. They're both standing near the back, Tristan listening and Axel looking around like he's searching for someone.

Who do you want to see, Axel?

For a full two minutes, I observe. Finally, he ducks his head.

Tristan nods at me when we make eye contact. I'm not sure if the cops did call him, but Lia said they were going to. It wouldn't be a surprise to Tristan, since he was the one who told me to report the tire.

Axel seems to notice Tristan's little greeting to me, but he's less friendly. He gives me a tight smile and looks on. I'm not the person he was searching for, either.

That's actually a relief.

I finally give up trying to locate the person who slashed my tire and focus on my classmates.

It's not like I would notice if they walked right up to me anyway. I only saw a silhouette.

Justin, Mariella, and Tayley are near the front with their families. A few of their friends surround them. Jessie and Katy are just behind.

"This is heartbreaking," Mom whispers.

Syd takes my hand as Debbie's mom cries loudly on her husband's shoulder. Debbie might have been horrible to a lot of people, but she was their daughter, and my heart aches for them.

I dip my head and take a moment to remember something good about them both. Debbie shared her chips with me in middle school. They were my favorite flavor—salt and vinegar.

I once saw Kason helping a little kid hit a hockey puck while at the park with his family.

If they were killed because they were not nice people, I wonder if their killer stopped to think that their worst moments weren't *all* they were.

Probably not.

The mayor ends on a positive note, telling us to keep Debbie and Kason with us always. He says they'll live on in their family and friends.

Then he lights a candle and says a prayer. A chorus of "amens" drifts through the streets before it's whisked away by a gust of wind. I tug the zipper of my coat up and stuff my hands in my pockets.

I look up, openmouthed, as tiny snowflakes float down from the sky.

The sky clouded over in a heartbeat, and Debbie's mom cries harder. In fact, it's hard to see anyone who's not crying. I link arms with Syd and take a breath.

The image of Debbie's head flicks into my mind as I look at the picture of her on an easel. In the photo, she's smiling and her hair is styled in thick waves. I try to burn that photo into my memory. That's what I want to see when I think of her, happy and smiling.

Some people start to filter into Ruby's, and others close in on Debbie and Kason's families to offer their condolences in person.

"Can I go to Puck's with Syd, *please?*" I ask.

"We're going to Ruby's," Dad replies.

"I know but can Syd and I not? Everyone from school is going to Puck's, and I kinda feel like I should be with them."

We should be where Debbie and Kason would have been. They both loved Puck's. Kason would eat baskets of fries, and Debbie always had a banana milkshake and fried chicken strips.

"I don't like the idea of your being somewhere else, Izzy."

"Please. We won't go anywhere other than Puck's."

Our parents exchange glances.

"What if I walk the girls there and pick them up from the door when they're ready?" Syd's dad suggests.

"Deal," Syd replies.

"Okay, but you do not leave until one of us comes back for you," Dad replies.

"Done and done. Thank you." I turn to my sister. "Ruby's or Puck's?"

"Hey, Lia," Tristan says. His eyes drift to me and then back to my sister.

Lia turns and gives him a hug. "Hey, I'm pumped to run into you, even like this. How are you?"

Axel is no longer with him, I see. Where did he sneak off to? He's probably gone home. It's not like he has anyone here to hang around with—he's admitted that much.

I wonder if under all the anger he's lonely.

Tristan shrugs, gesturing to the stand where the candle is flickering, almost blowing out in the wind and light snow.

Lia sighs. "Sorry. Silly question."

"Do you want to grab a drink and catch up?" he asks.

Dad clears his throat.

Tristan does a double take, as if he thinks Dad has forgotten who he is. "I'm happy to go with your family, if that's all right." He makes brief eye contact with me again.

He says the right thing, and I think he understands that my parents don't want Lia walking off with anyone, but I can tell from the frown that he's hurt. Dad has let Lia go off with Tristan hundreds of times before.

Dad nods. "It would be nice for you to join us, Tristan. We haven't seen you in a while."

Tristan smiles. My parents, Lia, and Syd's mom head to Ruby's, but Tristan hangs back for a moment. "Hey, Iz. All okay now?"

"Yeah. Did the cops call you?"

"Officer Duggan dropped in on his way home."

"Thanks again for changing my tire."

"Anytime." Frowning, he adds, "Well, hopefully you won't need that again."

"Yeah, that would be terrible. I mean, good that I don't need your help for that . . . you know what I mean?" My eyes widen. "You do know what I mean, right?"

Why can't I be cool?

Laughing, he replies, "I do."

"I'm going to Puck's with Syd. See you later."

I wave and he disappears into Ruby's. I'm kinda surprised that Lia didn't hang around when I was talking to Tristan. She never liked when I talked with her friends. We shared a lot growing up, because we're close in age, so she always wanted to keep her friends to herself.

Syd is smirking at me, her green eyes reflecting my mortification.

"Don't say a word," I warn.

"Come on, girls, let's get you to Puck's," Syd's dad, Graeme Webb, says. "Remember, do not leave until I come back."

"We got it, Dad," she replies. Her voice sounds like an eye roll.

He watches us go inside, and then he leaves to join the others at Ruby's.

Puck's is packed again, like it was the day after the deaths. Matthew is lighting the candles, but the pictures are gone.

"Hi, Justin," I say, stopping at his table. There is no one else with him yet or I probably would have chickened out.

Syd carries on, going to grab us a booth and probably order shakes. I really wish she would just stand with me; it looks so damn suspicious when she leaves us to it.

He looks up and leans back against his chair. "Can you sit a minute?"

This is new.

"Okay," I reply, taking the seat opposite him. *Be cool.*

"Look, I'm sorry for the other day. You caught a lot of attitude from me. I was having a crappy day, you know?"

"Understandable."

"I'm still sorry. I'm not usually a massive jerk."

"I know that, too. Forget it, Justin. I have."

"The cops said the killer posted that meme." He plays with a sachet of sugar. "I reposted it."

I feel my eyes widen. "The cops said that?"

"Well, not directly but it's obvious."

"Lots of people reposted it, but the cops think it was someone with a grudge against Debbie and Kason. I mean, they're looking into who they've had issues with and questioning their friends and family. The meme was just to find out . . . well, you know."

To find out the worst way to kill them. Or the best, I guess.

He nods, staring at the packet of sugar.

He's not convinced of that.

Well, neither am I.

Maybe Justin also believes they were killed because of their fear rather than a grudge.

"What are you thinking, Justin?"

He nods. "There's someone who had a beef with K."

"Who?"

"Jessie Gardner."

"Jessie?" I blurt out. "That doesn't make sense. She's one of you."

Jessie can mostly be seen following Tayley and Mariella around when they call her. When she's not needed, she hangs out with Katy.

"One of us," he says with amusement in his voice.

I don't react.

"Why did Jessie hate him? They always seemed to get along."

He taps the sugar on the table, and I want to slam my hand over it to stop him. "They got along too well. He was stringing her along for a year, maybe a bit more. He knew she was in love with him and used that to get what he wanted, if you know what I mean."

"Yeah, I got it."

"Anyway, she was pretty messed up about it and kept calling K, up to seventy times a day."

"Why would Jessie want Debbie dead?"

"Jessie was insanely jealous of everyone who got with K. D was all over him recently."

"Have you told the cops? I mean, they must have asked you if there's anyone you think held a grudge."

He frowns, twiddling the sugar sachet. "I mean, it's just a theory. I don't think we need to be dropping her in it just yet."

"Justin, she could be a murderer."

"It's so easy from the outside, Izzy. What if this was happening to your friends?"

"Why would you mention her if you think she's innocent?"

"I dunno. I'm just throwing thoughts around. She's seventeen, Iz."

"So was Ted Bundy at one point."

My phone buzzes in my pocket. It'll be Syd telling me to hurry up. Or telling me to go for it.

"I'm going to talk to her and clear it up," he says.

"I'll come with you."

"What?"

I fold my arms. "You brought me in on this by telling me. I'm coming with you."

Justin's eye twitches, and he looks at me like some alien has taken up residence in my body. Okay, so I might be talking brave and making demands, but my heart is pounding so hard I might faint.

"All right. Meet me at seven-thirty Monday morning, before school starts."

"You have to go to the cops if she doesn't have an alibi. You can't keep this a secret just to protect her."

He nods. "Agreed."

"Right." I take a long breath. "I'm going back to Syd."

"See you later."

My legs are like jelly as I make my way across the restaurant. Miyah sends me a text, a GIF of someone crying, which she's captioned "Day 8,372,625 stuck at home." Slight exaggeration.

I send a quick reply, telling her I'll visit as soon as I can, and slide into the booth opposite Syd.

She has our milkshakes already, and she's all smiles. "Well?"

I roll my eyes. "Calm yourself. It was about Debbie and Kason."

"I still want to know."

"Justin said Jessie might have a motive."

Syd's mouth pops open. "I heard Jessie ranting on the phone in the bathroom last month. Remember I told you she was crying, like, hysterical crying."

"What was she saying?"

"I thought I'd misheard but maybe I hadn't."

"Misheard what? Syd!"

"She said she wanted to kill *him*."

"Kason?"

"She just said 'him.' Her voice was all over the place. 'I hate him so much. I want to kill him with my own hands.'" Syd shrugs. "It might just be something she said; she was real upset. But now he's dead . . ."

"Yeah," I whisper. "He's dead and Jessie's just made it to the top of the suspect list."

twenty-two

IZZY

Justin wasn't joking when he said we should meet early. I told my parents that I had to work on a project with him in the school library. They trailed me to school, through yet another snowstorm, on their way to the airport to drop Lia off.

I have never been so relieved to see her leave town.

School starts in thirty minutes, so only a few students and staff are in.

The clock in the car flicks from 7:27 to 7:28. I'm meeting Justin in two minutes. The path is coated in white, and I can see only about three feet ahead, but I know where it is.

The weather really isn't my friend today. I shove my shoulder against the door as the wind tries to trap me inside.

Tucking my chin into my chest to avoid the snowy onslaught, I let the car door go, and it closes by itself. I'm running before even checking that the little padlock button on the key fob actually locked my car.

The thick haze of white makes it impossible to see. The wind whistles, sends a gust that almost sweeps me clean off my feet. I stop to plant my feet in the snow, leaning against a tree to anchor me.

The storm is supposed to let up sometime around nine a.m. If it continues like this, school will probably close.

A gust of wind slams into my body. My shoulder hits the side of the building, and then I'm thrown to the ground. I hit it facedown, as if the wind formed hands and pushed me from behind.

Or someone else was there.

Justin?

I leap to my feet and turn around, expecting to see someone standing in front of me, but there's nothing. That doesn't mean there wasn't—all they had to do was retreat five steps and disappear. My rough breathing mixes with the howling wind.

Pressing my back to the wall, I look in every direction, straining my eyes to see if there's even the outline of a person.

Nothing. No one. Just me and the snow.

Justin wouldn't do that and leave. We're supposed to meet. There wasn't anyone there at all.

I turn and run. My feet awkwardly slide as I go. If anyone could see me, they would probably film it for *America's Funniest Home Videos*.

The door near the library comes into view and I slam, quite literally, into another person.

"Whoa, Izzy."

It's Justin. I bounce off him and almost fall down again. I'm soaked and freezing. My heart is racing too fast. *It was just the wind, calm down.* "I need to get inside," I say in a rush.

Chuckling, he opens the door and holds it for me. "Are you okay?" he asks.

I push my hood down and brush snow off my knees. "Fine," I reply, omitting the part about the wind pushing me over. It sounds ridiculous.

The heat is on, blasting hot air from a noisy vent rattling above us. I sink into the warmth as my hair blows in my face. Mrs. Lockett is sitting behind the desk, glasses perched on her nose, gray hair in a bun, reading Charles Dickens.

She peers up and mutters "Good morning" before going back to her book.

"How do you know Jessie will be here?" I whisper as we head down the stacks. "This seems like an odd place for her to hang out."

"Not when you're trying to hide something."

"What would she be hiding?"

"K."

"She used to hide from Kason? But he's dead now. This doesn't make sense."

"I never said she was hiding *from* him."

Huh? "I'm going to need you to explain this."

"They would meet here . . . after he broke things off with her."

"She kept seeing him after he told her to back off? *In the library?*"

Justin shrugs. "I don't get it either, but she was obsessed with him. And not in a cute way, either."

Never did I think I would hear Justin use the word *cute*.

We walk deeper into the library. "Will she be here now, though? Kason's dead."

"She's always here. It's become her spot. I found her crying here a couple times when he'd found someone else and left her hanging."

"But it's different now."

"Izzy, if she's anywhere, it'll be here."

I hope he's right, because I got up early and walked through a blizzard to get to this building and find Jessie.

Justin looks down each stack, which seems weird, since he said she goes to the back.

"What are you looking for?"

He glances at me like that shouldn't need an explanation. Well, it does.

"Other people. You want anyone to overhear this? We're about to accuse her of murder."

"Um, no, we're not."

"She hated them both."

"No, only Debbie. She love-hated Kason."

Justin scoffs. "That's not a thing."

I'd argue but I can't be bothered. It's totally a thing. Jessie probably wanted to stay away from Kason because of the way he treated her, but she was in love with him and couldn't walk away.

Justin turns to me. "She's not here."

I cross my arms because duh. Why would she come to sit at the back of the library after finding out the guy she's crazy about is dead? I wouldn't even come to school.

"She's always here," he mutters to himself.

This is getting weird.

"Justin, she probably couldn't face coming in today. Let's just go." I turn to leave when something on the floor against the far wall catches my eye. "Wait, what's that?"

We crouch down and I hook it around my finger. Lifting it in front of me, I examine the brown leather bracelet.

"It's a guy's," Justin says. "We should hand it in. Someone's probably looking for it."

"Do you think it was Kason's?" I ask.

"Why?"

"Look at the clasp. There's a K engraved on it."

Justin almost headbutts me as he takes a closer look. I'm being totally cool with having him this close to me. On the outside, at least. "I never saw him wear it. Maybe Jessie bought this but didn't get a chance to give it to him. He had one that his parents brought him back from Italy. Black leather."

"Would he accept a gift from her?"

"I want to say no because he knew how she felt and he didn't reciprocate, but . . ."

But he didn't care enough to stop sleeping with her, so why would he turn down a gift?

"Oh my God, did Mrs. Lockett seriously not know they were hooking up in the library? There are books here. Who would do that?"

"Izzy, the only time she leaves her chair during school hours is to get coffee."

I stand up and pass the bracelet to Justin.

"What am I supposed to do with this?" he asks.

"Give it back to her."

"Why me?"

"You're her friend."

He hesitates before following me, and I feel his irritation as we walk out of the library. He wanted answers. This time Mrs. Lockett doesn't look up as we pass her.

"Should we try calling her, to check that she's okay?" I ask.

"Yeah, you should do that. And give her the bracelet."

"Why me?" I ask, pushing his hand away as he tries to give me the bracelet.

"I'm K's best friend. She's not exactly a fan of mine."

"Everyone's a fan of yours, Justin," I blurt out before I can stop myself.

He shakes his head. "Things aren't perfect for me either, Iz. Having your parents die when you're twelve doesn't exactly make for a great life. My parents weren't—" He breaks off. "It's just . . . half the time I feel like I'm sinking."

On that note, he walks away and leaves me with way more questions than I had before. His parents weren't what? Good parents? I knew that he lived with his aunt and uncle . . . but what was he going to say?

I don't know anything about his life, really. Only that he's good at hockey and he's super popular. There's so much more to him, and my heart aches at the possibility of his parents mistreating him.

Whatever he's not saying, it's not good.

Great one, Izzy. I bite my lip, wanting to slap myself. I didn't handle that very well.

First bell rings, so I head to find Syd and try to forget Justin and Jessie.

I find Syd quickly, running toward me along the corridor. Her eyes are wide, and she's holding her phone out. This better not be another video of a cat riding a robot vacuum cleaner.

"Jessie's *missing*!"

I blink. "What?"

"She's missing, Izzy. Her parents reported her *missing*! She didn't come home last night."

"No way." I grab her phone and read the missing person report that's been posted. She was last seen by Katy outside Ruby's. "This is bad."

"Uh, yeah. Was she at the vigil last night? She definitely wasn't at Puck's."

"She was there, but I didn't see her afterward either."

I look up as Justin runs around the corner. "Have you heard?"

"Just now. Was she there last night?"

"Not at Puck's, but she was at the vigil. She went home with her mom."

"Not her dad, too?"

"He's not around," he replies, digging his phone out of his pocket. "I'm going to try calling her. Who cares if she doesn't like me." He hangs up a few seconds later. "Voicemail."

"Do you think it's the killer?" Syd asks, her big eyes bulging.

Justin looks at me. "Do you think she's the killer and knows the cops are on to her?"

I throw my hands up. "Why are you two asking me? I have *no* clue."

"We're just throwing ideas around," Syd says.

"Would she physically be able to drown Kason, though?"

I ask. "I know she's about the same height as him, but he worked out. . . ."

Syd shrugs. "Don't you get super strong in moments like that?"

"Adrenaline, sure, but he would have the same. He'd be fighting back as hard as he could," I reply.

"I've got to go to the guidance office," Syd says. "But this is just too much." I watch Syd walk off with her phone to her ear.

"Do you think she's dead?" I ask Justin. "We shouldn't assume she's the killer."

His shoulders sag. "It doesn't look good, whatever's happening. She's either a cold-blooded murderer or a victim."

"God."

"I've gotta go, Iz. Keep safe."

I jump at the bell as Justin walks away. We completely missed homeroom.

In first period, Axel is waiting. I take my seat beside him and smile.

"Morning, Izzy."

"Ooh, he's friendly today."

His smile shows perfect teeth. His face smiles. Wow. "You're a delight as usual."

"Did you hear about Jessie?"

"Yep. I didn't do it, before you ask."

I roll my eyes. "You're ridiculous."

"She lives a couple blocks away," he says. "I noticed the cops at her house on my way here, so I figured something had happened."

"What was her fear?" I ask.

He shrugs. "I don't look at those."

"You don't look at them? After everything that's happened?"

He shrugs, keeping his eyes down. "Doesn't matter *how* they die."

"How can you say that?"

"Whatever method, you're still dead."

"Axel," I breathe.

What is he hiding? There's a lot of pain mixed up with that anger. I wish he would let me in.

He shakes his head. "Forget it. Where are we with project Poe?"

I can't forget it.

twenty-three

IZZY

I'm sitting at the desk, waiting for an epiphany. You know, that moment when everything makes sense and you no longer have questions.

No matter how many times I go over what happened and what I know about the potential suspects, I come up blank.

Debbie and Kason were murdered, and Jessie is missing.

She could be the killer or the third victim.

Axel is waiting for his motive to be revealed: he said the cops would find out how much he hated Kason.

I can't forget that he might be right about being set up. He's a loner who doesn't care about authority and is pretty hostile to everyone. If I were going to pick someone to pin my crime on, it would be him.

That would be easy. But I can't get my head around it. Axel seems so much more than his hard exterior to me.

While he's reading and making notes beside me, I check for

Jessie's post. People have been removing them, but I have screen-shots of *all* of them.

My lips part on a gasp as I reach the repost of Jessie's fear. She's afraid of being stabbed.

Axel looks across, but he doesn't say anything. He's proven that he wouldn't care anyway.

Could Jessie be lying somewhere now with stab wounds?

I wish I knew her well enough to know where to look. She could be anywhere in town. She might even be safe and plotting her next murder. It's not actually clear which side she's on at this point.

Justin said she was unstable because of Kason, but it's a bit of a leap from that to murderous. Besides, she was hurting herself and not trying to hurt others.

I shake the thoughts out of my head, knowing they'll resur-face soon enough. For the rest of the lesson, I try to focus, but the words on the page don't make sense.

"Izzy?" Syd says, poking my arm. "Come on!"

I startle and look up. She must have come in to find me but I didn't notice her. "Oh."

The class is over, and the last few people are filing out. Axel has already left.

"You okay?" she asks. "When I didn't see you leave class, I came in. You're usually one of the first out."

"I'm worried about Jessie."

"They'll find her."

"Alive?" I ask, packing my stuff in my bag.

"For all we know, she could be the killer—you said that

yourself," Syd says. "I think they're organizing a search party. Jessie lives up near the industrial area. I overheard Mariella telling Tayley. There are some unused units, and the river runs alongside."

I nod, trying not to imagine Jessie's body lying somewhere. "How was guidance?" I ask.

She shrugs. "Fine. The usual."

The usual what?

"I'm going to skip next period," I tell her.

"Why?" she asks.

"I can't focus."

"What are you going to do?"

"Hang out in the library."

"Do you want company?"

"No, you go to class. I'll be fine," I tell her. An hour alone with my own thoughts could quite possibly be a disaster, but I can't concentrate in class.

I'm going to go and make a list of names and death fears, so I have all the information in one place. Something I imagine the cops have done, too. There's probably a board at the station with all that information on it.

I even brought a new notebook to school. It's empty and I've been having heated debates with myself about it. Should I make lists or not?

It's kinda creepy, even I know that. But I've got to do something. And I do love a list.

I keep my head down, hoping no one spots me. Everyone is in class now, and surely any staff not currently teaching will be preoccupied with Jessie's disappearance.

I walk into the library and notice that Mrs. Lockett isn't in her usual spot at the desk. She might be organizing books or in the office tutting about late returns.

Whatever she's doing, I'm glad she hasn't seen me. Not that she would know if I'm supposed to be in class anyway. I don't much feel like talking to anyone.

I go to the back and sit at a desk, as hidden away as I can get in here. Then I pull my pink notebook out of my bag and start making my long list. The popular kids I put in a column of their own. If Jessie is dead, that makes three popular victims.

It has to be someone who hates that clique. Clearly, they're meaner than I thought. Kason and Debbie have both behaved horribly. I don't know much about Jessie, but her jealousy probably didn't make her the kindest.

Axel hates them.

I'm not convinced that Jessie is physically strong enough to overpower Kason. She's a similar height but skinny.

My money would be on Axel winning a fight with Kason, though.

Thirty minutes later, I want to run straight into the snow. Listing people and deaths is sobering. There is no list joy. These aren't tasks I can tick off and feel that warm glow of achievement. These are people's lives.

One thing bothers me. Well, there's more than one, to be fair. . . . But why now?

I chew the end of my pen and try to think, but I'm distracted. Something isn't right.

Turning, I look over my shoulder, through the stacks. No one is here. It's just me and I assume Mrs. Lockett.

But I'm not afraid of Mrs. Lockett, so why is my pulse suddenly racing?

I stand and very slowly turn around, my eyes trying to take in everything at the same time. The stacks are clear. The front door is closed.

"Mrs. Lockett?" I call, and wait for a response.

There's not even a hint of her timid voice or scuffling feet on the tiled floor.

The killer wouldn't attack in a public place. I hope.

I move away from the desk and tiptoe to the aisle. Rows and rows of books are my only company in our little library. I'm near the classics section. I'm sure Poe is somewhere here, too. Surely no one would kill me with Jane Austen present?

Holding my breath, I listen for footsteps. Mrs. Lockett still isn't at her desk. Where could she be?

The whole world could have vanished and I wouldn't know.

I turn back to my table and try to shake the feeling of being watched, when a shadow is cast over the desk from behind me.

Gasping, I spin around, and Axel's pale eyes stare back at me.

"You skipped class," he said.

"Good Lord, you almost gave me a heart attack! Were you here all this time?" I ask, sitting down and flipping my notebook shut so he won't see his name on a suspect list.

"Obviously. What are you doing?" he replies.

"Couldn't focus with all the gossip flying around in class. It's all anyone can talk about, and the conspiracy theorists are out in force. Did you see Mrs. Lockett when you came in?"

"I passed her outside. She said something about going to the staff room to borrow coffee. Not sure how you borrow that." He sits down and leans back in the chair like he's at home. "What're you writing in that notebook?"

"Just stuff for class. Did you hate Jessie?"

"You really think I could kill someone, then be back at school, business as usual, the next day?"

Why does he think Jessie was murdered yesterday?

I shrug. "That's how plenty of serial killers get away with it."

"Why are you so involved? You know those who insert themselves into an investigation rocket up the suspect list."

"I do know that. So do you. Is that why you're staying out of it?" I ask.

He laughs unexpectedly, and I realize how cute he actually is. *Stop that.* "Touché. So, what do I have to do to convince you I didn't do this?"

"I didn't know you cared what I think. And aren't you better off asking the cops that?"

"I'm not a killer, Izzy."

As if the killer wouldn't proclaim that.

"Who do you think it is?" I ask.

"You're better off asking the cops that," he says, repeating my words with a smirk.

"I have asked but they won't tell me anything."

"They won't consult with a teenage girl about a murder investigation? Strange."

"You're not funny, Axel." Though he kinda is. I haven't heard him use sarcasm much. "Why are you here?"

He shrugs. "I like the quiet."

All right, that I can believe. But he seems like the kind of person who would skip a whole day and go home rather than just skip a class. I've never seen him with a book that hasn't been assigned by a teacher.

What could he really be doing in here?

Axel pops up as if he's materializing from thin air.

twenty-four

FEAR

I flex my hand, curling it around. My wrist twinges as I close my car door and walk in the shadows. Jessie put up a decent fight, but she didn't last long, and I craved more the second her body went slack. It's addictive.

Within an hour, I'd taken her, killed her, and dumped her.

That's why I'm excited for tonight. My heart thuds against my rib cage as I watch her. Number four.

Julia Stone.

It didn't take long to figure out where she lives. She posts multiple selfies from her home, often boasting about how she has it all to herself because her parents are workaholics. She talks about going to school, the time she needs to leave by, the clubs she does afterward. Never tell the world your routine; it's idiotic.

I counted three mentions of her parents being away in the first fifteen posts I scrolled through. It's almost as if the girl's trying to get herself kidnapped.

If a killer knows you like to run every morning from five to six o'clock, when do you think you're most at risk?

Some people have no common sense. Damn morons. Their lives are played out on the internet for everyone to see. A virtual world exposing them to more than online bullying and an unhealthy obsession with how they look.

I grit my teeth. They do all this, put themselves at risk daily, and still have perfect lives. What did I do wrong, growing up? Absolutely nothing, yet my childhood was a nightmare that Rock Bay turned a blind eye to.

I scowl as I watch her outside her house. It's unlikely anyone would recognize Julia on the street. With the number of filters she puts over her photos, she looks like a human doll.

She's currently talking to a guy by her car and laughing obnoxiously at everything he's saying. She's in her private girls' school uniform with her black braids tied into a large bun. A pleated skirt and a blue shirt that she's untucked to look cool at the end of the day. Probably because she was meeting up with this guy. I've never seen him before, so I don't think he's from town.

The plan is in place. Now I just need to execute it.

I wait across the street, hidden by trees and new snow that falls more heavily by the second. The one variable that I can never plan for. Though it's worked in my favor so far, as if nature knows that I'm owed.

God, if she invites him in, I'm going to have to wait.

Hurry up!

The thought makes the knot in my stomach twist angrily. I want to cave his face in for interfering. Everything is already set. This has to happen now. I've got a room ready for her, and I have a one-way mirror affixed to the wall so I can watch until she's so starved she's too weak to fight.

As she takes her last breath, I'll enter the room to be with her. I want to be the last thing she sees. I want to watch as she finally fades, knowing I'm the one responsible for it.

It's the ultimate high.

Revenge is great, but fear is sweeter.

Finally, Julia says goodbye. The guy gets into his truck and drives away. She stands on the street and waves until he's out of sight.

Then she does something unexpected: rather than going into her house, she walks off down the sidewalk.

Interesting.

Where are you going, Julia?

It's early afternoon but a storm has hit, so the sky is dark and gloomy.

She must be meeting someone. I can't let her reach them, or this is over for tonight.

I creep along the sidewalk, watching as she puts in her earbuds and bobs her head.

Silly girl.

Pulling my hood over my head, I stalk her like a predator. She has no idea that I'm here, right across the street from her. Snow pelts my face, but it's barely an inconvenience as the anticipation of grabbing her builds higher and higher.

Here goes . . .

She won't hear me approach, so I run across the road at full speed until I slam into her back. I take a chloroformed cloth out of my pocket, my hand whips around to her mouth, and I listen to the muffled scream against my palm.

Adrenaline and hatred pump through my heart, spurring me on.

She turns slack in my arms, her head dropping onto my chest. I sigh with relief. I needed this.

Fear has you now.

I scoop her into my arms and dash back across the road. Awkwardly, because I'm holding her legs, too, I open the back door of my SUV and put her inside.

I don't know why she uses so many filters in her pictures; she's much prettier without them. Her black skin is smooth over high cheekbones and full lips. Her eyes are framed with long lashes and a thin layer of eyeliner.

I stroke her hair and smile.

twenty-five

IZZY

I manage to just barely focus on work in the morning. But while I'm eating my chicken salad wrap at lunchtime, we get the news.

My phone beeps; in fact, almost all the phones in the room do.

I read the notification, a message with a link, sent from Justin.

The cafeteria falls silent as word sweeps the room.

One day after Jessie was reported missing, she's been found dead.

Looking up, I notice Syd staring at me as if I have the answers.

She glances down at her phone, then back at me. "Can you believe this?"

"I think I can, actually," I mumble as my blood runs cold.

So, Jessie isn't the killer. She's the third victim.

This guy just went serial.

As I'm scrolling through the article, Axel sits down at the table, putting his tray next to mine as if this is completely normal.

"Axel?"

"I'm flattered you remembered."

Is he lost?

"Didn't you hear?" Syd asks him.

Voices in the cafeteria resume, but they're mumbled and quieter than usual. Everyone is talking about Jessie but trying to talk without people at surrounding tables hearing.

"What? Is it Jessie?"

"Good guess," I say, and I slide my phone toward him.

I watch with curiosity as his eyes flit back and forth while he reads the article on the screen. His forehead is pinched, but there is no other expression or emotion. He looks like he's reading a car magazine.

BREAKING NEWS:
Body of missing seventeen-year-old Jessie Gardner found in field.

"Shit," he mutters. "What happened to her?"

"They haven't released those details yet," I reply, taking my phone back. "But her fear was being stabbed."

He slumps back in his seat. "School has to be canceled now, right? The cops have to drop that *everyone's safe* bull now."

That's what he's thinking about? Our classmate was probably stabbed to death! "They might not have much choice," I reply tightly.

"Do you think there will be a town curfew?" Syd asks.

"I don't know, but if anyone asks you to meet them anywhere, do *not* go."

Axel eyes me suspiciously. "Why would you say that?"

I lick my lips as heat prickles my scalp. "Why would Kason leave the party or Jessie be out so early in the morning? The killer is getting them alone somehow."

"Or killers," Axel adds.

"Now, there's something I don't want to think about," I reply.

"What are we thinking now that Jessie is . . . you know?" Syd asks.

"Justin," Axel says. "With Kason gone, he's the star."

"What does he get out of Debbie and Jessie's deaths?"

"They both dated Kason, right?"

"Well, yeah, but that doesn't mean he was jealous. He was dating that Gemma last week," I say.

"It seems like someone who doesn't like the popular clique is doing this. Like a cull of mean girls . . . and boys," Syd says with absolutely no tact.

"Well, that suspect list is long," Axel replies.

"Not really," I say. "It has to be someone who really hates them and is strong enough. Kason would have fought, and that dude was built."

Axel looks at me. "You're back to thinking I could have done this, I see."

"I didn't say that."

His eyes tighten in the corners. "You didn't need to. Don't worry, I'm sure you're not alone. It's always the ones without a big circle of friends and a happy home, right?"

"That's not true. Though, to be fair, I've never thought you definitely didn't do it."

"Really, Izzy, what the—"

"I'm kidding, Axel."

Kind of. I do flit between believing in his innocence and keeping him high on my list. He seems more lost than homicidal to me.

Justin walks past our table, does a double take at Axel, and heads out of the cafeteria.

"He looked guilty just then," Axel says.

"How?"

"He just does. Looking over here like he's suspicious of *us*."

"You think he suspects one of us?" Syd asks.

"One or all. Don't worry, it's only Justin. There's not a lot going on inside his head. It's just ice and naked women."

I turn my nose up. "Gross."

We change the subject, because a couple of teachers enter the cafeteria and pace the room like they're watching for something. So we eat in relative silence, and Axel leaves the second he's finished.

When lunch is done, Syd and I go to class. Even with the arrival of the cops on campus, school so far hasn't been canceled.

They must think that we're safer here, and I actually agree. We're in large numbers rather than all going off in separate directions.

No one does any work, though. All through Spanish class, I twiddle my thumbs. Then, in last period, I quietly drum on the table while waiting for the bell. All I want to do is go home and lock my door.

Finally, the bell rings and we're free. Syd isn't waiting for me when I reach my car, but we did say we'd both go straight home.

I get in, start the engine, and peel out. I don't get far, though.

Everyone seems to be leaving at the same time—there's a line of cars to get out of the lot. People are honking, as if that's going to make it go any faster.

I dial Miyah while I wait.

"Hey, Iz. You doing okay?" I smile at her bright voice.

"I'm on my way home. You with your dad?"

"Yep. I guess you're calling because of Jessie," she whispers.

"Uh-huh. You shared the meme, Miyah. I'm worried you could be a target."

"No danger of that. The only thing I'm allowed to do alone is pee."

"Good."

"It's really not, but I appreciate the love, Iz."

"You're practically my sister."

"I'll be careful. You better be, too. I know you can't help getting involved, but make sure you're never alone. Not reposting doesn't mean you're safe."

"I know," I say. "Traffic's moving now. I'll catch up later."

"Love you," she says and ends the call.

Turning up my radio, I listen to news of Jessie. Her untimely death floats through my car. All the deaths have been a constant on the local radio stations.

No new information. Only that she was last seen at ten p.m. by her parents and then found at nine-thirty this morning. The news took about three hours to get out. The cops would have told Jessie's parents first, of course.

There is still nothing on how she was killed. No confirmation that her death fear was used. That is what everyone suspects, and the news station reports that she was afraid of being stabbed. They're also quick to reiterate that we don't know for sure.

Mom and Dad both text me to lock the door at home after school—as if I don't usually do that.

I'm not allowed to leave.

I don't want to leave.

Mom will be home earlier today, but I'll still be home alone for an hour.

The line in front of me clears, and I pull out of campus. The first flecks of fresh snow hit my windshield, and my wipers instantly bat them away.

Taking my foot off the gas, I crawl along as the snow pelts to the ground. It's only taken five minutes for the storm to really kick in.

I flick my headlights up, but that does very little to help. All I can see is a thick blanket of white hitting my car. Leaning forward in my seat, I squint and ease off the gas.

Another car rolls up behind me. I look up to the mirror and then back to the storm. The car keeps the tiniest distance, definitely a touch too close. Grinding my teeth, I try to ignore it and focus solely on what little I can see of the road in front of me.

What is this jerk's problem?

He creeps closer, but I can't see him in the mirror at all. We're almost bumper to bumper. I take a breath that's supposed to settle the rolling anxiety. It doesn't work. There are ditches on either side of this road; I can't afford to lose focus.

Does this asshole want to force me off the road?

We're both going to crash if he's not careful.

My palms turn slick around the steering wheel.

He inches closer until I can see the outline of his windshield. I wish I could see who's in there so I could report them. They're too close for me to see a license plate.

I can't allow my eyes to leave the sliver of road I can actually see for longer than a heartbeat, though. Who would drive like this in the middle of a storm?

I want to beep the horn, but it's not safe to let go of the wheel.

The car revs, making me jump. I cling harder to the steering wheel, but it causes the car to jolt. Gasping, I turn into the skid as my tires slide under me.

Fear drips down my spine as I picture my car facedown in the ditch.

When my car straightens out, I ease back squarely onto my side of the road and apply the brake.

The car that was behind me pulls to the other side of the road and speeds away sharply.

My eyes flit to the car, the road, and back as I come to a complete stop.

Against the black-tinted back seat window, hands press against glass.

No . . .

Oh God.

I do a double take, but the hands are gone. And so is the car.

I definitely saw that. It wasn't my overactive imagination.

With a pounding heart, I try to come up with a description

of the car. A gray SUV—that's about all I've got. The snow isn't helping.

My fingers shake as I grab my phone and dial.

"Nine-one-one, what's your emergency?"

I take a breath. "I think I've just seen someone being kidnapped."

twenty-six

IZZY

I'm home barely two minutes when Sheriff Rosetta and Officer Duggan knock on the door. I've confirmed that Syd is home safe. Mom and Dad are on their way, but their commute will be close to an hour in this weather. A blanket of snow has already settled on my car.

I let the officers in, shivering at the two-second bite from the snowstorm. Sheriff looks over his shoulder as I slam the door, probably thinking that I don't want the neighbors to see that he's here.

"Would you like something to drink?" I ask.

They both ask for coffee and stay mostly silent while I make it. I notice they look around the kitchen as if they've never seen it before. They've both been inside my house. It's a small town, and Dad invites most people to our cookouts.

When I've made the coffee, I join them at the kitchen table.

"We've spoken to your parents, and they're happy for us to talk to you about what you saw," Sheriff Rosetta says.

I nod. "Yeah, my dad said he would tell you that it's okay."

"Can you take us through it?"

"I was on my way home and kept slowing down because of the storm. Then this car came up behind me, way too fast for the conditions. It was like they were in a hurry. They stayed back for a few minutes and then went past me." I take a breath. "I saw two hands, like more of the sides actually and some fingers." I hold both wrists together, palms touching, and show them. "The hands weren't flat to the glass . . . as if they couldn't because they were tied."

Sheriff nods. "And did you see who was in the car?"

"No, the windows were tinted. It was a gray SUV. An old one. I didn't get the license, and I couldn't see the driver. It all happened so fast, and the snow was really coming down."

He nods and smiles. "It's okay. You're doing well. Do you know the make and model of the car?"

"No. It wasn't huge, and it didn't have smooth, curved lines like the ones made now. That's why I think it was quite old. It was definitely a pale gray, though. I remember the windows were a lot darker than the paintwork."

Officer Duggan scribbles down a note with one hand while drinking his coffee with the other.

"I know you said you didn't see the driver, but could you tell if they were male or female?"

"No. I'm sorry."

"All right."

"Do you think the killer has someone else?" I ask.

The sheriff clears his throat. "Let's not speculate."

So, yes.

"I wanted to ask about Jessie," I say.

"Unfortunately, we can't give you any details, Izzy. You know that."

"Yeah, I do, but . . . was she in a lot of pain?"

I can see the debate in his eyes. "I don't think she suffered for long." He pauses, then says, "We're going to stay with you until your parents arrive, Izzy, okay?"

My spine stiffens. Now, why would he do that? We have locks.

"You think I'm in danger."

I'm not asking him.

The sheriff blinks twice. "We have no reason to believe you are, but we're not taking any chances."

He's lying. Why is he worried about me? I didn't repost that meme. The killer has no idea of my death fear.

But the killer has seen me looking at his car, and maybe he knows I saw the person in the back.

Would he care? I couldn't see anything with those tinted windows. Though he must know that I'm somewhat involved, having found Debbie and all.

I raise my eyes to the sheriff. "You're worried that he saw me looking at his car."

"Izzy, there's no reason to panic," says Officer Duggan.

"Easy for you to say."

Maybe I should have left town with Lia.

"Even if this person did see you," Sheriff says, "they might not recognize you. We're going to be cautious, but like Officer Duggan said, we're not going to panic."

"Should I still go to school?"

"There's no reason to stay home. That being said, if anyone new contacts you, do tell us."

Does he think the killer might contact me? God, I hope not.

"Will you close the school? You've got three dead students!"

"We can't say, Izzy. The investigation is ongoing. None of the murders have happened on school grounds. We do believe you're safe at school."

"Has anyone else been reported missing?"

"Izzy . . ."

I pout. "Right, you can't tell me."

They haven't. Not yet anyway. He wouldn't be sitting in my kitchen drinking coffee if there was a recently reported missing teen.

"Are you calling everyone who reposted that meme to see if they're home and safe?" I ask.

He smiles. "You would make quite the detective."

Not the first time I've heard that. "You are doing that. Good."

I should tell them about Axel. But there's no way he could've left school and kidnapped someone in that short amount of time. Right?

twenty-seven

FEAR

I jam my fingers into my eye sockets, as Julia's constant dramatic screaming is giving me a banging headache. She's spent the last hour solidly hollering for help, as if people actually come by here.

We're too far out even for the regular dog walkers or joggers.

There's a reason I chose this barn. I'm not an idiot. I plan perfect murders.

I watch her through the mirror as she sits against the wall, head tilted to the ceiling—or heaven—screaming that she wants to go home. Her eyes are squeezed closed, and her mouth is downturned in an ugly cry.

I can't ever imagine *wanting* to go home. I would rather have starved in that tiny room she's currently wishing she could escape from.

She has *no* idea.

I pass her phone from hand to hand as I observe her. An hour ago, she sat down. Before that she was running about, whacking the door and pushing the walls as if they would cave in.

This was more satisfying in my mind, but now I'm stuck babysitting the screaming victim. How long until she gives up?

Julia's parents are overseas, and I've managed to keep them at bay with a text message. They only attempted to call once, so two minutes later I sent a message apologizing, saying I was taking a shower when they called and about to go to bed.

They haven't tried since, but I don't know how long they will leave it. Will they be happy to only receive texts from her? This is the part I have no control over, and it both scares and excites me. How long before she's reported missing and the cops go looking for her?

I'd join the search, but it would look too suspicious, since I don't know her.

In the morning, I'll call the school and say she's sick. I'll leave a message, pretending to be a relative.

I can imagine them listening to the message and wishing her well.

She'll probably be dead by the end of the week, and revenge will be served.

I found varying information on the internet on how long it takes to starve to death when I was doing my research. All dependent on the person. I guess time will tell if Julia goes in days or weeks.

It's an experiment I would like to try again, see if the process takes longer with water left for them. If I could only find someone else reposting about starving.

Only take those who repost. That's the rule.

Not everyone has a public account, and that irritates the hell out of me.

Julia closes her eyes, and a tear rolls down her face.

I can't remember the last time I cried. I used to as a kid, but I learned fast that it didn't get me anywhere. They liked my tears, my pain, and my fear. Especially my fear.

That's not important now.

They're dead, and I'm not.

Watching her wake up was like watching your team win the Super Bowl. I looked on with interest, my heart beating faster and faster, as she realized what'd happened.

It seemed to happen slowly and then all at once. She lifted her head, blinked hard a few times, looked around. Then she was up on her feet and running full force toward the door.

I stood on the other side of it, drinking in her screams.

The satisfaction of that one has long worn off. She's so loud.

I should get a notebook and document what happens. Growing up, he was always scribbling notes, things I'd done wrong, things he wanted to do.

When he died, I found a couple of notes he'd kept. Or maybe he just forgot to throw them away.

One of them is here, pinned to the wall. A constant reminder of why I'm doing what I'm doing. His messy scrawl: *Kid has no respect and needs drowning.*

Needs drowning. As if that's an acceptable punishment for a bit of backtalk.

I don't know where he thought of it, but he did it once. I'd been home late from school and gave him attitude when questioned why, apparently. He ran a sink of water and blindsided me.

My stomach flames at the memory, still feeling the burn of

my lungs as they stung without any oxygen. I probably could have taken him. I worked out even then—to keep me sane—but I was still too scared to fight back.

No, I didn't start fighting back until I embraced my desire for revenge.

twenty-eight

IZZY

I don't want to be at school, but I'm probably safer here than anywhere else. My parents are at work, so being home alone isn't a good idea.

Syd's dad insisted she stay home today, though, so the day is going to drag. It's weird being here without her.

I'm not alone for long, though, as Justin and Axel walk into AP English together. Well, not *together,* just at the same time. They both have identical scowls and are looking at each other like they want to throw down.

Axel takes a seat beside me, scraping the chair as he goes, but he doesn't say a word.

I glance to the side. "Morning, Axel."

Yesterday he came and sat next to me at lunch, and now he's pretending that I don't exist.

"Mornin'," he grunts.

"Are you okay?"

"Mmm."

"I'd hate to see you in a mood, then."

His chest expands in a deep breath, and he closes his eyes as he calms himself down.

"What's going on?"

He shrugs. "Lack of sleep, school pressure, murderer in town. You know, the usual."

I'm not convinced that he's at all bothered by school pressure. "Home stuff okay?"

It's a risky question, as we never talk about that.

"We don't need to do this, okay?" he snips.

"Do what?"

"The friendly thing. We've gone almost four years without it."

So does that response mean something's wrong at home? Is he trying to tell me in a really backward way that he wants us to be friends? "Let me know when you've calmed down. We're working on our presentation, and I don't want to do it alone."

I scowl at my full notebook on Poe and seethe over Axel's attitude. One minute he's okay with me, and the next he's acting like we're mortal enemies. Does he want to be friends or not? Perhaps a better question should be Why do I care?

"All right, I'm sorry, Iz," he says a few minutes later.

He's literally never called me Iz before. Why the hell now? I don't think he's ever apologized, either.

I peek over again. He's turned toward me, slightly frowning, and I think I can see the hint of a bruise on his cheek. "Do you want to talk?"

"Not really," he grunts.

"Are you going to anyway?"

He shakes his head. "It's nothing."

I wonder if it's about the cops and he won't tell me because he doesn't trust me. Maybe he doesn't trust anyone. Though he did tell me they'd find out how much he hated Kason. I'm dying to know that.

He turns away, and I know the chance to talk has now gone. Axel is a mystery; there's a darkness in him that I see behind his eyes. It's not just his less-than-fluffy personality.

While Axel and I work, on semi-good terms, I feel Justin watching us. He sits two rows back, though he might as well have his chair touching mine. That might just be because the class has fewer students than usual, as some, like Syd, didn't turn up.

Yesterday has me paranoid. I don't like that there are people missing today. They're probably all home, but that doesn't stop me from stressing that they're actually *missing*. The very first thing I did this morning was check the news. There has been nothing new.

I'm certain of what I saw, driving home yesterday. Why was the person in the back not reported missing?

"I saw something on my drive home yesterday," I whisper.

Axel looks at me out of the corner of his eye, not even bothering to turn his head. "You saw lots of things, I would imagine."

"I see you've got your sense of humor back."

He smirks. "What did you see, Izzy?"

I'm back to Izzy.

"On my way home, I saw someone being kidnapped. The aftermath, actually, not the act."

He blinks very slowly two times. "You saw *what?*"

I lean closer and, in hushed tones, I tell him everything that happened.

He barely reacts. No alarm in his pretty eyes and no increased breathing. If it was him, surely there would be something to give it away?

"The sheriff wouldn't have stayed with you if he didn't think you were in danger. Not while there's a killer out there," he says as I finish my story.

"Right."

"No one's missing," he adds.

"No. No one has been *reported* missing. How many kids out there don't have someone who cares where they are?"

His eyes grow darker. A reaction to something, at last. "Far too many. What are you doing now, then?"

"No clue. There's tumbleweed in my head when it comes to my next move."

Axel potentially has a motive, Mariella is acting extra mean, and Justin is suddenly talking to me. The more I learn, the more confused I am. How many more suspects are out there?

"Izzy without a plan—I didn't think I'd ever see it."

"I probably shouldn't have any plans. The cops are investigating. I should stay out of it, pretend it's not happening."

He tilts his head to the side. "Why *do* you get involved?"

"Because I found her," I say. It's as simple as that. I don't think I'm some super amateur sleuth, I don't hunger for the truth, I don't think the cops are doing a bad job. I just want to know why

I found one of my peers dead on the side of the road. Why did I have to see that? I can't let it go.

"You need to talk to someone about that." he says.

"I've been offered regular guidance, and my parents told me they'll make an appointment with our family therapist. I don't feel like it yet."

"You have a family therapist?"

I roll my eyes. "We don't all go together."

"I bet you all bake Christmas cookies together and sit around playing board games, too."

"Why is that a problem for you?"

"It's not," he mutters, scribbling something down in his notebook.

I take it he doesn't bake cookies with his family. Or didn't. I know that he lived with Tristan for a while, and both of Tristan's parents are dead.

I wish I could ask him what his home life is like. I doubt he would tell me, but Tristan might. Axel is hiding a lot. Maybe if I knew him better, it would be easier to see his innocence. Besides blinking, he didn't react to my telling him about the kidnapping thing. The killer would have been rattled.

When the bell rings, Axel grabs his pen and notebook and flees the room like it's on fire. I move much slower to my next class, my head running wild with theories.

School without Syd passes as painfully slowly as I thought it would. But I'm finally free and walking to my car in the lot. Snow showers to the ground, spiraling in the wind. It's getting worse.

As I reach my car, I get a text, but it's way too cold to look at it right now. I get in and whack the heat up before I read it.

Miyah: *Bored out of my mind. Staying at school until Mom picks me up. Spanish club. There's a club for that! Ugh! I miss u.*

Me: *Ur school has a club for everything. When are u free?*

Miyah: *Dad says when the killer's caught. Ur coming to the party this weekend, right?? U can't miss it!*

Uncle Samar's fiftieth birthday. It'll be a massive party at their house.

Me: *About to drive. Obvs I'll be there*

Miyah: *:D*

I pull into our drive, and I'm not surprised to see Mom's car already there. I overheard her and Dad talking about her working from home in the afternoons, so I'm never here alone.

That does nothing to keep me calm about the situation. They tell me not to get ahead of myself while guarding me. Mixed messages much?

I knock quickly to let her know I'm back, then I leave her to it.

After grabbing a snack, I go upstairs to call Tristan.

He answers on the third ring. "Izzy?"

"Hey, Tristan."

"Everything okay? Do you need a ride?"

A ride? Oh, he told me to call him if I needed a lift. Okay, that's sweet.

"No, I'm home. I just wanted to see how you are."

How unconvincing was that? I wince at how awkward I am. Why can't I have Lia's confidence?

"Really?" he asks.

"Okay, no. Well, I do care if you're okay. Obviously. Um." *Oh God, shoot me now.* "I wanted to ask you about Axel."

My question is met with silence. "Axel?" he finally asks.

"Yeah. We're working on a partner project at school, and he's kind of confusing. One minute he's hot and the next as cold as the damn snow outside. I was just thinking if I could understand him, maybe we could get on better."

Silence hangs down the line. Then he says, "Can we meet somewhere?"

My hand tightens around my cell. He wants to *meet.*

twenty-nine

IZZY

"Iz, you still there?" Tristan asks. "Can we meet at Puck's for dinner? This isn't exactly a conversation we should have over the phone."

I clear my throat. "It's a dinner conversation?"

"It's an in-person conversation, and I'm hungry."

Surely he would ask to meet somewhere less people-y if he was luring me to my death?

My heart beats harder. "Mom would never let me go out alone right now. You could come here?"

I want to see what he does when he's invited over.

"Fair enough. I'll be there in fifteen."

My hand tightens around my cell. "You're not at work?"

"Weather's too bad to go out again."

"O-okay. See you soon."

Tristan hangs up first, and I look at my phone. That could be totally innocent, but he's *never* asked me to meet him before. He's

Lia's friend. But Lia and the rest of their gang have all moved away to college. He wouldn't come over knowing my mom was here if he wanted to kill me, though. Plus, why would he do it in my home? That's not how this killer has been working.

If he even thinks about attacking me, I'm going to scratch the crap out of him and embed his DNA under my fingernails.

I run down the stairs and tell Mom that Tristan is coming over. She nods, waving me away and returning to her call.

Tristan said he's hungry, so I chuck a pizza in the oven, chips in a bowl, and unscrew a jar of Dad's homemade salsa. That'll have to do.

Nothing says *please don't kill me* like a pizza.

Good Lord, what is wrong with me?

He's right on time: fifteen minutes later, he knocks. I rush to the door, because the snow is coming down hard, and Tristan jumps into the house.

Mom walks out of her office at the same time. She didn't say she was going to do that, but I knew she would. "Hey, Tristan. Iz, I need to run to the store before the storm gets worse. Your dad is working late, and we might not be going anywhere later."

"The storm is supposed to be bad for a few days," Tristan says. "Fishing is now postponed until after the weekend."

"I heard that, too." She turns to me. "You do not leave this house."

I hold up my hands. "I know the rules."

"You'll still be here when I get back?" she asks Tristan. "I shouldn't be more than an hour."

"I'll stay until you're back."

It's fun listening to Mom and Tristan talking about baby-sitting me. Not. Clearly my mom trusts Tristan. She did with Lia for four years.

"Thank you." She grabs her purse and coat and runs from the house to her car.

"She thinks I'm four."

He laughs. "You're lucky to have someone who cares."

"I'm sorry," I say, wincing at how often I put my foot in my mouth.

"Don't be."

I bite my lip. Why can't I just be normal around him? "So, I'm not a great chef. Pizza will have to do," I say.

He kicks off his shoes and follows me into the kitchen. "You didn't need to feed me, Iz."

"You're hungry and doing me a favor," I say. "Soda?"

"Water, please."

I grab a Coke and a bottle of water, and we sit while the pizza cooks. Tristan dips a chip.

"I missed this salsa," he says, going for a second one.

"Do you miss high school?" I ask.

"Not school, necessarily. Though I promise you it's easier than work." He smiles. "I miss friends."

"Do you keep in contact?"

"I do but Insta isn't the same. I suppose you could say I've dropped off the grid a bit. Besides working, I don't do much."

"Why is that?"

He ducks his head, and I notice his cheeks redden. "Embarrassment. All my crew from school are off making something of their life. I'm still here, taking over my dad's company, working the boats."

"That's nothing to be embarrassed about."

"Enough about me. You wanted to know about Axel."

"I wouldn't have asked about you if I didn't want to know."

That's not strictly true. I would have asked to be polite.

"Thanks, Iz. So . . . what's Axel done to you?" he asks on a sigh.

That's interesting. Why would he think that? *Done* something, not *said* something.

"Nothing. Why would you ask that?"

He shakes his head. "I just mean his attitude. He's got a temper, but he's harmless."

I gulp down a mouthful of soda. "Right. I've been getting a lot of the attitude. Is he always like that?"

"Pretty much. Always has been. Like I mentioned before, we're not close. Our grandma was about the only one in the family who actually gave a shit about us."

"Your parents?" I ask. Of course, I know they both died last year, but that's about all I know about them.

"My parents weren't around much. Raising kids didn't come naturally to them." He scowls into the jar of salsa. "I had food and a roof over my head, but I knew I wasn't loved. Axel moved in with us when he was eight, after his mom died."

"Whoa, that's heavy. What happened to her?"

"She overdosed while Axel was at school. He found her when he got home. His dad was serving a life sentence in prison, so he had nowhere else to go."

"He found her," I whisper, trying to imagine the horror of

that. No wonder he's angry at the world and pushing people away. "That's awful. All of it. I'm sorry you both went through stuff like that."

He smiles but it quickly falls away. "Axel moved out of my house at the beginning of December, after hearing that his dad died in prison. He lost my parents and his dad in a matter of months."

"So he does live alone."

"In a crappy apartment on the outskirts of town."

"Why did he move out? It was just you two then, right?"

"I don't know, really. Yeah, it was just the two of us in the end. He's had to deal with a lot of loss recently. I guess he felt like being alone."

"I don't know what to say."

The oven beeps.

"You don't need to say anything, just understand that he's not being a dick for no reason. He has a lot of anger."

I get up from the table. "I'll get the pizza."

Tristan and I eat on the sofa while watching *The Witcher* on Netflix. We occasionally stop when I have another question about Axel. Like how does he afford his own place? Tristan's answer? He doesn't know.

I finish my pizza and take a slurp of soda.

As Tristan is about to grab another slice, we hear a feral scream from outside. My heart stops as I look at Tristan with wide eyes. At the same time, we leap to our feet.

"What the heck was that?" I ask, running to the window after Tristan.

"Sounded like someone screaming."

Someone or something.

We try to look through the storm, but the snow is coming down like clouds falling from the sky.

"Help!" The scream comes again.

Tristan runs to the door and flings it open. Neither of us care about shoes or coats as we step onto my porch.

"Hello?" Tristan shouts.

"Oh my God! Help!"

"Where are you?" I yell, shielding my eyes from the snow in a futile attempt to see better. "Follow my voice. We can't see you."

I squint through the snow. A second later, a petite figure comes into view. The girl, probably my age, trembles as she staggers toward us.

Her hands are tied.

thirty

IZZY

"Help me," she pleads, dropping to the ground, her knees disappearing into the snow.

It's her. The girl in the car.

"Oh my God! Call the cops, Izzy," Tristan shouts, running toward her.

I spin around and dash back in the house to call as he picks her up and brings her inside.

Tristan moves quickly, wrapping a blanket from the back of the sofa around the girl's soaking body while I speak to the sheriff.

She sobs into his chest as he holds her up. His eyes are wide as he looks at me as if I know what to do.

I end the call. "Sheriff's on his way."

Tristan rubs the girl's back as if he's trying to get some heat into her.

"What happened?" he asks.

"I—I was taken."

"By who?"

Trembling, she shakes her head, her tears dripping from her jaw. "Didn't see his face."

"Where is he now?" Tristan asks, glancing back to the window. "Iz, lock that door."

I leap forward, almost losing my footing and crashing to the floor, and run to the door to bolt the thing. Could the killer be chasing her? Did he see where she went? I turn the lock and lean against the door like a terrible human barricade.

"It's okay now," he says. "Come and sit down."

She sits on my sofa. "My hands."

Tristan opens the blanket. "Who would do this? Let me untie it," he replies.

My eyes widen as she raises her hands.

She turns her head to me as he awkwardly works on her bound wrists. "Could I have some coffee, please? God I would love a coffee. I was t-taken . . ."

"You're safe now," I reply numbly. "I'll make coffee."

I walk into the kitchen, being sure to leave the door wide open so I can hear what they talk about.

"Where were you taken from?" Tristan asks her.

She sniffs. "I was walking to my car yesterday afternoon, and someone grabbed me from behind. I passed out, and when I woke up, I was in a car, tied and blindfolded."

My hands shake from the adrenaline rush—and the cold, hard fear—so it takes me longer to make the coffee.

"Did you see anyone or anything that could help the cops?"

"No," she sobs. "I thought he was going to kill me."

"Shhh, he didn't, and you're safe now. It was definitely a man?"

"Oh. Well . . . I—I can't be sure, but I think so."

I walk back into the room and hand her a coffee.

The rope is on the floor by Tristan's feet.

"Thanks," she says, wrapping her free hands around the mug.

"Of course," I say. "My name's Izzy," I add. "Sorry, I didn't ask your name."

"Julia Stone."

"Why do I recognize you?"

She looks blankly at me. Then her head tilts, like she's trying to figure it out, too.

"Amiyah. Do you go to school with her?" I ask.

She sits straighter. "Yes, I have a couple of classes with her. I think we've been at a couple of parties together before. I recognize you, too."

I smile at her, wanting her to feel safe now. "Miyah's my cousin. Where are your parents?"

"They travel for work. They're in Tokyo right now."

"Julia, did you share that fear meme?" I ask.

She gulps. "Yes."

"What was your fear?" I ask, sitting next to her.

Tristan shoots me a look like I shouldn't be asking her that right now. But I don't follow her, and she doesn't follow me.

"Starving to death."

I close my eyes and take a breath. I try not to imagine what her fate would've been if she hadn't escaped.

When I open my eyes, Tristan is looking at Julia openmouthed.

He shakes it off. "The cops will be here soon. Is there any family you want us to call?"

"M-my grandparents are thirty minutes away," she says. "I don't know where my phone is."

"You can use mine," I tell her, handing it over.

Tristan and I walk to the window to watch for the cops while Julia makes her call. She instantly breaks down as she speaks to her grandparents. Loud sobs make her words almost impossible to understand.

"Should I intervene?" I ask.

Tristan shakes his head as we watch her wipe her eyes with her free hand. "No, she probably needs to hear their voices right now. Are you okay?"

"She could have died."

He grabs my hand, and I look up into his eyes. "But she didn't. She's here now and she's safe. It's going to be okay, Iz."

I'm not so sure. Being kidnapped surely isn't something you forget. How will she ever be okay? Nothing will be the same for her.

"Should I call your mom and dad? Your mom's due home soon, but we should call, right?" He lets go of me.

Oh crap, I didn't even think about that.

I run my hand through my hair. "Um. Yeah, probably."

"Are you sure you're all right?" he asks. "You're pale. Do you need to sit?"

"I should've made myself a coffee, too," I say.

"Sit with her. I'll make the calls and get you a drink."

"Thanks," I murmur, and go sit with Julia as she hangs up and puts my phone aside.

I instinctively wrap an arm around her, and she leans into me.

"You're warm," she says, almost to herself.

She's still frozen to the bone. "I should get you some spare clothes or you'll never warm up. I could get you some cozy sweats."

"I nearly died," she says, either ignoring my question or not hearing me at all.

I open my mouth twice before realizing I don't know what to say.

Her big, bloodshot eyes stare up at me, waiting.

"You got away, Julia. You're so strong and you're going to be okay. No one is going to hurt you now. Okay?"

"He was going to starve me, wasn't he?"

I dip my chin. "Don't think about that now. How did you get away?"

"He took me to some barn in a field near Whites Industrial Estate. My hands were tied together, and I was in this little room. I managed to shake my head enough to get the blindfold off. Then I worked on busting the lock on the door. I thought I'd broken my arm when I was slamming against the door."

She lifts her sleeve, and her whole arm is an ugly shade of purple.

"As soon as I was free, I ran back into town. The storm rolled in, I could barely see anything, and I couldn't hear anyone. I just started screaming, and then I heard you and . . ."

"Tristan."

Tears well in her eyes again. "Thank you for helping me."

"No need to thank us."

Tristan walks into the living room as sirens blast outside.

"Help is here," I tell her.

Sheriff Rosetta and just about the entire force walk through my door as Tristan opens it up. Two paramedics are close behind. I stand back as they tend to Julia. Besides her hands and her arm, I don't think she was hurt physically.

Tristan, Julia, and I are taken into the kitchen. We sit down at the table, and Officer Duggan flips his notebook open. "Your parents home?" he asks me.

"Mom went to the store. Tristan called her and my dad, so they'll be here soon."

"All right, I'll start with Tristan, then," Sheriff says.

"Can I get her something to change into?" I ask.

He nods. "Julia, Izzy is going to get you something to wear. When you remove your clothing, can you put the items in this bag? I'll need the blanket, too."

"Yeah, that's mine but, whatever, take it," I say, running to the laundry room, where I know I have some clean sweats waiting to be taken to my room.

Mom arrives minutes later, followed by Julia's grandparents. Once Tristan is done, I give my statement.

It's late by the time the cops leave. Julia's grandparents go with her to the hospital, where she can be checked out properly. Tristan and I told them everything, but I don't like how the sheriff watched us. As if he was suspicious of us. But what were we supposed to do, leave her out there?

Mom and Dad are in the kitchen, trying to have a private conversation. Tristan pulls on his coat and lifts a brow.

"So, tonight wasn't exactly what I thought it would be," he says, stuffing his hands in his pockets and trying to lighten the mood.

"Pizza and Netflix was as much excitement as I'd planned. I can't believe Julia . . ."

"I know. But, hey, the pizza part of today was nice."

I nod. "Yeah, it was. I'm so grateful that you were here. I don't know what I would have done if I was alone. And thanks for telling me about Axel and your home life. It couldn't have been easy."

"No, there aren't many people I tell. You're a good listener, Iz. I just hope you don't go too hard on Axel."

I wonder if he'd ever open up to me the way Tristan has.

"I won't. I'll have a full day at school tomorrow and make friends with him in every class."

"Don't make skipping a regular thing like Axel does."

"Huh?"

He shakes his head. "I've seen him in town early way too often. It's like you guys think school should finish after lunch. He's smart as hell, much smarter than me, but it won't count for much if he doesn't graduate."

"Axel skips the last two periods a lot?"

Tristan shrugs. "Not every week, I don't think, but more than he should. Why?"

"No reason. I just don't notice him absent much."

"Do you look?"

I wince. "Well, no."

He laughs and slides his phone into his pocket.

Why would Axel skip so much? What could he possibly be doing during that time?

"You going to be okay getting home after everything this afternoon?" I ask.

He smiles. "I think I'll manage."

"This person has killed a guy, too."

"I know. I appreciate your caring. I'll be fine, Iz. You make sure you're careful."

I'm not sure being careful is enough.

Not when I have classes with Axel.

thirty-one
FEAR

She's gone!

Gritting my teeth, I slam my fist into the wooden wall that used to separate me from Julia.

How could she have gotten out? How could *I* have let this happen?

The door is bashed in, lock broken. I don't know how she found so much physical strength. I should have reinforced the door, put two locks on it. It's not a mistake I will make again.

Growling, I shake my throbbing hand and pace back and forth.

This is the first time I've been able to come back since she turned up in town. The cops have had this area covered since then. Their tape rattles in the wind around the small barn.

They've also searched the one next to it, but they haven't found my base. It's too far away, hidden in trees and kept secret from the world.

I don't leave anything personal behind in this one. I'm careful, and I wear gloves. It's okay.

I should have made a room inside the base to do this. I was too eager, and this was the only option that could hold a person. Only it couldn't. I grit my teeth at my mistake. How could I have been so stupid?

You're better than this.

Rubbing my forehead with my gloved hand, I breathe slowly and purposefully through my nose.

Okay. I need a new plan. I have the base that I can use to do this again. When the cops aren't swarming town, I'll go and get the materials I need. It won't take long to build a wall.

Next time I will have better security. I'll make sure I bring them in on a Friday so I can stay over the weekend. Two days should be long enough to weaken them. Maybe I can even get Julia again.

My mouth salivates as I imagine taking the same person again. It'd be my biggest challenge, because she is sure to have family watching her like a hawk, but I like a challenge. I want them all to know what it's like to be petrified for your life.

With everyone I take, I feel a soothing in my soul.

I grew up fearing *everything,* and now I fear *nothing.* Not even the cops. If they were smart, they would have found me by now. Nothing can stop death.

Slamming the barn door, I walk around the back and into the small wooded area behind it. There isn't much here, mostly overgrown shrubs and a few gnarly trees, but in the middle is something that I visit often.

I stop by the spot and rake the snow out of the way with my foot as more starts to fall from the gray clouds. It won't take long for the snow to cover my tracks again, as five inches has been forecast.

Buried beneath my feet is Victim Zero.

The cops haven't found the dead body buried on this site. It's five feet from the small tree they've tied the police tape around.

No one perfects anything without a little practice. My childhood may have hardened me to many things, but I wasn't sure that I would be able to kill, to take someone's life with my own hands.

I was wrong.

I can do it, and I do it well.

The drifter under the ground put up a decent fight, but he was no match in the end. He lived alone on the streets, out of town but not far enough. The image of his big, fearful eyes when he woke and realized what I was about to do is burned onto my retina.

It's not something I will ever forget.

Crouching, I touch the hard, frosted moss and mud that covers his body.

The first kill is never your best. You're nervous and unsure if you're going to do it right. I experienced an incredible low for two days. I was unable to sleep and felt physically sick. But that was replaced with a feeling of intense power, and I need that high again.

I look at the ground and try to picture his dirty face. My practice victim. I don't know his name. It doesn't matter.

I cover the patch back up so it looks the same as the rest of the ground, stand, and breathe in the crisp scent of fresh snow as it drops on Zero, a fresh blanket to cover my tracks.

There is still so much work to be done.

For starters, what am I going to do with my little Izzy?

thirty-two

IZZY

The next morning, Mom drops me off at school, since I'm no longer allowed to be alone, ever. She's probably considered asking Syd to follow me to the bathroom.

I spent two hours on the phone to Miyah last night. She seriously freaked about me and Tristan finding Julia. Then she freaked some more because I had Tristan over.

Snow is lying thick on the ground, and even more is in the forecast. There hasn't been a winter storm alert yet, but it wouldn't surprise me if one came.

I walk into the building, and it's like someone announced that the queen has arrived. If synchronized staring was a thing, my classmates would win gold. They even stop talking as they spot me.

So, I guess word got out about me and Tristan finding Julia.

"Oh my God!" Syd says, linking her arm in mine and tugging me around the corner. "There you are! I've been *dying*. Dad tried to get me to stay home, but there was no way. We cut a deal, and I have to call him as I leave the building and get in my car. Then I have to go straight to his office, since I can't go home alone."

"Take a breath, Syd."

"Yesterday was insane! I can't believe she escaped. I can't believe you rescued her, Iz. You're a hero!"

"Not really. I just opened my door."

She rolls her eyes. "So modest."

As we walk the halls, I'm met with even more stares.

I duck my head as my cheeks heat. I'm not used to attention. People never look at me. Why do people crave this? It sucks.

"How long before people get bored of watching me?" I ask.

"Um . . . never," Syd says, sighing. "You're so involved in this, and *everyone* knows. You can't keep secrets in this town. You tell a person something in confidence, and it's hit the town square before you've even left school."

"Someone here is good at keeping secrets," I tell her.

"Well, the killer is hardly going to advertise that news. Sucks that you can't go anywhere on your own, either. We're going to be in lockdown until this psycho is caught."

"My parents are freaking out. Mom kept crying when the cops left. She was half mad and half proud of me for helping Julia."

"Well, duh. The killer could have followed her into your house."

I shake my head. "I couldn't leave her out there, could I?

Tristan was with me. Anyway, I think I'm just going to go to the library this morning."

"You're skipping again?"

"I don't feel like sitting in class, being stared at like a caged animal. I hate zoos."

"Okay. You know I'll cover for you."

"Thanks."

We part ways, Syd to homeroom and then first period. Me to the library to hide.

Mrs. Lockett looks up from the front desk when I walk in. She sips her mint-scented tea, smiles, and goes back to Charles Dickens. I think that's the only author I've ever seen her read.

I sit down at an open table and take my pink notebook out.

Then I take out a textbook, so it looks like I'm studying.

I flip the page and pore over the list of names I've made. I add Julia to it. Would the killer try to take her again? That seems incredibly risky, since her family will surely be with her every second of the day.

Julia is from a different school, so that alters things a little. Though Miyah is popular and Julia has been at parties with her—and evidently me—before. Julia isn't necessarily a popular girl just because of that. I mean, I'm not and I go to parties. Thanks to Syd.

If Julia doesn't hang around with the in crowd at her school, my theory is *way* off.

Could the killer be choosing people purely based on their fear rather than working off a personal hit list?

God, that makes sense. It also makes it harder to find him. Unless, of course, I've already found him, and his name is Axel.

Tristan said that he sometimes leaves school early.

No way could it be him, though. I mean, he sits beside me in class!

I should have gone to first period to see if he's in today. His car wasn't here, but I only saw half the lot as Mom dropped me by the front doors . . . and I wasn't looking.

Justin.

Axel.

There could be other suspects, but right now I have nothing for anyone else. The killer might not even go to this school or be an ex-student here. Now that they've attempted to kill someone from St. Mary's, I'm kind of walking around blind.

I make more lists. I have lists for days. Lists of victims, potential victims, possible suspects, motives, and finally a list of places I'd rather be than here.

Second period rolls around. Suddenly, someone sits opposite me and I startle, almost knocking my pens on the floor.

I raise my head, do a double take, and slam my notebook shut.

My heart races overtime.

Swallowing, I say, "Axel. What are you doing here?"

"I missed my partner in first period. Didn't think you'd be here."

"You came looking for me?"

I'm sure my voice sounds like I've swallowed helium.

"I saw you first thing, so I knew you were here. Why did you skip?"

"Wasn't feeling it."

His icy eyes light up as if he senses a lie. "Really?"

I nod, keeping my smile light as I pretend that he's not driving me insane. "This whole thing is making it impossible for me to focus."

"The whole murder thing, you mean?"

How easily he says "murder."

"Yep."

"You saved that girl. It's all anyone can talk about."

My stomach clamps down so hard I feel sick. She could have died. "Uh-huh. Julia is her name. She was petrified. She's so lucky that she managed to get away."

"Where was she?" he asks, tilting his head.

I think you might know that one.

"Said she was in an abandoned barn. Managed to get free and ran into town."

"And you just happened to hear?"

I feel like we're playing a game of chess, waiting for the other to make a move before we can countermove.

"I didn't *just happen* to hear. She was screaming outside my house. We opened the door and called out. Then there she was."

"We?"

I blink twice, debating whether to tell him Tristan was with me. He might know and be testing me. "Your cousin was over."

His head rears backward.

Nope, he didn't know that.

"Tristan was at your house? Why?"

"He's a friend," I reply.

"Of your sister's, right? I didn't know you two had become besties."

"That's not exactly what we are. He used to come around quite a bit when Lia lived at home. My parents like him, too."

"Your parents were home with you?"

"Why all the questions?" I ask, laughing nervously.

"Just trying to help you out. You should watch Tristan."

My heart skips a beat. "And why is that?"

"He's an asshole."

"I mean, he would probably say the same about you."

Axel chuckles. "He would definitely say that. Tristan is the type of guy to call you his best mate while stabbing you in the back. He'd probably tell the cops I'm the murderer just to get me out of his life for good."

"Man, there's no love lost between you two, is there?"

Axel looks down. "He's just not the hero you and that kidnapped chick think, that's all."

Is he referring to his upbringing? Maybe Axel is mad because Tristan didn't defend him. But they're both victims. Tristan is only a year older—how could he have protected him? I wish he'd elaborate.

"What did he do to you?" I ask.

"He hasn't done anything to me."

I'm right: Tristan didn't do anything, and *that's* the problem. I'm half scared that Axel might be a killer and half want to give him a big hug.

"Are you going to second period?" I ask.

"No. I think I'm done with school for the day."

"What, you're leaving now?"

"Why not? No one is doing any work. I have better things to do. The teachers don't seem to care, so why should I?"

"What better things do you have going on?"

"Nosy, aren't you? You're acting weird with me."

"You're *always* acting weird with me. Let's forget it. We need to finish our assignment. We have the presentation soon. If you're leaving now, we could meet after school. Your place?"

His face falls. "You want to come to my place?"

"Sure. We need to finish this. I'm sure my mom would drop me off."

"What happened to your car?"

"Nothing. My parents are paranoid."

"So, they're going to let you come to my house?"

"You're a classmate, so . . . sure."

I really hope my voice sounds as calm as I'm trying to make it . . . and this might take a lot of convincing, because my parents won't be happy.

"Why don't we do it here, now?"

"You said you were leaving."

"I can stay."

Why do I like bickering with him?

"Do you not like people coming over? I love having friends at my house."

He grits his teeth. "I'll come to you, then."

"So, you don't. Like people in your space, I mean."

Could that be because I'll see something he wants to keep hidden?

"No, I don't. Why are you being pushy?"

I shrug. "Curiosity. Did you figure out the thing you were scared the cops would find?"

"Huh?"

"You told me the cops would find out how much you hated Kason."

"Oh, that. Yeah, they already did. It's cool."

What?

"When did this happen?" I ask.

"When they questioned me. Izzy, back off. You're not actually working this case. You're a seventeen-year-old high school student. Stay in your lane."

I narrow my eyes. "I found Debbie, material probably belonging to the killer, and Julia. Forgive me if I can't let this go!" I snap. Not to mention having my tire slashed and someone watching me.

An alert pops up on my phone.

"Oh, great," I mutter, looking out as the snow falls harder and faster than predicted. We now have a severe snowstorm warning.

"Looks like none of us have to stay here today," Axel says at the same time the principal makes an announcement over the speakers.

School is canceled, and I have no car here to get home.

thirty-three

IZZY

"You're wasting time," Axel says, pacing and clenching his hands. He's frustrated with me because I won't immediately leave.

I turn away from him, pressing my phone harder to my ear. It's hard to hear Mom with the call cutting out, and Axel is no help.

"... Sydney ... lock up ... to no one ... soon as I can ..."

She's stuck at work, trying to see if the roads are open, as the snow dropped from nowhere, it seems. "Okay. Mom? I can barely hear. I'll see you later."

I hang up.

"Are you ready yet?" he asks, pinching the bridge of his nose.

"You could have left already!"

"No, I can't. You didn't bring your car."

"That doesn't affect *your* getting home," I say, listening to Syd's phone go to voicemail.

Oh, come on. I need you to pick up.

"I should just leave you, then?" he asks, lifting an eyebrow.

I would prefer that. I think.

Syd doesn't answer. I grab my bag, unease swirling in my stomach. She might be waiting for me in the parking lot.

Dad is out of town for the day. He might not be able to safely drive home.

Mrs. Lockett is collecting her things as we head toward the door.

We don't have long to leave campus before the storm is too bad and we have to stay.

There's a plan for that, of course, but I don't want to be here.

Axel waits by the front door of the library.

"Come on, Iz. If we don't go now . . ."

"Yeah, I know, but I can't get ahold of Syd."

"I can take you home! Jeez, just let me help you!"

Absolutely *no* way.

"That's fine. I'll get her in a minute."

"Why are you being so awkward?"

Behind him the storm is picking up, turning the whole land-scape pure, brilliant white.

"I'm not being awkward. Ugh, I can't get stuck."

He shrugs. "So, let's *go*."

I'm going to have to chance it and hope Syd is waiting for me. Only a few people are still here. I get my things from my locker while Axel frowns at me. I zip my coat all the way to my chin and pull my hood over my head. Axel doesn't bother with his hood.

He opens the door, and we dash outside. Snow pelts us, hurtling down from the sky like an attack. I try to cover my face, but I can barely see as it is.

Axel grabs my free hand and drags me along.

We're heading in the right direction for the parking lot, so I let him. Besides, if it weren't for him, I would probably be blown off my feet.

Bitterly cold wind stings my hands and legs. We're soaked through within seconds of being outside.

Axel pulls us around the corner. He would move much faster without me. To our left, I can see headlights out on the road as people scram to get off campus.

"Axel," I shout as a gust of wind almost knocks me to the ground.

I can't remember a storm ever hitting so quickly.

He doesn't hear me shouting, but he does pick up the pace as if he also understands how bad this is. It's dangerous to drive, and the longer we wait, the less chance we have of leaving at all.

I want Syd to go without me. If she doesn't, she'll be stuck here.

Why didn't we get more warning? It wasn't supposed to be this bad.

Axel takes my hand again, and we run into the storm.

When we reach the lot, I can just about make out the one car left.

Syd has gone, thankfully.

"Get in, Iz!" Axel shouts.

I stop when he lets go of me and cringe at the water seeping up my calves.

Wait, is that a good idea? I'd be a fool to get in a car with him even if I can't quite bring myself to really believe he's a murderer.

"Isabel, get in the damn car!"

"I'm going back inside. You get home."

He comes back around the car, and I take a step toward the school.

"What's wrong? I'm trying to help!"

"Why do you leave school early?" I shout over the howling wind.

"What?"

"You heard me."

"Why are you asking that *now*? Get in!"

I brush snow off my eyelashes. "Why?"

"I hate it here! Plenty of people skip, now get in."

"Did you skip the day Julia went missing?"

I can't see much, but I can see his jaw dropping. "I can't believe it. You *do* think I'm the one murdering people."

"No . . . I don't know. It's just . . . you're shady and you skip a lot."

"I can't believe you. You always seemed so cool! Go back inside if you don't trust me. But this is your last chance to get a ride home."

Why is he still offering me a ride when I confessed to thinking he's a cold-blooded killer?

That's not normal, right?

"Hello?" a voice shouts through the snow.

I turn to see Lara walking toward us with her hands shielding her eyes. "Come inside, it's too dangerous to drive now."

Axel narrows his eyes at me.

"Axel, no. She's right, we have to get inside. Don't be stupid."

Without a word, he gets into his car.

"What is he doing?" Lara asks.

"He won't listen."

"Come on, Izzy, get back inside. I'm sure Axel is sensible enough not to drive in the snow."

We walk against the wind, leaning in so we're not pushed to the ground. Lara shuts the door behind us. I turn and look out the window.

Axel has the lights on, but he's not leaving.

"I should go back out and see if I can get him to come in," Lara says.

I grab her wrist. "No." Letting her go, I add, "It's dangerous. He's probably sulking and doesn't want to admit that you're right."

"Is something going on?"

"Why would you ask that?"

"You seem on edge. Do you need to talk?"

"It's just . . ." I pause, the events of the past week washing over me. "Um, the storm, you know? I'm freaking out a little that I can't get home. My parents probably can't, either."

"It's going to be okay, Izzy. This isn't the first time we've had to camp out at school for a while. Head to the cafeteria. Principal Beckett is there with a couple other students who walked or cycled in today. We're going to figure out how to get everyone home safely as soon as the weather will allow."

"Okay, but aren't you coming, too?"

"I need to get something from my office first. I'll keep an eye on Axel's car. I'm sure he'll admit defeat and come back soon."

I smile and it's probably a poor shot at looking confident.

Lara doesn't call me out for being on edge again, so I walk away, keeping one eye on the window.

Suddenly, Axel's car lights shut off.

thirty-four

IZZY

I sit in the cafeteria with a couple other students and wait. All underclassmen except me, and Axel outside. In his car. Unless he got out when he turned the lights off, but he would have made it inside by now.

Chewing on my nails, I obsessively watch the door to see if he's going to come in.

So where is he? He could have gone somewhere else in the school. I did tell him I suspected him as the killer and then refused a ride. It probably hasn't made him want to be anywhere near me right now. Though he did still tell me he'd take me home.

He's either a crazy murderer or super forgiving.

"Izzy, do you have any other clothes here?" Principal Beckett asks.

"Um, yeah. Gym stuff," I reply, shivering and longing for my cozy leggings and a sweatshirt.

"You can go to the gym and get changed."

I stand up. "Have you heard anything about when it'll be safe to leave?"

She shakes her head. "Not yet but the blizzard is supposed to pass quickly. We're going to make hot cocoa and have a snack now, though."

I smile because that's what she wants from me right now. Besides, the storm isn't her fault, and she's just trying to put us at ease.

"Come right back, please," she adds as I walk away.

"Will do," I say. She doesn't have to tell me twice.

It's weird being in school when the halls are empty. There's usually laughter, voices, people running around and throwing a ball. The hockey team would be walking around like they're national heroes, and the rest of us would be rolling our eyes at them.

Now there's nothing. It's like the school is dead.

I push into the changing room and get into my sweats. Rolling my clothes and coat up, I stick them in my bag. I'll have to get the coat back out and hang it up in the cafeteria, but there's no way I'm holding it and having it drip all over me.

I leave the changing room dry and warm and head toward the cafeteria. Hot cocoa does sound quite nice, actually. On my way, I text Mom, Dad, and Syd, asking how they are and letting them know I'm safe at school.

A bang from behind me steals my breath. I whip around and scan the empty hallway.

Everyone is supposed to be in the cafeteria. Maybe it's a teacher making sure everyone is where they need to be.

I back up, my hearing on high alert. I could probably hear a snowflake land.

Footsteps tread lightly somewhere off in the distance, around one of the corners.

"Hello," I call.

The noise stops.

"Hello?"

Nothing.

A teacher would reply.

Unless they've already gone and can no longer hear me. I glance back down the corridor. I'm about halfway to the turn, and then it's just a minute's walk from there. I step to the side, one step closer to seeing the cafeteria door.

Along the corridor, I hear another footstep. Just one, like the person is taking a step closer to hear whether I've left or not.

"Axel?" I call out. "Is that you?"

I take another step, my heart thudding so hard I can hear it. "If that's you, come to the cafeteria. I won't bother you."

Another step back while keeping my eyes in the direction of the noise. Wouldn't Axel answer me? Maybe it's not him. Maybe that's what he wants me to think.

The footsteps start, this time one after the other in quick succession.

Toward me.

I turn and sprint. My heart thumps so hard I think I might collapse on the floor.

Raising my palm, I slam into the lockers at the end of the wall. Shoving myself off, I change direction and fly along the corridor with adrenaline coursing through my veins.

The footsteps thud loudly behind me.

I cry out, pushing myself to run as fast as I can as I finally see the door to the cafeteria.

Tears prickle at the back of my eyes as I stumble in.

Principal Beckett's eyes land on me, and her face falls. "Izzy, is everything okay?"

"No. I heard someone in the hallway. They chased me!" I say, pointing. No one is there.

She frowns. "You heard what?"

"Footsteps. Footsteps *chasing* me!"

"Well, there are a few teachers searching the school. They probably didn't hear you." She points to a metal cart. "Hot cocoa, help yourself to a cup."

"The person ran. They were chasing me."

"Izzy, I don't see anyone, but I'll check it out."

"I . . ."

"It's okay. The school can be eerie when it's empty, especially during a storm. Go and get a drink; you'll feel better once you've warmed up. I'll take a look around, okay?"

She probably thinks I'm an idiot.

I shake off the uneasy feeling in my stomach—well, I try to—and grab a Styrofoam cup. We're not trying to save the planet today, I see.

Someone out there wanted to scare the crap out of me, and they succeeded. It was probably Axel getting payback.

A few students talk about me but pretend not to. They lean closer together; one tries to glance over casually.

The first sip burns my tongue, but the creamy chocolate is

very welcome. My fingers are still slightly numb. At least my heart rate is calming down now.

Lara walks into the room. She looks around and then heads to me. "Axel won't come in. Do you have his number to text? I'm not sure his car is the best place for him to be."

I'm not sure I'm the best person to persuade him.

"I'll try," I say, unlocking my phone. "Did you go out there?"

"No, it's too dangerous. Though someone might have to soon if he doesn't respond to you. Let me know if he replies. I need to speak with Helen."

I want to ask who Helen is, but she walks over to Principal Beckett and that pretty much answers that one for me.

It's weird to think that teachers have real names.

I compose a quick text to Axel.

Me: *Come in. Please, it's dangerous. I'll explain everything.*

All right, that might be a little lie. I'm not going to tell him everything that Tristan has told me, but I will tell him that he's made himself look guilty by skipping school. Not to mention there's some kind of evidence connecting him to Kason.

Evidence I'm dying to see.

Right now, I just want him to be safe in school. The rest can be figured out after.

Axel: *You think I'm a killer.*

Me: *No, I don't. Some things point toward you, but I don't buy it. Please come in so we can talk.*

Axel: *What makes you think I'm not already in the building?*

I sit up straighter and glance around the room. Maybe it was him in the hallway. He's annoyed at me, so he could have done that to freak me out.

Me: *Where are you? We're supposed to be in the cafeteria. Come join me.*

Minutes pass. I keep my eyes on the cafeteria door closest to the main entrance where he'd come in from. No Axel and no reply.

What is he doing?

I stand as Lara and Principal Beckett walk over.

"Axel said he's come in. Well, he *implied* it."

"Okay, let me check."

"He must have been the one chasing me."

Principal Beckett smiles, still not convinced. "We'll find him, Izzy. Take a seat."

I wait for them to leave, then I make sure Mrs. Lockett is busy with other students. Once I'm sure she's distracted, I slip out of the cafeteria.

Tiptoeing, I keep near the walls and flick my phone on silent. Still nothing from Axel.

Lara and Principal Beckett split up; one goes right and the other left. They actually *split up.*

I'm definitely not the idiot.

I follow Lara because Principal Beckett is holding a chunky flashlight that is about the size of her forearm. Lara only has her phone, and that's nowhere near good enough to be used as a weapon.

She walks toward the computer labs.

I take another look at my phone. Nothing.

I don't like this.

Me: *Axel, are you okay?*

Maybe if he thinks I'm worried about him, he'll reply.

Two minutes tick by, so I don't think he cares if I'm worried.

I creep along, trailing Lara. If she catches me, I won't know how to explain myself.

She turns a corner, and that's when the hallway is drenched in darkness.

thirty-five
IZZY

Oh God. This is bad.

I press my back against the wall and glue my lips together so I don't make a sound.

Blackouts are common during bad storms. But they don't usually happen while we're trying to find a missing person in the school. Not to mention a missing murder suspect.

The generator usually kicks in within seconds, too. Which should happen about now.

I slow my rapid breathing as I feel a tightness in my stomach. All I hear is my own breath.

Why is the generator not working? It doesn't usually take this long.

"Lara?" I call. "It's Izzy!"

She wasn't too far away from me when the lights went out, so unless she went through a classroom and then outside, she should be able to hear me.

"Lara?" I say, wincing at the possibility that I'm revealing my location to Axel, too.

Okay. Think, Izzy.

Lara isn't answering, so I have to do this myself. I can't rely on someone else to fix this for me.

Touching the wall beside me, I follow it back in the direction I came from. I know the layout of the school, so I know how to get to the cafeteria from here in the dark. If I can't see, then neither can Axel.

I've got this.

I move slowly, every step light and controlled. My wild heart tries to get me to curl up in a ball and wait for someone to come to my rescue, but I won't do that. It's time for me to be brave.

Being brave isn't feeling too good right now, but that's not going to stop me.

I press on, making my way toward the cafeteria. When I get there, I'm not leaving ever again.

Holding my other hand out when I think the corner is coming up, I strain my eyes to see . . . well, anything. The storm has made it impossible for light to shine through the windows.

My left hand brushes the cold wall, and my right comes into contact with something warm.

A person.

I gasp and drop my hand.

"Who's that?" I ask, my eyes widening but still seeing nothing. "Who's there? Lara? Axel?"

I step back when the person says nothing.

232 | NATASHA PRESTON

"Who is it?" I demand.

A scream rips up my throat when I'm shoved backward. My head slams into the floor, making me feel instantly sick.

Groaning, I grab the back of my head and roll over. I need to get away.

My vision blurs even in the dark, but I push myself up and run.

I sprint as fast as I can, but my legs feel heavy and my head is pounding.

Someone pushed me.

The *killer* pushed me.

I whimper as I try to escape, not knowing if he's following me or not. Wouldn't he have just killed me right then if he wanted to?

My racing pulse rushes in my ears, making it impossible to hear anything. I don't know if he's chasing me, but I'm disoriented and dizzy. He could easily catch me, so what is he waiting for?

Maybe I'm not the person he's looking for in here.

Who is the target?

Axel was with me until I went into the school. There's no way he would know who was stuck inside.

The strobe lighting above me flicks on. I blink heavily as the bright light burns my eyes.

It takes me a minute, but my vision sharpens and I'm able to see clearly.

No one is around me.

Breathing heavily, I push the door to the girl's restroom and stumble inside.

I slide to the floor and put my head between my knees.

You're fine, you're fine, I repeat over and over.

Axel wouldn't do this, surely?

Why would he go from killing popular people based on their fear to terrorizing a school? It doesn't fit. Something is off.

So what *is* going on?

He could just be playing a trick on me.

Though he's risking getting in trouble, because the teachers are obviously going to get involved. Not that being in trouble has ever seemed to concern him before. I pull out my phone with trembling hands and send Axel a message.

Me: *Truce?*

I stare at the screen and wait.

Axel: *Truce? I've done nothing to you! What are you talking about?*

Is he serious? Scowling, I tap a reply.

Me: *Where are you?*

Axel: *Home.*

Oh, really?

Could he be home? He didn't actually tell me he was in the school . . . he just implied that he *could* be.

I want to believe him.

This has to stop.

I push myself to my feet, run out of the bathroom and toward the main entrance.

The light from the generator doesn't seem as bright now, and it's not hurting my eyes anymore. My head is still throbbing from the fall, though.

I run past the cafeteria so that none of the teachers will see me.

What I do see, however, is Justin's locker, dented and wide open. I slow to a stop and glance both ways down the hall. Then I creep up to the locker.

Who would want to break into Justin's locker?

Axel had an issue with Kason. Though, as Kason's best friend, maybe Justin was involved.

I peek into the gray locker. The first thing I notice is evidence of Justin's love for hockey. Pictures, stickers, and banners line every side. He has a few textbooks, an old, battered copy of *Lord of the Flies,* a travel mug that is probably growing things on the inside, and a picture of him and Debbie.

Wait. They're kissing in the photo.

When did that happen?

I rifle through the rest of the locker, but if there was something incriminating in here, it was taken.

By who?

thirty-six

IZZY

Within an hour, everything has changed. I'm now sitting in an interview room in the police station with my parents. The sheriff and Officer Duggan are opposite me.

I've gone over everything I know. Twice.

Which is basically that Axel is missing and was probably the one responsible for breaking into Justin's locker, and that some-one pushed me over, to which the sheriff asked if I could have just bumped into another person and fallen in the dark. *No.*

My head is fine, though. Lara checked me at school, and they checked me again here.

"You think this Axel is responsible?" Sheriff asks, furrowing his brows.

I should have counted, but I think this is the third time he's asked me that.

"Well, no. I don't know, but there are things that don't add up. I mean, he hated them; he had time to kidnap Julia, because he's been skipping school; he's weird about death; he disappeared during a storm when he should have been at school; and he hasn't been seen since. That's all suspicious. There's just something that's off. He's smart but this would take a lot of planning, and he's in school every day. There are times when this couldn't have been him."

He shakes his head. "We have someone heading to his apartment now. But I'm more concerned that you seem to be getting yourself quite involved."

My jaw drops. "It's not by choice!"

All right, not *entirely* by choice. I would much rather have never seen Debbie's body. If I hadn't, I wouldn't be here now.

Mom and Dad sit so still I'm not entirely sure they're breathing. I'm sure they're too mad to move.

They've done nothing but listen, and I know they're not happy with what they've heard.

"Why didn't you come forward with this information before?"

"Well, there have been a lot of rumors flying around. Axel doesn't get along with Justin and his crew. It wasn't really surprising for any of them to throw accusations around."

"Next time tell us, and we'll decide if it's important."

I nod, abashed. "Okay. Are you looking at the security camera footage to see who pushed me? It could be the killer."

Dad's fists tighten on his lap.

"We will investigate, Izzy."

"Can we take our daughter home now?" Dad asks. He smiles but his voice is tense.

I'm likely grounded. For the rest of my life.

"Yes," Sheriff replies. "If you think of anything else, Izzy, I want you to call immediately."

"I will," I reply.

Mom and Dad usher me out to the car as if I'm a three-year-old and give me the silent treatment.

For six minutes and thirteen seconds. Then they explode, demanding to know "what on earth I think I was doing."

I mean, it's not like I thought I was doing anything.

So, I might have gotten myself a little more involved than I should have, but that doesn't mean I've put myself in danger like they're thinking.

Unless, of course, Axel is the killer and he knows that not only do I suspect him but I've also told the cops.

They lecture me the whole drive home about my poor choices. Then I'm allowed to go to my room alone. Where I'll probably have to stay until I'm thirty.

That also means no party at Miyah's tomorrow. That one makes me feel awful, because my parents will miss out, too.

I lie on my bed and call Miyah to give her the bad news.

She answers almost right away.

"I have to tell you something," I say.

"No. No way you're missing my dad's birthday party! Come on, Iz."

"I can't help it. I'm grounded, probably forever. No exaggeration."

"Iz," she groans, stringing my name out for about five seconds.

"I'm sorry."

I launch into the whole story, including being pushed, and she doesn't say a word—unlike her—for the entire time I speak.

When I'm done, she finally says, "What were you thinking? Are you okay?"

"I was thinking that I want to know who killed Debbie and Kason. And, yeah, I'm okay."

"God, Iz. The killer could have touched you tonight. You need to wait for the cops to figure out what's going on!"

"I know I acted recklessly, but the more I find out, the more I need to know. Now I'm kinda confused, because there's no link, that I can figure out, between Axel and Julia."

She groans again.

"How well do you know her?" I ask.

"I bet you were told to leave this alone."

"By the cops and my parents. What's your point?"

Laughing, she says, "Fine. I know her fairly well. She's lovely, really sweet and helpful. She doesn't live in town, but she's been to a few festivals and things. She often volunteers for town clean-ups. Even did the sketchy part that the rest of us refused."

Axel's apartment is in that part of town. Everything is a bit rougher around the edges over there.

"She's popular?"

"Sure. Why is that important?"

"I thought that's what this was about. Debbie and Kason were, too."

"Thought? I just said she *is* popular. That should strengthen your theory."

"It would have if they went to the same school. I don't think this has anything to do with who they are. I think it's about what they're scared of."

I bite my lip as I think about how many people told this asshole their biggest fear.

"Iz, are you still there? Maybe the best thing for you is to come to the party. It'll take your mind off this craziness, and you'll be around family."

"Not much I can do, Miyah. I'm grounded. You're still not allowed out alone, right?"

She sighs hard. "Not allowed to go anywhere without a chaperone."

"Good."

"I'm sorry?"

"You're not safe. You reposted the meme, and the killer clearly doesn't care what school you go to. Why aren't you taking this more seriously?"

"Not you, too. I'm fine. I'm careful and stay with other people. We have alarms everywhere. Our whole house is one giant gadget."

"Don't sneak out."

"I'm not stupid, Iz." She sighs. "So, you've heard nothing from Axel since he told you he was home? Do you think you will?"

She's deflecting here. Miyah is fierce, and I admire that so much, but it does sometimes get her into trouble.

"I honestly don't know. I just can't believe he would do something like this."

"You don't believe it as in you're shocked or you think he's innocent?"

That's a good question.

"The evidence suggests—"

"I'm not talking about the evidence," she says, cutting me off. "I'm talking about what you feel. You've always had good gut instincts. What are they telling you here?"

"That there's something sketchy about Axel, but I'm not sold on his being a cold-blooded killer. There's something . . . intriguing and kinda sad about him. In a good way, not a crazy murder spree way."

"Okay, that wasn't as decisive as I was hoping."

"Tell me about it. Look, I've got to go. I haven't lost my phone yet, and I don't want to give them an excuse."

"Okay. Try to get your parents to let you come tomorrow. My dad will be so sad if you miss it."

"Will do," I reply, though I know there is absolutely no way they're going to give in.

thirty-seven

FEAR

I hide in the shadows, moving around town unseen. It's shockingly easy, considering that the cops are hunting a serial killer. Idiots.

My SUV is parked a block away, beside an empty house, not far from Izzy's house. I would love to see her expression if she realized how close I was to her. How close I am to her a lot of the time.

Not today, though. She's usually hanging out in town on Saturdays, but I haven't seen her once.

Footsteps ahead crunch in the snow. I sink behind a bush and peek around the corner.

What do we have here?

Yes.

She's bold, I'll give her that. Amiyah Dalal is walking along the road in a shiny silver parka and pink winter hat. Her long hair blows in the wind, and she holds her head high, as if she owns the street. Pretty girl.

Cousin to *the* Izzy Tindall.

The two couldn't be more different, both in appearance and in attitude.

Izzy wouldn't be outside alone. Amiyah is creeping along the street at night, thinking that she will never be caught . . . or hunted.

Surely her parents wouldn't have let her go out alone? She doesn't strike me as the type to follow the rules, so I bet no one knows she's out here tonight. No one but me.

She's heading toward Izzy's house, but I can't be certain that that's where she's going.

Amiyah looks around. I duck my head and wait for her to turn back. Could she be starting to feel nervous out here?

I haven't yet decided if she's brave or stupid. I dive into my pocket for the things I need. Pulling out the little bottle of chloroform, I dampen a rag, and my chest expands. After the first time, I use only a small amount. You don't want them to be out of it for long. It's no fun that way.

It's time. Finding her out here was a gift. I wasn't looking, not for her anyway.

Her fear is one that has haunted me for years. Since I was fifteen and took a car on a joyride for the first and only time. I remember the saliva that flew from the corners of his mouth as he threatened to drag me behind the jeep he'd just found me driving.

I lived in constant fear.

This town will, too.

Amiyah continues. Just a little farther and she'll reach the drive where my SUV is parked, back behind the overgrown bushes.

I lean forward so I'm crouching on my toes, ready to leap.

Almost there.

She places her next step, and I run.

I hurtle toward her so fast she doesn't even have time to turn around before my hand is over her mouth and nose. She screams into the rag as the poison turns her body limp in seconds.

With my pulse thudding and adrenaline searing through my veins, I catch her and disappear along the side of my car.

Houses line both sides of the road, and still I manage to take her.

Miyah is petite, barely weighing one hundred pounds, so it doesn't take a lot to move her. I couldn't be in a more perfect place to do this, a block from Izzy. It's not enough, though; I want to drive right past her house. She's on the corner, so I'll drive around past the side of her house and then drive away toward the old industrial estate.

She's getting close, and knowing her sharp little mind, she could figure this out. I don't want to stop yet—I'm only just getting started—and Izzy knows too much. If she would just look a little harder, she would really see me.

I should hate her, but I don't. She's always been all right . . . and she didn't share the post. If anyone would condemn what happened to me as a child, it's her.

The constant battle between my mission and my rule not to touch anyone who hasn't reposted the meme is giving me a headache. I could take Miyah to the industrial estate, and she probably wouldn't be found for a while.

So why do I need to make any of this about Izzy?

Yet here I am, pulling over a block away from her house in the dead of night to send her a warning. Miyah will act as a message to a girl I don't want to hurt.

My eye twitches at the admission.

Why should I care about anyone in this town?

I don't. I *hate* them all.

I carry Miyah to the back of my car, put her down, and use rope to tie her hands above her head. Gripping the rope, I make a knot around the tow bar. My heart dances with so much excitement I almost slip the knot undone.

Miyah's forehead creases, and she rolls her head to the side. "Wh-wha . . ."

"Shhh," I say, and her dark eyes fly open.

She looks around, mouth dropping, and tugs on her hands. I can tell that she's still disoriented, because she tries to scream but nothing much comes out.

A look of pure, unfiltered horror flashes on her face, and I drink it in.

"We're going for a drive."

"No," she rasps, frantically tugging on the rope. "No! Help! Help me! Help!"

I'm sure she thinks she's screaming louder than she is. I can only just hear her, and I'm close enough to feel her breath on my cheek.

I stand and shake my head. "No one can hear you."

Her tiny screeches for help don't let up as I get into the SUV, but even I can't hear as the wind whistles through the branches beside us. I close my door and start the engine.

Gripping the steering wheel, I kick the stick into D and put my foot down.

The car glides along the snow as I drive around the block and head toward Izzy's house. Snow hits the windshield hard, coming down like a cloak to disguise what I'm doing. Two blocks ahead of us, I see the first streetlight flick to life. They'll all be on soon.

I push the pedal and actually hear her for mere a second before a bump in the road on the corner near Izzy's knocks her out.

She goes silent, but I can still just see her body trailing in the mirror, and I give myself to the monster inside.

thirty-eight

IZZY

I spend a very slow Saturday locked in the house.

I heard Dad on the phone with the cops this afternoon. Apparently, there's nothing new they can tell us. Which means Axel wasn't home when the cops went to check, and he hasn't been found.

Nothing has turned up on the security footage.

Or nothing they want to tell us about anyway.

Where could Axel be?

It's now late evening. My parents refused to go to the party without me. They said there'd be other parties, though I'm not sure Uncle Samar will feel that way. They're downstairs watching a movie, and I'm in my room, scrolling mindlessly through social media.

My TV is playing in the background, but I can't focus on anything.

I go to text Miyah when I see my window swing open beside me.

A scream rips up my throat, but before I can make a noise,

Justin climbs in with his hands up in surrender. "Shhh," he hushes. "I just need to talk to you."

Scrambling to my feet, I back up, my eyes darting between the door and him. He'd get there first.

"Izzy, I'm not going to hurt you, I swear."

"That's exactly what you would say if you *were* going to hurt me."

"You saw my locker," he says, lowering his arms. "That's what I want to talk to you about."

He might claim to not want to hurt me, but my heart is still beating wildly, as if I'm in danger. The first time Justin has ever been in my room, and I just want to throw him out. "You have my number. Why couldn't you just text?"

"I heard about you getting locked in and Axel going missing. Tayley saw you outside the police station. I assumed you were grounded, and I don't know if you lose your phone when you're grounded, too. The last thing I wanted was your parents to see my texts."

"You couldn't have asked Syd if I still had my phone?"

"And have her question why I want to contact you? No thanks. This is between us. Will you relax? I'm not going to do anything."

"I'm good, thanks."

"Can we sit down? I just want to talk."

"My parents are downstairs."

"Why do you think I came in through the window? Why do you have it open?"

"I didn't realize it was unlocked," I tell him. "Don't worry, I'll be locking it when you go out, though."

He smiles for a second.

I should be happy that he's here.

"Tell me why you're here, Justin. I don't know who broke into your locker."

"No, but you think it was Axel, too."

"Why do you think it's him?"

"Because he went missing at school. His car was still in the lot when I went past this morning."

What I don't understand is how he got home without his car in that storm. Unless he hid at school until it was over and somehow managed to walk without anyone seeing him.

Why wouldn't he come back for his car?

I suppose he wouldn't need it if he also has a gray SUV.

Still, it doesn't make sense that he walked home from school in a bad storm. It still doesn't make sense that he could be a killer.

I'm doing it again. This is for the cops to figure out.

"Right, we have the same theory. Why did you need to come and see me again?"

A similar theory anyway.

He lifts one eyebrow, looking cocky and, I hate to admit, cute while he's doing it. "Debbie and I had a secret thing. I told you she was into Kason and then that picture of the two of us turns up in my locker."

"I don't really care who you dated."

Which is a big fat lie. Though the more time I spend around Justin, the more confused about him I am. I thought I had the biggest crush. He seemed so perfect.

"I'm not stupid," I add. "Your locker was the only one broken into, so I know someone was looking for something. They found it, didn't they?"

He sighs. "It was a burner phone."

"Original."

He grins but continues. "It was K's. There were messages between him and Axel."

"On a burner phone?"

Justin winces. "K sold some weed here and there."

Of course he did.

"They've never been friends, but toward the end, their rivalry got worse. When Axel slept with Jessie, K lost it."

"Axel slept with Jessie?" He didn't tell me that. "Wait, but Kason didn't want to be with Jessie."

"No but she was in love with him and was trying to make him jealous. He didn't want her, but he loved that she was always on the sidelines waiting for him."

"Your friend was a real asshole, Justin."

"He wasn't *all* the time."

That doesn't make the things he did okay, but I'm not getting caught up debating that with Justin right now.

"So, there are messages on this phone between him and Axel?"

"Yeah, threatening messages on both sides. Nasty stuff."

"Death threats?" I ask.

"More than one."

I rub the ache between my eyes. "Why didn't you show the cops this? Axel could have been arrested before he took off."

"There's incriminating stuff about K on there."

"But he can't get into trouble. *He's dead.*"

"And his mom wants to run for Congress. That would never happen if this got out. Imagine asking people to vote for you when your seventeen-year-old son is revealed to be a drug dealer."

"She's running for Congress?"

"They were planning to announce the campaign, but then K was killed. I spoke to his mom to find out if she's going ahead. If she wasn't, I was going to turn this in."

"Where did you talk to her about it?"

"Just along the dock. I saw them laying down flowers for K."

"Was Axel around? Could he have heard that conversation and put it together?"

Justin shrugs. "I didn't see him, but I wasn't paying attention to anyone else."

"Would he have known you'd have the burner?"

"He would know the cops didn't find it in K's room or locker. And there's no one else K would have trusted with it."

God, this is a mess.

My head hurts and it has nothing to do with being shoved to the floor yesterday.

"So, he broke into your locker and took it," I say. "I suppose it doesn't matter, since you weren't going to show the cops anyway."

He shrugs. "Maybe. We don't know what *he's* planning, though."

I blow out a breath.

"You really need to keep your window closed, Iz."

I nod. "I will. But tell me more about the Debbie thing. I'm fuzzy on that."

"We were seeing each other on the down low for a while."

"Why?"

"I don't know. We liked each other, but neither of us wanted to date. She liked K but hated how he treated women, and I wasn't up for anything serious. I have to keep my head in the game if I want to play in college. Tayley made it clear she wanted to get with me, and I couldn't be bothered with the drama if she knew I was hooking up with Debbie. It was just easier to keep it quiet."

"The pic looked kinda intimate."

"We were messing around. Neither of us wanted more than what we'd agreed. I liked her; she was cool."

"Okay."

So, both Debbie and Jessie wanted Kason. Debbie was seeing Justin in secret, and Tayley was hot for him.

Has their whole group hooked up with each other?

I don't even want to ask where Mariella fits into this. She's been super quiet recently. I've heard nothing since Mariella was a bitch in Puck's.

I thought this would bother me more than it does. My whole time at Rock Bay High has been spent wishing Justin would notice me. What's wrong with me?

"What are you going to do about the burner cell?" I ask.

"Nothing. I can't tell anyone. I told Principal Beckett that nothing was taken."

"Did she believe that?"

He shrugs. "She let it go."

Not the same thing but okay.

We both look toward my door as we hear footsteps along the hall.

"Hide!" I whisper-yell at him, waving my hands like a lunatic.

Justin drops to the floor like a ninja, barely making a sound, and rolls under my bed.

Okay, wow.

That is not his first time.

I *really* hope there's no stray underwear or "I heart Justin Rae" notes under there.

I sit down and pretend to be watching TV when the door opens.

"Are you all right?" Mom asks.

My heart thumps at the knowledge that I need to be very convincing now.

"Fine."

"Dad and I are turning in. Don't stay up too late."

"I won't. 'Night."

"'Night, love," she replies, and closes the door.

Justin rolls back out a second later.

"I'm thinking of going to Axel's apartment," he whispers.

"That's a horrible idea. In fact, that's the worst idea I've ever heard. From anyone. *Ever,*" I reply quietly.

"You don't agree, I get it. But this dude might've killed two of my friends, and I have to know why."

"One, he's not there. Two, why now? Three, are you *stupid?*"

"One, he might be. Two, because now is the only time I can get away from my folks. Three, maybe, but I can't sleep properly until I know why he murdered my friends."

I grab his wrist as he turns away. "Wait. I don't think this had anything to do with them. I think they were random. Granted, the killer probably thought he'd won the lottery when K reposted that meme. But I think he's working off a list of fears he wants to execute, not people."

"What?"

"Julia doesn't fit. She was popular but kind. She didn't live in town or go to our school. But maybe her fear fit his fantasy, same as Kason and Debbie's."

"Well, I'm about to be something he fears."

I tug him harder as he tries to leave again. Is he aware that he's seventeen and not an adult in the mafia? "No way. I can't let you do this."

"They're my *friends*. What would you do if this was Syd or Miyah?"

I don't have an argument for that. If someone hurt my best friend or my cousin, I would kill them with my bare hands.

He pulls out of my grip. "See. I have to go. I'll be careful . . . and I have a hockey stick with me."

I clench my fists, my stomach churning. "I'm coming with you," I say with instant regret.

thirty-nine

IZZY

Justin folds his arms over his chest. "You're not coming with me. I don't need protecting."

I suspect he adds "by a girl" in his head but he's too smart to say it aloud.

"Safety in numbers, Justin. Besides, Axel has reached out to me before. If we see him, and hopefully we won't, I might be able to reason with him."

"If he's murdered two people and kidnapped another, I don't think he's going to be massively reasonable, do you?"

I think Axel is currently more reasonable than Justin.

"Stop arguing with me. The longer we leave this, the more likely we are to be caught."

"Izzy . . ."

"No. You had to know that I would insist on coming, too."

"Not really. You barely ever say a word. How would I know that you'd be so brave? I kind of just wanted someone to know where I'd gone. In case . . ."

I grab my fleece jacket and wave my hand at him. "I don't know what to do with that, so I'm going to ignore it. Come on, let's go and find us a killer."

"Keeping this light, I see. I like it."

I silence my phone and zip it into the pocket. "I'll change my mind if I don't."

"You *should* change your mind."

"How many hockey sticks do you have in your car?" I ask, grabbing one of my spare pairs of snow boots from my closet.

"Five or six."

"Good."

I might end up using one on Justin if he keeps arguing with me.

We climb out my window, I push it shut, and we shimmy down the drainpipe.

My fingers dig into the plastic as I hold on for dear life.

I grit my teeth, placing my foot lower, and then I'm close enough to the ground. If we pull this off the wall, my parents are going to send me to a boarding school.

Letting go, I drop to my feet, bending my knees to land gracefully. I can't believe I just did that without getting injured.

A warmth spreads through my stomach. This might be stupidity, but at least I'm finally strong enough to go for it. I do have to slow my breathing, though, because it's embarrassing how out of shape I am. But I did it.

No more sitting back and being rescued. No more lists or speculating. I'm doing something about it. Besides, we'll be careful and stay out of sight. Axel wouldn't come back now, not with the cops all over his apartment. It's riskier for him to go there than it is for us.

Justin smirks at my grin. "Getting a taste for it, huh?"

"Adrenaline rush. Look, my hands are shaking." I hold them up, and my fingers tremble. "I'm sure it'll wear off and I'll be petrified in a minute."

He watches me curiously. "You've never snuck out before, have you?"

"No. I would definitely get caught. I'm already planning how to contact my friends after my parents catch me and send me away to a boarding school in England."

"We won't be long. They'll never know."

"Oh my God, how do I get back up there?"

"Go through the door, Izzy."

My face falls. "Why didn't we do that just then?"

He freezes as he thinks about it. "It's habit with me. What's your excuse?"

"Habit? How often do you sneak into people's houses?"

His second smirk tells me that he does this a lot.

"I don't want to know. Come on."

It's not supposed to snow again, but the dark sky is overcast. That works in our favor; hopefully no one will see us.

We keep close to the wall as we walk around to the front of my house. The frost bites at my skin. I should have put on gloves and a hat. There's no time to think about my wardrobe, though. I just need to crack on with this incredibly dumb thing.

Maybe I *can* reason with Axel and no one else will get hurt. I think I'm the closest thing to a friend he has at school. Or sort of. I really don't think he would hurt me.

"Where did you park?" I whisper.

"Just around the block."

"Why? My parents don't know your car."

He gives me a sideways glare. "Forgive me for trying not to get you into trouble."

We creep along the bushes at the side of my house.

"Run," he whisper-shouts, grabbing my wrist.

Our feet crunch in the powdery snow on the ground as we run down the sidewalk, and the starless sky threatens to drop some more.

I struggle to keep up with him, since he's an athlete and my idea of exercise is a jog to the fridge. Wind stings my cheeks as we dash to get into the warmth of his car.

Justin unlocks his car, and I dive inside.

Gently closing the doors, I lie back against the seat and blow out a long breath. I just snuck out of my house.

He cranks the heat up and pulls onto the road.

"Do you think Axel will show up? The cops haven't been able to find him."

"The cops have been at his house since yesterday. I watched the last car leave just a while ago. If he's going back, it'll be now."

"I feel like you should have told me this *before* I got in the car," I say. "Do you really think the cops won't have someone watching the house? He's a suspect in a murder investigation. There will be an unmarked car there."

He frowns and his hands tighten around the steering wheel. "You're right. We'll drive past and park around the block."

"Justin, what are you really hoping for?"

"What?"

"You know what I mean. There's no reason for you to go there. The cops will be on it."

He scoffs. "Are you sure? They haven't found anything yet. The only reason they suspect Axel is because he's a bit moody, had a fight with Kason, and went missing from school."

"Considering that they don't even have that on anyone else, I would say it's a good place to start. Don't you think?"

"I don't know, Iz. Three of my friends are dead, and that freak is hiding something."

"Maybe."

"What, you don't think he could be the one doing this?"

"Do you think he would be able to?"

"We never know what someone is capable of. He lives alone, no one around to see what he's doing or plotting. I bet he spends every evening planning revenge."

"Revenge for what, though?"

"I don't know. None of us do, because we know nothing about him . . . other than that he's creepy and a loner. Why did you come if you think he's innocent?"

Honestly, I'm questioning that myself. Am I more worried about Justin being in danger or Justin hurting Axel if he finds him? We don't know that Axel is guilty, and Justin is, understandably, angry over his friends' deaths.

I get that Axel isn't the friendliest, and he could definitely hold his own, but could he hurt and kill people? I'm not sure I'm convinced.

We drive through town, and large houses with picket fences give way to old apartment blocks and smaller houses in need of renovation.

"He's in that building on the left," he says. "Top right window."

I look out at the dark window at the top. There's a light on in the unit below him. Nothing from the other two units.

Justin drives by. There are cars parked in the lot and all along the street, but I don't see anyone inside them.

"The cops are either hiding or they're not there. Do you think they know something we don't?"

"They've already found him?"

"Do you think he might be dead?" I ask, and my stomach gives a squeeze.

"Maybe."

I hope not.

He pulls the car into a free spot outside a pharmacy. The convenience store next to it is boarded up, probably because the third business has no windows left. Beyond Axel's building and these businesses there is nothing.

"Where are we going?" I ask, peering into the darkness.

"Around the back of his building. His back window looks out across a field and a river."

I've been in a rowboat along that river. In the summer, it's full of people swimming and rowing. Though we usually stick closer to the town square side, where there's a little beach.

"Are you ready, Iz?" Justin is clutching his hockey stick.

"I suppose."

"You'll be fine."

"Yeah," I whisper.

We get out of his car and walk in the shadows of the apartment blocks. The river is completely frozen over. No boats come along here in the winter, not like at the port. Snow sits on top of the ice, and the river is distinguishable only because the level is slightly lower than the narrow walkway.

Justin and I move slowly, placing our feet in the crunchy snow very deliberately. The walkway has bumps and dips that my feet sink into or roll off as we walk.

I can't see much, because the streetlights are at the front of the buildings, but I can see the vapors of my breath dance in front of my face.

Finally, as snow sinks into the tops of my boots, we reach the corner of Axel's building.

Justin looks back at me and then tilts his head up. "Still no light on."

"Because he's not here!"

"Maybe we can get in."

"Do you think he would have left evidence behind? Do you think the cops would have? I doubt he has a little black book of targets tucked under his pillow."

"He killed my friends and screwed around with you," Justin says. "We have to do something. I can't sit at home and wait. No one thinks more like a pissed-off teen than us."

"How do we think like a serial killer, though?"

Justin sighs sharply, and I watch his irritation rise and vanish into the night. "Stay here and keep a lookout."

"Where are you going?"

"To see if I can get into his—"

I gasp. "Okay, I'm starting to think we're crazy. We can't go *inside* his apartment."

"My phone is on vibrate. Message me if anyone comes."

I grab his hand, but he pulls out of my grip and shakes his head. "I need to do this. For K and D."

"All right, but *hurry*. Get in and back out."

He waves his arm at me, half listening, and disappears through the front door. No lock. No security. Anyone could walk straight in there.

forty

IZZY

The FBI would give me a job in surveillance if they could see how thoroughly I'm watching the surrounding area. One black cat on the sidewalk, two cars on the road, and a bird flying overhead. That's what I've seen so far. I could even tell you the make and color of the cars.

Justin is safe with me on lookout. I don't know how safe he will be if Axel comes by, but I wouldn't let him go up. And with Justin and his hockey stick, it might be Axel in trouble anyway. I really don't think Axel would be that surprised to see me here.

I tug on my zipper, but it's already all the way up to my frozen nose. Frost seeps into my bones so deep it's going to take hours to warm up.

I pay no attention to the fact that I can no longer bend my fingers. I do my job as if Justin's life depends on it. Quite possibly, it does.

I watch as the cat leaps onto a fence and into the backyard of a boarded-up bungalow.

Snow falls heavier now, so it takes extra effort to look through it.

Come on, Justin.

I return my focus to the building, stopping before I get to the door because opposite me, by another corner of the apartment block, is the dark figure of a person, hooded and staring in my direction.

My breathing accelerates as I duck behind the wall.

With awkward, stiff fingers, I send a quick message to Justin: *HE'S HERE!*

I slide my phone back into my pocket and peer around the corner, my shoulders hunching as I prepare to come face to face with Axel.

But I'm not at all prepared, because when I lock my eyes on him, he's moved a few feet closer. I can just about see through the thick snow. Oh God.

My muscles lock. I want to check to see if Justin is coming out, but I can't take my eyes off . . . him. It's the right height to be Axel, but the hood is too low and it's too dark to be sure.

The snow beneath his black boots crunches as he takes another step. He's coming toward me, not the front door.

My lungs flatten and the vapors in front of my face disappear.

Go!

I spin around and run along the side of the building to the back, where we came from.

Where the hell is Justin?

He's breaking and entering, so surely he would be listening for messages from his lookout?

I try to make as little noise as possible, but the snow has

turned on me, and every step is obnoxiously loud, as if the snow is shouting "She's here" with every step I take.

Flakes hit my face as I run in the darkness back along the little walkway between the building and the river. I look over my shoulder and freeze. There's no one there.

Dread creeps up from my stomach.

Where is he? And where is Justin?

I slow my breathing so that I can listen to even the quietest sound. There are no footsteps.

Ahead of me is an alleyway between two buildings. If I go down there, I can reach Axel's front door quicker. I just want to get Justin and go home. I'm looking back and forth, in surveillance mode again—only this time it's much more petrifying.

I carefully lift my foot and place it slowly into the snow. My pulse thumps wildly as I retrace my earlier steps with as little sound as possible.

When I reach the alley, I glance down to see how far I need to get before I'm at the front of the building.

But I'm not alone. The hooded figure is standing halfway down, between me and safety. My stomach turns over.

It's too dark to see, but I try to look for anything familiar. The shape of him is disguised by a black coat and hood. A lot of people are around six feet.

I open my mouth, but my bravery deserts me almost instantly. Nothing comes out. I'm frozen in place and unable to speak.

He reacts, however. His head dips and he bends his knees.

Fear grabs me by the throat as I realize what he's about to do.

When he springs up again, he's running toward me.

A scream rips from my throat, but it sounds more like a muf-fled whisper than anything. Fear has also stolen my voice.

My feet slide as I turn on the spot and sprint as fast as I can through the snow lying in my way. I can hear him now. Loud footsteps that sound like they're getting closer by the second.

Snow pelts my face, collecting on my eyelashes and stinging my eyes.

I push myself harder, and that's when my ankle rolls under me. My pitiful scream erupts from my lips again as I fall side-ways, sliding from the walkway onto the frozen river.

Landing on my side, I roll onto my front and push myself up. Pain slices through my ankle as I put my weight down on my feet. I look over my shoulder to see him step down onto the river.

A sob bubbles from my mouth.

Without thought, I take off and I run as fast as I'm able to. Faster perhaps. Adrenaline courses through my heart, and I barely feel my injury.

I don't look back, but I hear him stepping purposefully on the ice. In my hurry to get away, I'm like a rookie ice skater.

Heavy pants erupt from my lungs in quick succession until they're all I can hear.

The solid yet slippery ground seems to move under me—it's like trying to run on the deck of a boat in rough seas.

Why would he be chasing me when he doesn't know my fear? Remembering something Axel said at school when all this started nearly knocks me off my feet: every way to go is bad. I didn't choose, so is he going to pick one?

I have to get out of here. Pushing myself faster, I still feel as if Axel is right on top of me, but after running for what feels like hours, I realize that I can only hear my footsteps scraping across the ice.

Knowing there's no way he could move without making a sound gives me a second to look around and find out where he is. I whip my head around, almost doing a double take, because I'm facing forward again in half a second.

No one is behind me. I turn my head again, making sure. Then I stop and scan my surroundings. I'm almost across the river and onto the other side, so far from Justin's car.

Where the hell has he gotten to?

This can't be Axel. Surely he wouldn't do this to me.

I strain my eyes looking through the wall of snow for the silhouette of a person. Axel or Justin. One of them will find me, and if the storm keeps up like it is, I won't know until I'm standing right in front of him.

Wiping snow from my face, I slowly back up toward the apartment blocks. I need to get to Justin's car.

My pulse thumps in my ears. Maybe Justin spooked Axel and he took off, knowing he was outnumbered.

I place my foot again, and even with the wind howling around me, I hear the faint crack of ice giving way beneath my feet.

I freeze and hold my breath as if that will make me weightless.

If I go into the water, I might not come out again.

Don't. Panic.

I lift my foot and carefully place it in front of me, and the ground holds. I step again, squeezing my hands into fists so that I don't give in to my instincts and run. That would be hugely stupid. Running increases the probability that I'll fall by at least a hundred thousand percent.

Crashing to the ground with the full weight of my body will likely cause the ice to break. I'm not drowning out there in freezing water.

I creep forward again, wincing while I pray for solid ice.

A sickening crack beneath me makes my stomach roll. I look down but can't see a thing in the dark with the storm swirling around me.

I'm halfway back now, and I could be the last person on earth. I'm consumed with the snow; it's all I can see, hear, feel, and smell.

With a knot in my stomach, I continue on, walking light and slow and leaving cracks in my wake.

I shiver as snow attacks my body, wind curling it around me like it's trying to swallow me whole. My feet shuffle forward until I hit the embankment. I cover my sob with my hand as I step onto the walkway, leaving the river behind.

Placing my free hand on the wall of the apartment block, I run, pushing my legs faster and harder than they're used to. I sprint down the side of the building, and as I turn the corner, I slam into a hard chest.

forty-one
IZZY

A scream tears from my throat, and I leap back.

Two strong hands catch me as I lose my footing and start to fall. "Izzy!"

"Justin! Oh my God, where were you?"

He looks over my shoulder, though I'm positive he can't see anything.

"Looking for you! Get in the car," he says.

No need to tell me twice. I run to his car even faster than he's able to. He unlocks it, and I dive into the car and peel off my soggy coat.

Justin gets in and whacks the heat up as soon as the car roars to life. "Are you okay? Who did you see?"

I'm so *not* okay. I take a few deep breaths.

"I couldn't see properly, but he was Axel's size. He started coming toward me, so I ran." I suck in a ragged breath as Justin drives. "He chased me across the river. I couldn't find you."

"Damn. Are you okay?"

"Fine," I reply, trying to ignore the hot pokers stabbing at my ankle. "Where were you?"

"I got your message and came straight out, but you were gone. I went looking for you."

"Did you see him?"

By the glow of the dash, I watch him shake his head. "Nothing. I only saw you when you ran into me."

"I listened for you, too. Thought you might call out for me."

"I didn't want Axel to know that I was there. I was hoping to surprise him."

"Yeah, well, the only person surprised tonight was me. One minute he was there and the next . . . gone."

"He's very good at that."

"You really didn't see him?" I ask.

I didn't lose visibility until I realized that Axel was gone. Justin should have had enough time to get out and run to the back of the apartment block.

"Nothing. He might have known I was there and ducked down the alley to the front of the building. He could've gotten away while I was running around the back."

"Can we never do anything like this again?"

He chuckles. "Fine with me. I didn't like not being able to find you. I was worried that . . ."

That Axel had killed me.

"I'm all right. Did you see anything in Axel's apartment?"

"It was bare. He has a bed, TV, desk, and kitchen. There was only one picture in a cracked frame—must've been him as a kid with his mom, Tristan, and I assume Tristan's parents."

"It was cracked?"

"Yeah, but it was sitting on his desk, in the middle and almost against the wall."

"Not somewhere it would have fallen?"

"Exactly. I don't know, maybe it was closer to the edge and fell so he moved it somewhere safe."

"Wouldn't he have changed the frame, then? Perhaps he got angry and smashed it on purpose."

"Then put it back?" he asks.

"Or slammed it down where it is and it cracked." Just like the ice cracking under my feet.

"Could've. I'd buy him smashing it more than it falling."

Axel's angry with a lot of people.

You're still not sure it's him.

Justin pulls up a block from my house.

"I'll walk you to your house," he says.

"You don't need to, it's just ahead."

"After what happened tonight, do you really think I'm letting you take one step alone?"

"I can take care of myself, but thanks."

He gets out of the car with me. I glance in the back as I close the door and notice a stack of books and a pink notebook. An odd color for Justin, but it could just look pink in the dark.

"Izzy," Justin says. His voice is just above a whisper and so completely hollow that I feel the goose bumps prickle across my skin.

I walk to the front of the car, and the image in front of me steals my breath.

"Is that what I think it is?" he asks.

In the glow of the streetlights, I clearly see tire tracks. Between them is a single track, one tarred with blood.

Panic seizes my heart.

I know this fear . . .

No!

"Oh my God. Miyah! Miyah!" I scream.

"Whoa, Izzy, shhh!"

"Miyah!"

"Izzy, what the hell is going on?" Justin grabs me as I take off along the road.

I don't get far as he wraps his strong arms around my waist.

"Miyah! Miyah! No! Miyah!"

Somewhere in the distance, I hear my parents shouting and Justin replying.

All I can think about is Axel having Miyah . . . dragging her behind his car.

"Miyah! He's got her! Let go, Justin! He's got her!" I thrash in his arms, but I might as well be standing still for all the good it's doing. He's far too strong for me to get away.

"Stop, Izzy. Talk to me."

"Isabel!" Dad shouts.

They sound closer now.

I turn as well as I can in Justin's death grip. "Axel has Miyah!" I scream as my legs give way. Justin catches me before I even fall an inch.

"What are you . . ." Dad trails off as he sees what's in the road. "Dear Lord, is that track . . . ?"

"It's Miyah," I say as vapors from my mouth give the words physical form. Inside I turn to ice and shatter.

Mom pulls me away from Justin, and this time he lets go. "Izzy, you can't think . . ."

"It was her fear," I whisper, staring at the bloody track.

Across the road, I see lights flicking on in the windows of neighbors' houses.

Justin is calling the cops, and as for me, I'm as frozen as the ground.

The world moves around me. I'm vaguely aware that Mom takes me and Justin inside, Dad stays outside talking to neighbors and calling Uncle Samar to see if Miyah is home. Nothing feels real. The world moves too slowly.

"Izzy, what's going on?" Mom asks. "Why do you think Miyah is in trouble? Who is this and what the hell were you doing outside at midnight?"

"That doesn't matter right now," I say, wiping my tears. "He has Miyah!"

She's fierce but can she survive *that*?

"Was Miyah the only one with that fear?" Justin asks.

"The only one I saw," I reply.

"Izzy!" Mom gasps.

When I look across at her, I notice her shaking hands. She's scared, too.

"Izzy was out because of me," Justin tells her. "That wasn't her fault, but we saw those tracks in the road and . . ."

Mom grips her heart and says between two big sobs, "You think it's our *Miyah*."

Justin raises his palms. "We can't be sure."

"I know," I say, collapsing onto the sofa. I am, though. It's my cousin.

The cops roll up minutes later. I count one car, then two, three, four.

"You two aren't going anywhere," Mom says as Justin and I look out the window from the sofa.

Sheriff Rosetta walks into my house and Dad trails behind, his face ashen.

"Dad," I say, standing.

He rubs the light stubble over his chin. "Miyah isn't at home."

forty-two

IZZY

Daylight streams through the window. I haven't slept. Dad spent all night out with my aunt and uncle. Officer Duggan went with them, too. The cops traced the tracks but found no sign of Miyah, Axel, or the car. The search for that particular SUV came up blank. It's not registered to anyone in town.

Now that it's morning, an official search is starting. Outside our house is a circus with neighbors and cops, forensic cops tracing the work that was done last night.

Amiyah is dead.

Those words rattle around in my head over and over, but they still don't make sense.

My beautiful, strong cousin.

Aunt Ellen and Uncle Samar won't accept it until there's a body. We've seen blood, skin, and hair in the road. She's missing and her worst fear was being dragged by a car.

What other conclusion can you reach?

She's gone.

• • •

Justin now sits beside me on a bench in the town square. It's pretty similar to the vigil for Debbie and Kason. Only this time it's my family who's devastated, and we're not mourning; we're volunteering to search for Miyah.

Mom and Dad stand with my aunt and uncle, talking to the cops. I've never seen such a police presence around our town before. I even overheard talk of cops being on campus next week.

"How are you doing?" Justin asks, finally speaking after five minutes of silence.

I wipe my sore, stinging eyes. "Not okay," I whisper.

"I'm so sorry, Iz."

I try to smile, but it's too much effort.

"We're going to find Axel. You know that, right? We'll find him, and he'll go to prison for the rest of his life."

"Did you hear how the cops were talking about him? He's a suspect, but they're not going full force. They think he might be innocent. We suspected Jessie once, and she turned out to be a victim."

Axel might be a victim.

"This is a bit different. There is evidence."

"Circumstantial, though. Anyone could have broken into your locker. His car might be at school because he was taken. Ditching school doesn't mean he's kidnapped anyone." I take a ragged breath. "He might get away with this."

"He won't, Izzy. Don't think like that."

"Amiyah is dead," I whisper.

He nods. "And he will pay for that."

Syd and her mom stop by my parents. She's curled into her mom, sobbing. I look away, unable to watch her heartbreak.

Justin puts his arm around my shoulders. "Please trust me."

"What?"

"Trust that we'll find Axel . . . and Amiyah."

We will need her body to bury. God, I'll have to attend her funeral. We were supposed to rent an apartment together in LA. She was going to start a clothing line, and I was going to work in advertising and have an office with a glass front.

We had it all planned. Now we have nothing.

The dream shatters in my mind, our beachside apartment turning to sand.

The sheriff starts coordinating a search. There are so many students here from both schools, and Officer Duggan seems to have the headache of making sure they're paired with plenty of adults.

I'm sure the cops would have preferred us to stay at home.

But that leaves us vulnerable there.

"Can I come with you?" Justin asks.

"Are you here alone?"

He nods. "My aunt will be here later."

"Come on, looks like we're getting started."

My aunt and uncle make a group with Julia and her parents. My parents and I team up with Syd and her mom, Justin making our group six.

"You two stay close," Dad says to Justin and me. He tilts his head toward Justin. "You're back with us, huh? I didn't catch your last name."

"Rae, sir. I have classes with Izzy. Kason, Debbie, and Jessie were my friends."

Dad nods, his cheeks turning pink a little when Justin mentions his dead friends. "I'm sorry to hear that."

"Thank you, sir."

"We're going to walk along the port to see if we can find . . ." He takes a breath to compose himself. "See if we can find Miyah."

Mom takes his hand, wiping a tear. They both loved Miyah like a daughter.

Small groups separate and walk in multiple directions.

Justin and I walk a little ahead of everyone as Syd still clings to her mom. I'm worried about her, but I have to focus on Miyah right now.

No one wants to say that she's definitely dead. There wasn't enough blood. That's my guess. The trail went along my road and out toward the industrial estate, but then it stopped, as if Axel stopped. Could she have died in just a few blocks? Surely he wouldn't have stopped if she was still alive. That was her fear, and that's how he needed to . . . kill her.

"No one will call it until they find her," I whisper so my parents behind us don't hear.

We look down into the icy river as we walk.

"We'll find her," he replies.

Where would he take her? He didn't hide Debbie or Kason. Why would he take Miyah somewhere else after she died?

"What do you think he's done with her?" I ask.

Justin shrugs, wincing. He doesn't like these questions. Probably because he doesn't think I want to hear his theories.

I try to separate Miyah from this. If I pretend it's someone else, I can think. But that's almost impossible to do. My mind wanders to dark places where I just see Miyah dead.

The cops have searched Axel's apartment, his cousin Tristan's apartment, his aunt and uncle's house, his car, and just about everywhere else linked to him.

Axel has disappeared, and so has Miyah.

The traitorous clouds leak snowflakes. The last thing we need is to have our visibility affected today. If we get a heavy snowfall, could she be buried like the neighbor's dog?

We walk away from town. I refuse to turn my head and look down my road. Next there are fields until we reach the industrial estate. We could walk past that and loop back via Axel's apartment in the shady part of town.

I don't know what route we've officially been given, though. We don't want to miss anything because I want to face Axel's place.

I look carefully at the compacted snow on either side of the roads and sidewalks. It's pristine, untouched. This is the route the car took after it stopped, unless he turned around.

If she was alive, she would try to get away, but there is no evidence that anyone has run along here. She could have stuck to the road, but wouldn't it make more sense to run toward the town square and wake someone up?

Ahead of us, walking our way, is Tristan. His head is down, shoulders slumped. He looks deflated.

Dad clears his throat. "Perhaps we should cross the road?"

"Why?" I ask.

Tristan looks up and stops. So do we.

Oh, that's why.

"Hey," he says quietly, looking alarmed.

"Hi," I reply.

"I'm sorry . . ."

Across the street, I see two people point Tristan out.

That must be horrible, to be condemned simply because you share DNA with someone.

"Thank you," Dad replies tightly. "We should keep moving."

Tristan takes a breath. "If there's anything I can . . ."

I don't know why Tristan stops talking, but I suspect it's the glances he's receiving behind me.

"I think your family has done enough," Justin says.

Dad ushers us past. "Let's go."

I turn to Tristan as we walk past him and mouth "Sorry." He shouldn't receive hate for this. The cops would have questioned him already. He will want Axel found, too.

"Justin," I scold.

"What? The guy's psycho cousin is killing people."

"*He's* not."

"How do we know? They could keep the crazy in the family."

No way. Could Tristan really be helping Axel? They were both neglected and abused by Tristan's parents. Is it even Axel, or could someone be framing him like he thought?

"Don't spread rumors like that. Tristan has done nothing. Besides, if there's something there, the cops will find it."

Justin shrugs. "I suppose. I don't like him, though."

Right, because you're automatically a murder suspect if Justin Rae doesn't like you.

He's only saying that because last year Tristan was the golden boy on the hockey team. My crush on Justin increasingly fades the more time I spend with him.

We continue walking slowly along the sidewalk.

"There's nothing," I say, half deflated and half hopeful, as we reach the end of the port.

"We're not the only ones looking," Dad says. "We'll find her and bring her home."

In what state?

The snow falls harder. Now we're all walking, bundled up with hoods over our heads and coats zipped to our chins. I don't want to go home until Miyah is back with us.

Dead or alive, she needs to be with her family.

"I need to use the bathroom," Syd says as we head toward the town square.

"All right," Dad says. "We'll stop at Ruby's and get a hot drink and use the restroom. Then we'll follow our path to the town square and see if there's anywhere else we should look." Everyone agrees.

Once inside Ruby's, Syd and I go straight to the bathroom. I lock the stall and close my eyes.

Please let us find her.

I don't actually need to use the toilet, but I needed a minute. I hear Syd flush and wash her hands.

"I'll wait outside, Iz," she says. Her voice is quiet and unsure. I've never heard that tone before.

" 'Kay," I reply.

Closing my eyes, I lay my head back against the door.

Where are you, Miyah?

When we were little, we made up our own language. Neither of us could remember it well, so it changed a lot. But we would often say the same random word at the same time.

Miyah said we were "psychedelic." I full-on belly-laughed for five minutes before I corrected her. I wish we were telepathic.

I gather myself, taking long breaths, and then open my eyes. As I open the door to the stall, someone's hand covers my mouth and I'm shoved backward.

forty-three

IZZY

My eyes widen in alarm, and I try to scream, but Tristan's hand covers my mouth tightly.

Justin is right: they're a murderous family.

I go to thrash away from him, but his grip is tight. "Shhh. It's me, Iz. It's okay. I had to talk to you. Calm down, I'd never hurt you. I'm going to let go."

He lowers his hand, and I push him away, stepping back so there's as much distance between us as possible.

"What the hell are you doing?" I snap.

"I'm sorry. I saw you guys coming in here."

"So, you thought, what? You'd attack me?"

"No." He shakes his head with a frown. "Jeez, Iz, that's not what I was doing. I need to talk to you, and there's no way your parents are going to let you anywhere near me."

"They don't blame you for Axel."

"Sure they do. Everyone does. Two guys on my crew quit,

and people stare at me like *I'm* the killer. I wouldn't hurt anyone. Please believe that."

"Where is he?"

"I don't know. He's not answering my calls or replying to my texts. I've tried, the cops have tried. But, look, he couldn't have done this."

"You said yourself he's got a temper."

"That doesn't make a person a murderer. He can be hot-headed and overreact, sure, but he's not dangerous. He's had it tough, but he wouldn't hurt anyone. I'm trying to find him. I *will* find him so I can figure this out."

"Where do you think he'd go?" I ask.

The door opens. Tristan and I both look in the direction of the noise.

"Izzy?" Mom calls out. "Are you in here?"

Tristan places his palms together, pleading with me, and mouths, "Don't say anything."

Sighing, I nod and call out to my mom, "Yeah, I'm here. I'm fine, just need a minute."

"Okay. Ruby's making our drinks now. We need to get back out there soon."

"All right."

We both listen to her close the door.

"Thank you," he says quietly.

I fold my arms. "That was for you, *not* Axel. You should find him and turn him in. You can't let him get away. What he's doing isn't okay."

"None of this is okay, I get that, Iz. But I'm scared for him. They'll pin it on him, even if he's innocent."

All right, I get that he doesn't want to believe his cousin is a cold-blooded killer, but how can you ignore everything that's happening?

"Have you seen the evidence against him, Tristan?"

"Yes, and nothing is solid. No fingerprints or DNA. There would be some of that somewhere." He takes a breath. "Look, I know it's a big ask, but please don't write him off. You know him better than you think you do. Take a minute. Do you really think he could kill people? And kill them the way this asshole is?"

I press my lips together, because, honestly, it doesn't fit Axel. But maybe it doesn't fit my *idea* of Axel. I've always known he was a loner and pretty much disliked the entire student body, but I thought that was in a high-and-mighty way. Like he wouldn't lower himself to our level.

"There are things I now know that make me question everything," I tell Tristan.

"That means he's more screwed up than you thought, not that he's evil."

I shake my head. "I need to leave. If I'm not back soon, my mom will come looking for me again."

Tristan sighs. "Please talk to me, Iz."

"Why do you care what I think? The cops won't arrest Axel just because I want them to, not if he's innocent. Please move."

He steps to the side and lets me open the door. I slip out awkwardly past him.

"Izzy, I care what you think, and I know you're the only

person I've met who gives people a second chance without holding on to their past."

I look over my shoulder.

"All I'm asking is that you don't condemn him before there's solid evidence. I believe he's innocent."

"You don't like him," I say, turning to face him. "Why are you fighting to prove that he didn't do this?"

"He makes it difficult to like him, sure, but that doesn't mean I don't love him. He's family and the only person besides our grandma who hasn't tried to beat me down. Axel didn't do this."

"I'll talk to you later," I tell him.

Tristan doesn't follow me out. I take my latte from Justin, who's waiting by the counter, and walk outside with my group.

I can't think about Tristan or Axel right now, I can't allow myself to consider Axel's innocence, because my cousin is still missing.

"Which way?" Syd asks, still sticking close to her mom.

It's at that moment that I spot the sheriff shout something to Officer Duggan. They both run to his car.

I hold my breath as they speed past us as quick as lightning. They get into the car and peel away. The to-go cups that were resting on the car roof fly off and into the snow.

No. They've found something.

forty-four

IZZY

Two hours after the cops sped off, I'm home and staring at the living room wall.

We're waiting for the news that will break us. Aunt Ellen and Uncle Samar are here with us, because they didn't want to go back to a silent house. Miyah is anything but silent. She brings surround sound and Technicolor wherever she goes.

I'm alone because my parents are trying to get my aunt and uncle to drink or eat something. They look shaken and scared.

My phone is beside me, occasionally beeping with messages from Lia. She wants to come home, but we keep telling her not to. She finally understands how great the danger is here, but that doesn't stop her from wanting to be with her family.

I hope she listens, because I can't lose her, too.

I go upstairs to grab a hoodie, because I feel cold despite the heat blasting.

As I walk into my room, I notice something odd. A drawer in my desk isn't shut properly. I'm sure I closed it last night after I wrote in my notebook. Oh God, the one I had been writing all my notes in about the murders, victims, and suspects.

Axel has seen me with it . . . Justin, too.

I walk slowly to my desk and pull out the drawer with one finger.

"Oh no," I whisper as I see pens, pencils, highlighters, a few Tootsie Rolls, and Post-it notes. Everything that should be hidden underneath my notebook.

No. Justin had one that looked just like mine in his car. A hoodie had been thrown over it, but it must have slid out while we were driving. He wouldn't have a pink notebook—he had mine.

Groaning, I put my head in my hands. No way. Could this be Justin? The notebook could be a coincidence. He didn't hate Kason, Debbie, and Jessie. They were his friends. But that friend group was so twisted, who knows?

Downstairs, someone knocks on the front door. I take a deep breath, not wanting to leave the safety of my room, where I can still pretend that Miyah is alive.

I step away from my desk and glance out the window. Something dark, either a person crouched down or an animal, runs from the bushes along the sidewalk, disappearing behind the neighbor's house. The cops are parked outside. It couldn't be Axel . . . or Justin.

I shake my head. We've been home for two hours, and the cops are watching. He wouldn't be that stupid.

It was probably the black Lab from down the street.

Still, I run downstairs. Sitting on the sofa are the sheriff,

Officer Duggan, and a woman I don't know. They all look up at me as I burst into the room.

"Izzy, are you okay?" Dad asks.

"I think I saw something out my window. Someone running from our bushes along the sidewalk. I saw a flash, and then it was gone. It could have been an animal. Also, my desk drawer was open and I'm sure I closed it."

I don't tell them that my notebook was taken, because I don't want to have to explain it to them. There would be a lot of questions if they knew I was doing my own investigating.

Sheriff and Officer Duggan stand. The sheriff nods to the woman, and then the two men run out of the house.

Mom holds out her hand. "Come and sit with us. This is Ruth."

I don't want to, but I go to my mom and sit next to her.

"What's happening?" I ask.

Aunt Ellen puts her hand on my knee, and we look at Ruth. She's dressed in a sharp suit, her hair is neat, her makeup perfect, and she sits straight. I don't think she's with the police department.

Despite her authoritative demeanor, she looks warm and kind. I know why she's here. She's the one who supports families when they receive terrible news.

"Please," Uncle Samar says. "Please just tell us where my baby is."

I squeeze my eyes closed.

"I'm so very sorry to tell you this," she says. "Amiyah's body was found in a field by the old industrial estate."

My body shrinks, curling into Mom's side.

Aunt Ellen's scream is something I will hear for the rest of my life—deafening and animalistic.

I sob as the words solidify in my mind. Miyah is dead. That's now a fact.

She was in a field.

Axel dumped her after he dragged her . . .

Ducking my head, I try to picture her smiling. I don't want to think about her being in agony, being petrified and crying out for help.

I sob, my heart breaking, until my throat hurts and my tears no longer fall. Is it possible to run out? I think I've reached my limit.

Uncle Samar and Aunt Ellen stay curled together on the sofa, clinging to each other. Mom and Dad are pretty much the same, but they're talking to Ruth about what happens next and when we can bring Miyah home to rest.

It's at that point that I get to my feet. "I need some water," I say.

I want to be alone in a place where there is no discussion of my beautiful cousin's dead body. I somehow manage to walk into the kitchen without collapsing.

Running the faucet, I grab a glass and fill it up, the water flowing over the glass before I stop it.

Justin wouldn't have chosen those three if he was the killer. That couldn't have been my notebook in his car. And my parents don't go through my drawers, so I know that it was safe there.

It has to be Axel. He must know that I'm on to him.

The notebook can't be why he killed Miyah, though. He's only just taken that.

What does he plan to do with it? I've given him a list of other suspects. Will he use that to set up either Justin or even Tristan . . . like he said Tristan would frame him? Axel must have an endgame.

He can't get away with taking my cousin from me.

My parents would go mad if they knew what I was doing, but I really don't care about much anymore. Miyah is dead, and nothing will bring her back. But I can fight for justice.

Axel is out there, and I'm going to find him. Right now. I take my phone out of my hoodie pocket and send him a message.

Me: *Please tell me it wasn't you?*

With trembling hands, I shove my phone down on the counter. I hope he reads it like I'm doubting what I know.

If he lets his ego lead, he will.

forty-five

FEAR

I stop by their headstone, where they rest side by side. The shared stone claims that they were a loving mother and father to one son.

They had one son, but they did anything but love.

My childhood was spent in fear of them while pretending everything was fine to the outside world.

They should never have had a child.

I don't remember shedding a single tear for either of them.

The first time I ever felt anything *real* was watching the life slowly ebb away from him. It was fascinating, a rush I've been desperate to re-create.

The adrenaline, the shake in my hands, the skittish pulse in my neck.

I've been chasing that high since November . . . and now I've finally found a way to capture it.

I can punish this town for turning a blind eye to my troubles and give in to the only experience that has ever felt real, both at the same time.

I scrape a thick layer of snow off the top of the headstone and watch it fall to the ground. She fell down the stairs, cracked her head on the bottom. The doctor said it would have been quick, but I'll never know for sure.

I like to imagine that it wasn't. I hope she thought about every awful thing she'd ever done to me on her way down.

Though, I don't think she thought it was awful. Everything was my fault. In her mind, she was fully justified.

"Hello," I say, my smile stretching.

I can't remember the number of times I wished for them to be in the ground. I would have taken the foster care system, but I couldn't do anything—because of fear.

I never usually talk to them. What is there left to say? But I feel stronger now.

I doubt they would be able to hear me from hell.

"You said I was weak, growing up. Well, look at me now. I'm in charge . . . and you two are rotting flesh."

I take a breath, inhaling the smell of snow and freedom. I can do anything, be anything, and no one will stop me. There are no limits, no rules, nothing between me and what *I* want.

This is *my* time to make things right.

I duck down and tuck my chin into my chest as I notice a few people walking to headstones with bunches of flowers. I need to remain unseen.

It never occurred to me to bring flowers here.

How would that look?

I'm beyond caring what anyone thinks of my family now.

All they had to do was look a little harder, see the fear in my eyes when I was with them, and they would have known. But no one wants to hear about something so horrific as adults abusing or neglecting kids.

"I've come to say goodbye, as this is the last time I will ever come to see you. So, I want to tell you how much I *hate* you. There will be no forgiveness, and I hope you're burning in hell."

There's space beside the devil for those who harm children.

My time is potentially almost up. I have to make my move, and if things don't go according to plan? I need to leave. I can start over somewhere else, no problem.

Some plan their endgame and plan it some more. They spend hours, days, weeks devising the perfect plot, only to have something crop up and then they find themselves locked behind steel bars.

Not me. I don't have one endgame plan—I have four. If there is one thing I've learned on this journey, it's that you need to be prepared to adapt to whatever comes. You can't predict how it will all go; people don't always behave how you want or expect.

Izzy was never supposed to be a part of the plan. I actually liked her.

How that one ends will depend on her. She has three options, and I'm ready for each of those.

Plan. Adapt. Repeat. It's how you survive. How you win.

The sky begins to darken along with my mind. My plans swirling around in my head, rehearsed and perfected. Each one of them. They sit in order of preference at the forefront of my mind, and I would be lying if I said I wasn't excited to see which one it's going to be.

I'll soon lose all light, so I need to get going. I still have a lot to do today. I need to eat.

I walk away without another glance at their headstone. If Mr. Franklin from the funeral home hadn't offered to supply the thing, we wouldn't have given them one. When we told him we couldn't get one, he assumed we couldn't afford it, not that we didn't want to.

I park a block away, next to an empty house, and walk in the shadows toward the square.

With a knot in my gut, I watch from the street with a takeout coffee from Ruby's as the town digests the news of Amiyah's body being found. It's been one day, so she's obviously still the center of attention.

It took the cops long enough. I thought they would find her yesterday. I'll have to remember to record the date. They did find her faster than they found Jessie, though.

They're getting better at this. But so am I. I want it more.

There's still so much to achieve. I've barely scratched the surface of fear.

I walk down the back of Puck's and along the alley. The sun has set, and the snow has stopped. It's peaceful.

Taking my burner phone out of my pocket, I scroll. Miyah's death was something else, but it's left an emptiness in my gut that makes me uneasy. The cops ramping up and the FBI getting involved have accelerated things. I need to finish this job as fast as I can and get away.

I kick a rock at my feet. My time here is limited. This town is toxic, but it's still home. I have to start over somewhere else, make friends, and be someone no one will suspect before I can continue. That will take years.

Or I could hide in the shadows, move around the country and take people whenever I feel like it.

I reach the end of the alley and step out into the artificial light, casting a shadow along the snow on the ground.

Yes. Fear is stepping out of the shadows, and he could be anywhere.

My hot breath is visible in front of me as I stroll along the sidewalk with a renewed purpose that makes my heart fly.

The town is in pain; children are being murdered. I walk along the street and watch every somber expression with interest. My steps are light, easy, free. I soak in their agony and begin to plan my next move.

And I'm not doing it without Izzy.

forty-six

IZZY

My room has been my own little prison all morning. Mom and Dad are refusing to let me out of the house, so I've been watching TV shows. Oh, and going insane from not knowing what's going on.

Axel still hasn't been located, and the longer he's out there, the worse it looks for him.

I find myself constantly looking out the window and checking my phone. Justin hasn't contacted me.

I'm still in shock and grieving for Miyah, and I don't want to end up wrongly accusing Justin of anything . . . but I have to know if he has my notebook.

If he was involved in Miyah's death, I *need* to know.

I stare at his name in my contacts—a relatively new addition. He might delete my number from his phone if I ask about my notebook. The truth is, Justin could be completely innocent. Who would suspect the friend of the murdered teens? It's always the hateful loner, never the bestie.

My finger hovers above the call button. I hate calling people—unless it's to speak to Syd . . . or Miyah. I push away the anguish I feel over losing my cousin and tap the screen.

I want to hang up immediately, but I don't, and Justin answers on the fifth ring.

"Hey, Iz. How're you doing?"

"Not great. Everything is . . ."

"Yeah," he replies. "I get it. Do you need me to do anything?"

"Not to do anything," I say. "But I had a question."

"Go on."

I take a breath and blurt it out. "I noticed something on your back seat. A notebook. And it looked like my missing one."

There's a moment of silence. "What? You think I stole your notebook."

"No."

"Then what are you saying?"

I bite my lip. "I don't know. It's pink and it was in my desk drawer."

"And you think I took it when I came to your room? You were with me the whole time. How would I have done that?"

"Can you just check? I'm not saying you've done anything, but there were things in that notebook about the murders."

"Things?"

"Just my thoughts and suspicions."

"Izzy, I—"

"Please, just check, Justin. If it is mine, then maybe Axel has planted it in your car."

He's quiet for a second as he thinks about it.

"You think this sick asshole is trying to pin his murders on me?"

"Maybe. I don't know. Please check."

"All right. My aunt's calling me for lunch, so I've gotta go. I'll text you."

Justin hangs up, and I lower my phone.

That's pretty much how I spend the rest of the day, sitting on my bed, waiting to hear from Justin.

I look out my window as the sky turns black. It's night, and there is no Miyah. I'll never sit outside at midnight in the summer and watch the stars with her again.

My heart leaps.

Leaning forward, I strain my eyes. Is that a person again? The same one?

Where the road bends, a figure stands, and it looks like they're watching my house. Though it's dark and I could be wrong.

Axel?

This time I don't want to call out or tell anyone. I don't know how hard the sheriff or Officer Duggan have been looking for him, and I don't really care at this point. The only thing that matters is he's here now, and my rage and heartache have given me the strength to create my own endgame.

My phone beeps. I strain my eyes but can't see the figure move or see the light of their cell.

A number I don't recognize flashes on my screen. I look down.

Private: *If you want the truth, follow me. Tell no one.*

So that's Axel out there, and he's here to take me.

He says he'll lead me to the truth. I do want the truth, more than anything. I want to know why my cousin is dead. She never did anything to anyone. It doesn't make sense, and I'm so *angry*.

Me: *Where are u, Axel?*

I know this already, but I want him to tell me.

Private: *You can see me.*

No. I close my eyes and breathe deeply. He didn't correct me when I used his name. That's all the confirmation I need. It's him and he's watching me.

I never shared my biggest fear, but a shiver runs down my spine at the thought of him already knowing how he wants to kill me.

Private: *I'm waiting, Izzy.*

He's very trusting. I could have called the cops. I should call the cops, they might even be back soon, but then he might go into hiding and we'll have no answers.

Taking another deep breath, I rest my hands on my windowsill.

Am I really going to do this?

"Izzy, are you okay?" Dad calls.

I push away from the window and walk back to my family in the living room. "I'm going to go to bed. I won't be able to sleep, but I just want some time to myself."

Mom nods. My whole family knows I'm the quiet one who needs to reflect on things alone.

"Okay," Mom says, giving me a tired smile.

I hear the doorbell when I reach my room. Looking out the window, I see that the sheriff's car is back. So instead of sneaking out straightaway, I wait a minute in case Mom or Dad decides to come up and tell me that nothing was found.

Placing my ear against my door, I listen for voices. They come sporadically, quiet enough for me to be confident that everyone is still downstairs.

Okay, Izzy. Time to fight for Miyah.

Me: *where do I need to go?*

I'm assuming he's not still standing in my backyard. That seems a bit risky, even for him. There are now two cops and, I think, an FBI agent in my house.

Private: *end of the docks, near the fish shop.*

"Shit," I breathe out. So, that's where he wants to kill me?

My coat is downstairs, so instead I pull on a second hoodie, a hat, gloves, and a scarf. And then I open my window and climb out like I did with Justin.

When my feet touch the ground, I turn and sprint down the sidewalk. No one saw me, but I can't take any chances. I need to get away.

My lungs burn as I run the whole way, passing the dock. When I get closer, I stop and lean against the cold brick exterior of a bank. Starting out of breath isn't going to be helpful. I breathe through my nose until I've calmed down.

Time to face this. I slip down the alleyway between buildings. He will probably be there already, and I don't want him to see me coming.

I tread carefully, since there is no lighting and I know sometimes trash is left out if the bins are full.

Rubbing my hands, I try to get them to stop shaking. I'm

petrified but all I can think about is Miyah and how scared she must've been. I'm doing this for her.

I walk along the dark alley and can just about see the exit up ahead. Then all I'll need to do is cross the road and I'll be there.

A shiver runs the length of my spine as I walk blindly toward a serial killer.

The world is silent. No traffic noise, no voices chatting, no door opening and closing. The town is asleep.

I lick my dry lips and place my feet carefully on the ground.

It's as dark out as the school was when I was pushed.

Don't think of that.

A sudden clash behind me makes me jump back. I press myself against the wall behind a huge trash can, my pulse racing a million miles an hour.

What the hell was that?

The noise was too loud for rats, but it could be a cat or a fox, maybe.

Or it could be Axel.

Very slowly, I peer around the side. My heart hammers in my chest. I wish Justin was with me this time.

There is nothing visible that could have made a noise.

Oh God. What if Axel is hiding behind a trash can up there just like me?

I look behind me, at the exit, and calculate that I could reach it in about ten seconds. That's if I don't trip over anything lying on the ground.

There's nothing I can see that would make me fall, not if I stick to the very middle of the walkway.

Wincing, I peer around the bin again.

Nothing.

I need to get out of here.

Go!

Spinning around, I sprint to the end of the alleyway and straight into the back of a person.

Oh God, oh God, oh God.

Stepping back, my mouth falls open. "Axel?" I whisper.

He turns and my breath catches.

My heart misses a beat when I come face to face with Tristan.

forty-seven

IZZY

"Izzy," Tristan says.

"Oh my God," I mutter, backing up.

It was Tristan this whole time. How could I not have seen that? He did it. He killed Debbie, Kason, Jessie, and *Miyah*. Then he set his cousin up to take the fall.

"How could you!" I shout.

"What? How could I? Izzy, what the hell are you talking about? Why are you here? It's danger—"

His eyes widen, going bigger than I thought was humanly possible.

Wait. This isn't what I think it is.

"Are you meeting Axel?" he asks.

"What is going on?" I demand. "Why are *you* here?"

"Axel," he says. "He sent a text and said he'd finally meet me. I told him to come home but he refused, said he'd only meet out in the open."

Oh God. "He's planning on killing us both tonight," I mumble, looking behind me and back to Tristan.

He shakes his head. "No, no, he wouldn't do that. I'm family. Maybe he thinks we're the only ones who will help him."

"He killed Miyah!"

"Jesus! Miyah's *dead*?" Tristan looks over his shoulder, down both ends of the road like he's waiting for Axel to stroll up and protest his innocence. "Izzy, I'm so sorry. What happened?"

"Your cousin happened! The cops were at my house. They came to tell us that her body was found in the field by the industrial estate."

He dips his head. "I didn't know Miyah, but Lia always told me all these funny things you'd all done together. Iz, I'm sorry."

"Tristan, we *have* to stop him."

His forehead creases as if he's in physical pain.

"I know you don't want to believe it, but you have to look at the facts. Tristan, please. I need you on my side," I plead.

He looks up, meeting my eyes. "If it's him, I won't let him hurt you. Maybe you should go home and let me deal with this. Where's your car?"

"I walked."

"You walked? Dammit, Izzy, what were you thinking?"

"Well, I was thinking that I wouldn't be in danger until I met up with him. Doesn't matter how I got here."

"Go home, Izzy," Tristan tells me. "I'll deal with this."

"Not a chance. I have to meet Axel."

He shakes his head. "It might not be him."

I cross my arms. "It's pure coincidence that we're both supposed to meet him here tonight?"

"When did you talk to him?"

Sighing at Tristan's bullshit, I grab my phone and show him the message.

"That's not his number. How do you know, for certain, that it's Axel?" he asks.

"You got a text from him?"

He looks around again. "From his number, yeah. Will you wait in my car, at least? I'll come, too. We'll see this son of a bitch together. Safely."

"Tristan, no, I—"

"Izzy, I'm *really* close to calling your parents. You're being reckless. Come on before he gets here."

Tristan grabs my wrist and tugs me toward him.

"No, I have to do this!"

"We're not standing out here."

"He *killed* Miyah."

"Okay. I get it, you want revenge. Can we at least wait in my car until he shows? Let's get the upper hand. Izzy!"

"Fine. Okay, we can wait in your car. I'm going to confront him, though."

"Yeah, I got that. You won't be doing it alone."

"Where's the car?"

He nods across the road. "In the lot. Come on."

Tristan looks around as we cross the road. I feel oddly calm, probably what the shock of Miyah has done to me, but he is seriously on edge.

Can't be easy knowing you're about to find out your cousin is a killer.

I get into his car and look ahead out the windshield. "Why isn't he showing up? I don't like this."

"Let me take you home, then."

I swallow. "I might never get another chance to confront him."

"What difference will it make? Miyah will still be dead. You don't have to be, too."

"Did Axel tell you a time to meet him? He just said where to me, and I came as soon as I could. You don't think he would have left already, do you?"

Tristan looks at me like I've grown another head. "You're not thinking straight. The Izzy I know would never be this reckless. I'm taking you home."

"No! Call him."

Groaning, Tristan pulls his phone from his pocket. "Fine, I . . ."

"What, what is it?"

"I have another text from him, received five minutes ago when I ran into you. I didn't hear it."

"What does it say?"

"Calm down, Iz." His shoulders sink. "He's at a barn our family used to own."

"A barn? Like the one Julia was held in?"

He opens his mouth and closes it like a fish. "No way. No."

"Yes, Tristan. Drive there."

"He can't have done this."

"Tristan!"

"You're impatient and not thinking anything through. Izzy, jeez."

I turn sideways so I can try to get through to him. "All right.

None of this is your fault. You couldn't possibly know what was going on. He moved out, probably so he could have privacy to plot. He killed my cousin, Tristan. Please drive."

With a shaky hand, he turns the key in the ignition and blows a long breath through his teeth.

"When we do this, you stay behind me at all times," he says.

"Sure."

"I mean it, Izzy."

"I know you do."

"The only reason I'm taking you is so you can say what you need, then we're turning him in. You talk and then get back in my car. You got it?"

I buckle up. "I got it. Take me to my cousin's killer."

forty-eight

IZZY

Tristan drives cautiously along the snowy roads. His hands are tight around the steering wheel, eyes tense.

"I'm sorry," I say, finally looking beyond my own hurt and anger to what he must be feeling. Tristan has lost everyone, and now he's lost Axel, too. They may not be close, but he's all Tristan has.

I can tell he's trying to keep it together, knowing what Axel has done.

He shakes his head. "Look what our childhood has done to Axel."

"He didn't have to kill people."

"He's messed up, and that's on my parents. Jeez, he's a kid and he needs help."

I really don't want to talk about what Axel needs right now. He's killed people. One of them was my people. Why should I care what help he needs?

"What's the plan when we get there?" I ask.

"You wait in the car while I talk to him."

"What? No way am I—"

He holds up his hand. "Slow down. I want to defuse the situation first, see if I can calm him down a bit. I hate that I'm taking you there. He's dangerous, Iz. The least I can do is make it as safe as possible for you."

"Do you think that can happen?"

"I have to try." He blows out a breath. "Lia would kill me if she knew what I was doing."

"Good thing she's not here." I look at him. "Tristan, why *are* you doing this?"

"Because if I don't, you'll go alone and get yourself killed."

"What if *you* get killed?"

"Some things are worth dying for. Isn't that why you're steaming ahead with your terrible idea? Avenging your cousin is worth the risk of death."

"I suppose you think that's the definition of stupidity."

"Bravery, actually. No offense, Iz, but I didn't think you had it in you."

"None taken. I didn't before today, either."

Tristan turns and drives along the old road toward the industrial estate. The roads are bad here, but one vehicle has made recent tracks along the freshly fallen snow.

"The barn is to the left up there. I can turn back at any moment. In fact, I would love to."

"No," I reply. "I'm doing this. Please don't get yourself killed, though."

"He's family. He won't kill me," Tristan replies, and I think he half believes it.

There is a dim light on inside the barn ahead. I clench my hands together.

For Miyah.

"When do we call the cops?" he asks.

"Soon. Just let me have this moment." Once he's arrested, there'll be courtrooms and jail cells and I'll never have the chance to get in his face and tell him what I think.

Tristan stops the car and cuts the engine. He taps his phone and looks up. "Nine-one-one is in. I'll hit dial the second you start talking. You only have a few minutes, so make them count."

I nod, wanting more time but knowing that's too foolish. We're literally five minutes from the station, and they'll get here faster than that when we tell them we know who the killer is— and that he's with us.

"Where is he?" I ask. "Do you think he wants us to go inside?"

"Probably. You stay in the car and lock the doors until I tell you to come in. I'll leave the keys in the ignition. If something happens, you get away."

"Tristan, no, I'll go in first."

"Over my dead body."

My jaw just about hits the seat I'm sitting on. "I can't believe you just said that."

"Stay here, Izzy," he replies firmly. "Do *not* move until I come get you."

I watch through narrowed eyes as he gets out of the car and taps the bottom of the window, telling me to lock up. I press the lock button.

Tristan squares his shoulders, puts his phone inside his jacket, and walks to the barn.

I see a sliver of light as he opens and closes the door.

Looking around through the windows, I check to make sure that I'm alone out here.

Snow-topped trees blow in the distance, and the wind softly howls around the car.

The landscape is pure white, and I could be the only person in the world alive.

"Come on, Tristan," I mutter to myself.

My parents will give me a little while, but then they'll check on me and realize that I've gone. I won't have long, because I can't ignore their calls and let them think that I could be dead, too.

Maybe I should go in now and get this over with.

What's taking him so long?

Anxiety curls in my chest, spreading to every cell in my body until I can barely breathe.

Tristan might be hurt.

Go inside, Izzy.

I'm not sure Tristan has anything to defend himself with, since he believes Axel won't hurt him.

I stare at the door, waiting for the first sign that I should go in.

In the silent night, a scream pierces the icy air.

I sit taller, my heart freezing.

"Axel, no!" comes Tristan's muffled cry.

No, he's going to kill him, too.

"We're family!"

I swing the car door open and sprint toward the building. Two steps are as many as I get when I hear glass shatter . . . and the light goes out.

I hesitate for a second, but Tristan brought me here to help me; there's no way I can leave him behind.

Summoning all my new courage, I push the barn door open and step inside. Why couldn't I have come here during the day?

My eyes adjust slightly, but I can still only make out shapes. Like a sofa and what is probably a table.

"Izzy! No!" Tristan shouts. His voice is rough and wavers. "Run!"

I shift to the side and try to see where he is.

I crouch down, shimmying toward what I think is a cabinet against the wall.

The room is silent. I can't even hear breathing.

"Tristan," I hiss, turning my head to the side in the hope that it will sound like I'm in a different location.

"Izzy," he groans. "Go."

"Where is he?" I ask, fully aware that Axel can hear me, too.

I gently pat the floor around me in the hope that something hard will be nearby. Axel will have a weapon, and Tristan came unprepared—now he's injured somewhere.

"I don't . . ." Tristan trails off and takes a sharp breath.

"Tristan!"

Oh God. I wince, trying to think quickly. What should I do? If I take out my phone, Axel will attack. If I tell Tristan to press call, Axel will finish the job, if he hasn't already.

I crawl forward and my hand bumps into something soft yet

solid. My throat tightens as I reach out and pat a skinny, solid chest.

Oh God, it's a person.

"Tristan!" I shout, shaking the body. "Tris . . ."

My face falls when I leave my hand over the rib cage and finally feel how hard and cold it is.

A scream rips from my mouth, and I push myself back, falling on my butt.

I dig the heels of my palms in my eyes. *Okay. It's okay. Breathe.*

That's not Tristan. Who is it?

I push myself to my feet and look around. Behind the sofa, near the wall running parallel to mine, a silhouette.

Axel.

"Y-you don't need to do this," I say. "He's your family."

I can just about make out his arm reaching to the side. He flicks a switch and light floods the room.

"Oh my God," I whisper as fear tightens its grip around my throat.

Tristan.

forty-nine

IZZY

No. No way. It's *him.*

It's been Tristan all this time. How could I not have seen it?

His lips spread in a slow smirk.

I glance down and come face to face with a pale, lifeless Justin.

Pressing my fist to my mouth, I gag and look away.

When did he do this? I spoke to Justin this morning.

If Tristan's the killer, then where's Axel? Has he hurt him, too?

"W-why?" I whisper, looking around the room for any sign that I'm mistaken and Tristan isn't the killer. There is no Axel.

Could he have killed him?

"Why?" he seethes. "Do you have any idea what it's like to live your entire life in fear? The people who are supposed to protect and love you are the ones hurting you. And this town, these people," he spits, baring his teeth. "They do *nothing.* They speak of my dad as if he were a hero."

"Trist—"

"Don't interrupt me!"

I raise my hands, my heart freezing in fear. "Sorry."

"No one cared about what I went through. Every day I would listen to friends talk about holidays and places their parents were taking them. I'd listen, burning in anger, as they bitched about their dad for grounding them or their mom for taking away their phone. As if that's the worst thing a parent could do to a child."

I'm guilty of those things, but that is what every child should have to complain about.

My phone is in my hoodie pocket, but I don't think I can unlock it and call without looking.

"What happened to you?" I ask, trying to show him that I'm on his side.

His eyes tighten. "Hell," he replies. "Lia asked me about my parents once. It was the only time she came to my house. I thought they were out, but they came home early. They shouted that I hadn't taken the trash out. When they realized she was there, they turned nice. Even apologized for yelling, said they'd both had a long day." He laughs but there is no humor to it.

"What did she ask you?"

"She asked if they were as bad as your parents."

"What?"

He rolls his eyes. "It was a dumb, off-the-cuff remark about them being nicer when company is over. As if that's what happens with everyone. I suppose it does, but she had no idea how much mine changed when we were alone. She thought it was a joke, but it wasn't."

My eyes prickle with tears at the thought of anyone suffering in that way. My parents may not be perfect, but they would *never* hurt us.

"Tristan," I whisper, my heart aching in genuine sympathy for a second.

No, I haven't forgotten what he's done, but I can feel sorry for what he endured as a kid.

He looks away but it's not enough of a distraction. Running right now is too risky when he thinks I'm on his side. I push away all thoughts of revenge for Miyah. That'll come.

There are a few things I need to know first.

"Can I ask about Axel?"

I clench my hands, waiting for his reply. It doesn't look good for Axel.

His eyes snap back. "Things got better when he moved in. For three whole days. My parents played happy family until their anger and hate got the better of them. Things just got worse from that point. Axel brought more stress. Two kids."

"What about the fears?" I ask.

He tilts his head. "I was wondering when you would ask that. Punishments. My parents called it discipline, but it was cruel torture. They beat us, used anything they could get their hands on, too. We were locked in cupboards, boxes. We were pushed downstairs, held under water, threatened, and starved."

His words slam into my chest and steal my breath. I feel a tear leak from my eye, and I kind of hate myself for it. He showed no mercy or kindness or empathy for Miyah.

"You don't need to cry for me."

I shake my head. "I'm sorry you went through that." It's on the tip of my tongue to tell him that it doesn't make what he's done now right. He doesn't get a free pass to hurt others because he was failed so horrifically.

"Tristan, what do you need?" I ask him.

What I need to know more than anything is what his endgame is. He has to know that this can't last. He will eventually be caught.

"I need everyone to know how bad it feels."

"We can do that together. I'll help you explain."

"No! No, that's not what I mean, Izzy. People are not going to care if I give them my sob story. *They don't care.*"

"I care," I say. "You were always good to me, even though I was just Lia's dumb little sister."

"You're not dumb."

I smile and almost feel sick doing it. I can't believe I'm smiling at Miyah's killer, but if I don't, he'll kill me, and this will all be for nothing. Having a face-off won't get me the answers I need, and it won't help me find Axel.

"How can I help you?" I ask, going for a different angle.

He blows out a breath. "You can sit down and have coffee with me."

Whatever I was expecting, it wasn't that. My mind spins so fast I think I might faint. What is he doing? I don't want to sit with him.

"Coffee?" With a killer.

"You've been good to me, Iz. You're the only one still here."

He's talking as if I was one of his close friends, and right now,

I'll take that. I can make him think that I'm with him, then it'll only sting more when I betray him shortly.

I don't really want to drink out of anything in this dingy little barn, but a bit of dust is the least of my concerns right now.

"Sit, Izzy. I'll make it."

I do what he tells me, but I make sure that I'm facing him. Justin is lying on the floor behind me. I don't know how long he's been dead, but his body is hard. I try to remember what I learned about rigor mortis, but the stages jumble in my brain. Cold and hard is eight to thirty-six hours dead, I *think*.

It's about ten hours since I spoke to him; he could have died just two hours after our conversation. I swallow a wave of nausea.

Tristan smiles. Does he really think that we're going to sit and have a nice chat? That I'm going to listen to what he has to say and tell him his actions are justified?

Tristan makes the coffee. I watch him add milk and stir, my stomach lurching. It's such a normal thing to do. I'll never understand how someone can kill and then go home to make dinner or do laundry. As if murder is a part of the daily routine.

He puts a coffee down on the table, smiles as if we're best friends, and sits opposite me. He didn't slip anything extra into my drink, so I pull it closer by the handle, trying to ignore the potent smell of death. It's getting worse as the shock wears off.

If I can stay here and keep him talking, it'll buy me some time to figure out how to get the cops here. My parents must have realized I'm gone by now, surely. This barn isn't far from where Julia escaped.

Everyone will assume Axel is responsible.

I wrap my hand around the mug.

"Can I ask about Justin?" Tears sting at the back of my eyes, and I blink them away. He can't know that I'm gutted Justin is dead.

His lip curls. "I was going to frame him, but the prick figured it out. He saw me standing near his car the day I killed Miyah. He must have found your notebook. I was counting on the cops getting there first. His car is full of junk."

I was the one who sent him looking for my notebook. Justin didn't tell Tristan how he really found it. He tried to protect me. I clear my throat.

"That doesn't make any sense. You can't frame him with that. The cops would take fingerprints from it and figure out that it was my notebook, not his."

Tristan's eyes turn hollow, and I know I should have kept that thought to myself.

"That's behind us now."

"What's behind us? *Oh my God.* My notebook is full of reposted fears and victim names. You knew and that's why you took it. You were framing *me,* too."

"I said it's behind us now."

"You planted it two days ago. What changed? Why me?"

The stench of Justin's dead body hits the back of my throat every time I open my mouth to speak.

Tristan rubs his jaw. "I knew it was going to be difficult to pin this on Justin, since he was friends with most of the victims." He rolls his eyes when he says "victims," as if he doesn't think that's the right word to describe them.

"So, you needed me?"

"It was perfect. You didn't like that crowd, and they didn't like you. Except for Justin. I could see you two getting closer, I even heard his friends comment on it in Ruby's, and that made it easier. You and Justin were seeing each other in secret. He knew how much you hated his friends, and he started hating them when he saw how badly they treated you. So, like the devoted boyfriend, he devised this plan with you. The perfect killing couple. Much more believable than one seventeen-year-old kid alone."

"Miyah," I whisper.

He waves his hand. "She had a thing for Justin, and no one comes between you two."

I want to throw my coffee in his face.

"How would you prove that?"

"I wouldn't need to. A few rumors around school and the cops would soon hear how she wanted her cousin's man."

He can't be serious.

I take a breath to ease the stewing anger in my gut.

Stay. Calm.

"What changed your mind? What did Justin do?"

"He came knocking on my door, asking if I'd put your note-book there. The fool was trying to be a hero, turning up alone. Idiot. I stabbed him."

I can tell from Justin's blood-soaked clothes.

"Anyway, I wasn't lying when I said you're the only one who's been kind. I didn't want to frame you, so I wasn't cut up when Justin confronted me. I'd switch to Plan B, anyway. Or edit Plan A."

He shrugs. "We'll pin it all on Justin. Make it look like a fight. We'll need a head injury, something that will explain why we didn't run for hours. Or there's Plan C."

He wants to give us both concussions so when the cops turn up, it looks like we were out of it for hours. I don't think I even want to know Plan C.

I need to get him off this course fast.

"Tristan, where's Axel? He's been missing since the big storm."

"He's away."

"What does that mean?"

Away isn't dead.

"He's in the closet."

There's a door near the old kitchen. Tristan must have locked him in there. How long has he been there for?

My heart thumps harder.

"What happened between you two?"

He turns his nose up as if he detests his cousin. "He was getting closer, figuring things out. He called me from his car, said he was stuck at school. I told him he'd have to wait until the storm passed. He was worried about being a sitting duck, as you'd just accused him. The way he said it, though, it was like he knew it was me and was probing."

"That doesn't mean he was sure. He's your family."

Tristan narrows his eyes. "Everything was worse when he came to live with us. He blamed me as much as my parents. Said I was older. *By a year!* One year older than him and I was supposed to protect him. How?" Tristan bares his teeth, his face reddening.

"You couldn't have done anything," I say to get him to calm down. "I'm sure he knew that. You were a child, Tristan. Both of you were. Will you let him talk with us, too?"

"You want him out here?"

He asks that as if he's now testing me.

"I think he can understand you as well as I can. I mean, he's experienced some of the same things, right?"

He nods.

"Axel isn't your enemy. He can be an ally."

"No," he says, shaking his head, but his eyes say something different. He's wondering how. He wants to know my plan.

So do I.

"Of course, he can."

"How can he possibly help me?"

My jaw drops as I realize where his mind is going. Plan C is Axel.

"No, that's not what I meant. You don't have to do this to him. I'm saying that he can back you up."

"What? With the cops? You think I should hand myself in? I'm getting away with this, Izzy. I told you about my plan with Justin. I'm owed this."

No, you're not.

"Where are you going to go?" I ask. "Aren't you scared that the cops would figure it out?"

"I'm not going anywhere." His smile widens.

I lean back against my chair as if his words have punched me. "You're going to stay in town?"

"This town is home."

"What are you going to do with Axel?"

He chuckles. "He'll be fine. Or maybe I'll kill him, too."

"You can't. He's your cousin."

How is he going to convince the cops that all three of us got concussions in some big fight—with Justin the killer?

The only way this would even remotely work is if there was one survivor, two max. But which two?

"He might be blood, but he's not innocent. How do you think my mom died, Izzy?"

My fingers curl around the mug. "It was an accident. She fell and hit her head."

He smirks. "That's what Axel told the cops."

My jaw falls open. "No! *He* did it?"

"He was here alone with her, collecting the last of his stuff. He said she was drunk and fell down the stairs."

"Was she drunk?"

He scoffs. "She was always drunk."

"Did Axel admit that he did it?"

"Of course not. He wouldn't admit anything, but he did it. They hated each other. He blamed her for everything. Axel's mom was a deadbeat and neglected him, but she never hurt him. My mom only took him in because she thought she would get money for it. Axel knew that."

"She took him in for money?" I whisper.

"Why else? My parents hated kids. But it wasn't nearly as much as she wanted. It bought her all the vodka she could drink, though."

I breathe long and deep through my nose. I need to take

control here. "Tristan, what do you think happened to your mom?"

"I think they argued. She didn't want him to move out until he was eighteen, as she would lose the money. He threatened to go to child services. They fought for days over it. I should have stayed home when he came to collect his crap."

"When did you move out?"

"After her funeral. Dad got worse."

Tristan was already eighteen by then. Why did he stay?

"Don't you want the truth from Axel's mouth?" I ask.

I need to get Axel out of that closet. If he's still alive, it will be two against one. Maybe Axel could distract him while I dial 911.

Tristan frowns. "I've *tried*. The coward denies it every time."

My eyes drift to the door. Is he okay in there? I hope he can hear us.

I need to see him and make sure.

"Stop looking for him," Tristan snaps.

"Look, I can help you get the answers you're looking for. Axel talks to me. After everything you've been through, you at the very least deserve the truth about your mom from him."

"Why do you want to help me? I killed your cousin and your classmates."

A fresh tidal wave of pain sweeps over me. I push it away. "I don't believe people are truly bad. There's always a reason. Always. You've told me yours. What you went through was awful, and punishing you won't do any good."

I hope he buys this, because I've never lied so much in my life.

He nods. "That's what I said to Axel."

Great, now I sound like a killer.

"Drink your coffee. I'll get Axel."

My eyes fly to Tristan.

"If you try to run or get help, I'll kill him."

"I understand," I say.

His threat slides off, because I'm not planning to escape alone.

Axel and I are about to take him down.

fifty

IZZY

I watch, transfixed, as Tristan drags Axel from the closet.

Axel stumbles, his legs sliding under him, like a foal learning to walk for the first time. There's a gash on the side of his head the length of my little finger and blood trailing from his head down to his collarbone.

That looks like a new wound. Did Tristan do that just before I came in? I can't see any other injuries, but he's unsteady on his feet and wincing as he stumbles, so there could be more.

He looks at me, and it takes a second for him to recognize me, but when he does, his mouth drops open. "Izzy," he mutters, slumping down in the seat Tristan shoved him into. "What . . . ?"

"Hi, Axel," I say. I want to ask how he is, but I don't want Tristan to think that I care. He needs to think I'm indifferent to what he's doing.

He nods, blinking hard like he's trying to clear the fog in his mind. He probably has a concussion and needs medical help.

Damn it, I don't think he'll be as much help as I was hoping.

My two-against-one plan begins to fade in my mind, and I scramble to think of another way to escape. Somehow, I have to get Axel out of here, too.

Axel rubs his pale forehead.

"I think he might need water, Tristan," I say.

"No," he growls.

"You want him to talk, right? He won't be able to do much of that without water."

Tristan glares in the direction of his cousin, and for a second I'm sure he's going to pounce and squeeze the life right out of him. His desire for answers trumps all, and he dips his head in a sharp nod. "You can get it, Izzy. I'll keep an eye on him."

Axel glances at me, and I don't know if it's the concussion or if he's confused, but there are a lot of questions in his dazed, icy stare.

He doesn't know why I walked in here rather than being dragged.

How long has he been in here? No one has seen him since he went missing from school during the storm.

It's going to be okay, I silently tell him with my eyes.

I stand and pick up the cleanest cup I can find. On the counter are a few spoons and plastic cups. Nothing that is going to be much help. The drawers are crooked and look like they will scrape if they're opened. Even if there's something in there that I can use as a weapon, I don't think I can do it without attracting attention.

Turning the faucet on, I fill the cup and hand it to Axel.

I watch him drain every last drop in five long gulps.

Tristan watches him like he wants to kill him.

I look between them both, wringing my hands as I wait to see who will talk first.

"Can I take a look at his head and clean him up a bit?" I ask Tristan, deciding that it's probably better if I'm the one who speaks. "It might help clear his mind."

I don't know why it would help, but I can't sit here with him all bloody and dazed. If there's a chance I can patch him up enough to help stop Tristan, I'm going to take it.

"I'll let you if he answers my first question honestly."

"He will. Axel?"

Axel nods, his jaw tense, but there's a fire in his eyes that makes me think he wants to take his cousin down. I can use that, because I don't think I'm strong enough on my own.

We can do this.

"Was my mom's death an accident?" Tristan asks.

I hold my breath for Axel's reply.

He doesn't speak. Instead, he slowly shakes his head and confirms Tristan's horrible theory that Axel was responsible for her death.

My breath catches in my throat, and for a second, I'm absolutely stunned.

"Okay," I say, standing to take Tristan's focus. "You knew it wasn't an accident, and you were right. Next, we need to get him cleaned up and ready to talk properly. You're owed an explanation about your mom."

From somewhere deep inside, I have found an assertive

version of Izzy. I didn't know I had such a trait, and there's no time to think about it and possibly freak myself out.

Tristan nods at me, openmouthed. If I thought his shock would last longer than a few seconds, I would make my move now. With Axel still kind of out of it, it's too risky.

He does seem to buy that I'm on his side, though, and that I can use. I'm going to get Axel as strong as I can, and then I'm going to wrap something hard around Tristan's head.

Axel sits up taller. His jaw squares with determination. "Your parents were *trash*."

Tristan sneers. "You're not going to piss me off that way, jack-ass. I hated them, too."

"You're even worse. You think what you're doing is justified?" Axel says. *That's it, Axel, get his attention.*

"Like you're an angel? Murder runs in the family, bro." Tristan laughs but his eyes are firing daggers at his cousin.

Tristan might not care about his parents, but he does care about what he's doing. He will defend himself and what he's done until his last breath.

Axel's chest expands like he's trying to make himself appear bigger, as if he's about to start a fight. "You belong behind bars. I can't believe you think you're going to get away with this. You're pathetic. Weak."

Shoving his chair out, Tristan stands. It's at that exact moment that I react, too.

I launch to my feet with my mug in my hand and slam it as hard as I can into Tristan's skull.

He cries out, stumbling backward and grabbing his head.

Gasping at what I've done, I step back.

Axel pushes himself to his feet as Tristan hits the floor hard. His eyes seem to lose focus.

Move, Izzy!

I spin on my heels and reach out for Axel. "Come on!"

Axel leans heavily against me as we run out of the barn and into the cold.

Snow angrily whirls around us as if nature is mad with what's been happening here.

"Come on," I say, gritting my teeth as we run toward town and help.

Tristan isn't dead and we have no idea how injured he is. He could be anywhere. He could come to and grab us at any moment.

Axel stops and slumps against the wall of a warehouse.

"We're not even halfway yet. We can't stop," I say, urging him forward.

"Go ahead."

"No way. I'm not leaving you here. He won't hesitate to kill you this time. You know that."

I tug on his arm.

"I'll hide."

"Axel, *please.*"

"I'm holding you back. He won't think I've stopped."

"Not even when two sets of footprints turn into one?"

It's bad enough that we're leaving a trail until we get to the road.

He groans, knowing I'm right, and pushes himself off the wall. "I'll go as fast as I can. When we reach the road, you run ahead."

"We'll find you somewhere to hide, then I'll go ahead. I'm not leaving you until you're safe."

He tilts his head like he's unsure why anyone would do that for him. It makes me like him a whole lot more.

Those terms are nonnegotiable. I'm not leaving him vulnerable, because Tristan knows we've betrayed him and there will be nothing I can say or do to get him on my side now.

We run again, slower this time, because Axel is in desperate need of medical attention.

I hold as much of him as I'm able to as we rush through the blanket of snow.

"Izzy!" Tristan's booming voice sends a shiver down my spine.

Axel looks at me. He grits his teeth. "Faster."

We pass the final warehouse, and we're out of the industrial zone.

"Stick to the hedges," I whisper as we crouch down behind one. "I can't see him." We're almost to the port, I can see the railing along the sidewalk that leads to the docks.

"It's okay, we're almost in town," I say, holding half his weight.

"You should go without me."

"Not happening. Talk to me, how long were you in that room?"

He hisses through his teeth as he limps. "Since the blizzard. He called when I was in my car in the lot. I couldn't get the engine started, and Tristan said he was coming past and would give me a ride."

"What happened then?"

"Nothing at first. Then I noticed a picture of you stuffed behind a backpack on his floor."

"Me?"

He grunts as he nods. "He got *real* defensive when I asked why he had it. I didn't think you were that close. I reached down to grab it, and that's when I saw something else. It was a list of fears with names beside. A line was through Debbie, Kason, and Jessie. Julia's was almost scribbled out so hard it ripped the paper, and I could barely see what it said."

"Oh my God. Who else is on the list?"

"I didn't get a good look before I realized it was him and he whacked me. Your name was circled. No fear, though. He definitely wants something from you, but I don't think it's to kill you."

I shudder at his words.

Maybe it wasn't his plan to kill me, but I doubt he would let me live now.

We follow the railing alongside the water because visibility is low. That's the one thing we have in our favor. Tristan can see our footprints, but he won't know how far away we are. Hopefully the flurry of snow falling heavily will hide our path.

"I can see the square," I say, moving us forward as fast as I can. Whatever Tristan had planned for me, I do not ever want to find out.

Axel leans on me harder. I think his ankle might be busted.

"Iz, what was that?" he asks, pulling us both to a stop.

"We have to keep—"

Axel spins around and shoves me back behind him.

Tristan is there. He grins, his lips stretching in a grim, thin line.

"Don't do this," Axel says.

Tristan doesn't respond. He bends his legs and leaps forward.

fifty-one

IZZY

"No!" I scream as Tristan punches Axel so hard he falls with a loud thud into the snow.

Tristan turns to me, narrowing his eyes.

I take a step back and raise my palms. "Please don't do this. We need to call someone or he's going to die."

"Don't worry, he never dies. Just like me. If there's one thing my parents did for us, it was make us invincible. We can't be touched." He looks down as Axel's eyes flutter. "Keeps getting in the way, though, doesn't he?"

"Tristan, we can fix this. What happened to you, it changed who you are." Wind howls around us. It's freezing here on the roadway, a thin metal railing between us and the frigid cold water below.

"It's just you and me now," he says, ignoring everything I just said.

"You can't do this," I say.

"I already have, Izzy. Now all I need to do is get away with it."

"It's not right. I'm sorry your parents were awful, but you've killed people."

Behind Tristan, Axel stands up, holding his head.

We all stop as headlights pierce the falling snow.

A slow smile tugs at Tristan's lips.

I strain my eyes and gasp when the driver comes into view.

"Syd, no!" I shout as she opens her door. Why is she here? "Get back in! Go!"

"Izzy, oh my God! What the hell is going on? What was that text—" She stops talking as she sees an injured Axel holding his bleeding head. "Izzy . . . What's going on?"

"We're all getting to know each other a bit more," Tristan says, then adds for my benefit, "Thanks for getting here so quickly."

Tristan texted Syd.

"What's going on?" she repeats, her eyes flitting between the three of us.

No, no. She can't be here. I have to get her away from him. He will do anything to stop her from getting help.

"Nothing. Go back home. We're just . . . talking about me and Axel being . . . together now."

"He killed Miyah!"

I shake my head. "No, he didn't. That was all a misunderstanding. Get back in your car and go home."

"Izzy," Tristan says, his lips now curling in amusement.

"What the hell is going on?" Syd shouts. "The truth!"

Panic swirls in my stomach. "Let her go," I say. "You don't need her. It's me and Axel you want."

He points at me. "Don't tell me what I want."

Syd steps closer, her eyes widening. "You," she says. "Tristan, *you're the killer.*"

He raises his palms high. The action lifts his shirt and reveals a gun that's tucked into his jeans. "Guilty."

"*Why?*" she breathes.

Axel grimaces and bends over. Tristan is distracted with Syd, so I go to Axel and put my arm around him to steady him.

"*Why?*" Tristan spits. "No one ever looks beyond their own perfect life. Things weren't perfect for everyone, Sydney. You have no idea what my life was like. I had to make them pay. I *had* to."

Syd is stunned. "Kason, Debbie, Jessie, and Miyah. What did they do to you?"

"Nothing. God, this isn't about them. It's all of you. Everyone in this dead-end town who turns a blind eye and pretends. You're all the same. You pretend to care, but if it's even slightly uncomfortable, you don't want to know."

Axel looks at me, trying not to lean on me as heavily as I can tell he wants.

"We need to get help," he says, blinking hard.

I reach for my phone but it's gone. It must have slipped out of my pocket. "We're going to have to take him down."

Axel tries to stand independently, but his eyes lose focus and he sways.

Syd, obviously realizing that Axel and I are trying to come up with a plan, keeps Tristan talking. She asks him to explain what he means, what he's been through.

"Get Syd's phone from the car and call 911," I whisper to

Axel. "Leave the call on so everything that happens is documented. Syd and I will grab him."

"Izzy, no offense but . . ."

"We can do it. Two against one. Syd is also freakishly strong, and I've been working out."

I don't tell him that I've only been working out since January first, because that won't fill him with confidence. But I'm not weak, and Tristan might attack my best friend. That alone is enough to make me as strong as Thor.

I shift my weight from foot to foot and take a long breath. Okay, time to fight for our lives.

Leaping forward, I grab Tristan around the chest, keeping his hands tucked in so he can't shoot.

Tristan shouts out and spins around. My legs fly out as I go with him, almost kicking Syd.

"Izzy!" Syd shouts, jumping forward.

Tristan thrashes and throws me off. My back slams against the railing, stealing my breath. I push myself up, dripping as the snow seeps into every inch of my clothing. Tristan bares his teeth like a crazed animal, and I wonder if this version of him is the last thing that Miyah saw.

Gripping the railing to steady myself, I straighten my back and try to ignore the shooting pain burning along my spine.

"Tristan!" I shout as he pulls something from his pocket and launches at Syd.

Her scream cuts through my heart as Tristan plunges a knife into her stomach.

The world stops spinning. "No!"

Axel pulls me toward him. "Run, Izzy! We need to go!"

I reach for her. "Syd! Syd!"

She falls into the snow and clutches the knife wound, her long hair in her face as she looks up. Her body shudders and a gurgling sound bubbles from her mouth.

"Syd! No!"

"Get into the car, Izzy!" Axel bellows. "Now!"

I struggle in his grip as Tristan moves over Syd. He drops to his knees beside her head. "Big mistake to come, but props for rushing to your bestie's rescue."

"Syd!" I scream.

Tristan reaches over, placing his hand on top of the knife in her stomach as Axel finds unbelievable strength from somewhere to move me closer to Syd's car.

I see a flash of black as Syd reaches into Tristan's pocket; then she holds something against his head. A gun. Tristan's eyes go wide. He pushes down at the same time I hear a deafening *bang*.

Syd's arm drops to the side, and her eyes go still.

"Get in!" Axel shouts as Tristan groans on the ground, holding the side of his neck.

I scream and scream until I hear ringing in my ears.

"He's not dead!" I shout, my eyes fixed on Syd.

She's gone. He's taken her, too. My cousin and my best friend.

Axel shoves me into the passenger seat and slams the door.

I gasp for a breath.

Wincing, Axel puts his foot down and we peel down the road. I turn and stare out the back window at my beautiful Syd bleeding out and Tristan rolling onto his back.

"Axel . . ."

"I'm getting us to the station. It's going to be okay."

"No, it won't," I reply, sinking down into the seat. "I want Syd. I want her back."

I turn around and pull my feet up on the seat and hug my knees. We pass the big town sign that says THANK YOU FOR VISIT-ING ROCK BAY—WE HOPE YOU ENJOYED YOUR STAY.

"A-Axel? You missed the turn."

I glance sideways as his smirk grows.

How is he able to drive with his bad foot?

"Axel? Where are we going?"

I grab the door handle at the same time he presses the lock button.

Fear ripples down my spine.

"Axel?" I croak.

"It's like Tristan said, Izzy. Murder really does run in the family."

ACKNOWLEDGMENTS

It takes a whole team to publish a book, and my team starts with my husband and sons. Thank you for always being there.

Ariella and Molly, you are both a dream to work with. I don't know what I'd do without you. Thank you, thank you, thank you!

To my wonderful team at Random House, who have worked hard on editing, cover design, marketing, etc., without you this book wouldn't be here, and I can't thank you enough. Wendy, Ali, Kathy, Alison, Candice, Colleen, and anyone else who's touched this book, you are my rock stars!

I want to say a special thank-you to booksellers, bloggers, vloggers, "booktokers," and all of you who spend so much time promoting, recommending, and reviewing my books. I appreciate it so much.

And to you, the reader, thank you for supporting my writing. I'm sure we'll talk about the endings soon . . . haha!

Don't miss another
heart-stopping read from

THE QUEEN OF THRILLERS!

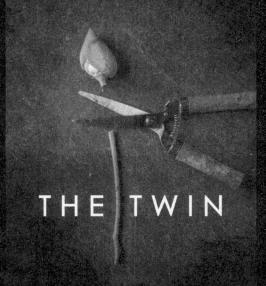

Copyright © 2020 by Natasha Preston. Cover art copyright © 2020 by Marie Carr/
Arcangel. Published by Delacorte Press, an imprint of Random House Children's Books,
a division of Penguin Random House LLC, New York.

1

I dig the tips of my yellow-painted fingernails into the firm leather seat as Dad drives us home on the verge of breaking the speed limit. He's anxious to get back, but I would rather he slowed down. My stomach dips, and I hold my breath, squeezing my eyes closed as he takes a sharp corner.

With my muscles locked into place, I raise my eyes to the rearview mirror. Thankfully, Dad's eyes are fixed on the road, but there's a tightness to them that's unsettling. He's a good driver, and I trust him with my life, but I'm not a fan of this speed.

The car, a black Mercedes, is immaculate and still smells brand-new a year on, so I'm surprised that he's driving so fast on dusty country roads.

Everything is going to be different now, and he seems to be in a hurry to start our new life.

It's not right. We need to slow down, savor the ease of what our lives used to be, because the new one waiting for us in just five minutes, I don't want. Things weren't perfect before, but I want my old life back.

The one where Mom was still alive.

It's spring, her favorite season. Flowers have begun to brighten our town, turning the landscape from a dull green to a rainbow of color. It's my favorite time of year, too, when the sun shows itself and the temperature warms enough so you don't need a coat.

I'm always happier in spring. But right now, it might as well be winter again. I don't feel my mood lifting, and I definitely don't care that I'm not wearing a stupid coat.

My twin sister, Iris, is in the front passenger seat. She's staring out the window, occasionally starting a short conversation. It's more than I've done. There's been nothing but silence from me. It's not because I don't care; it's because I don't know what to say. There are no words for what has happened.

Everything I think of seems dumb and insignificant. Nothing is big enough to fill the enormous void left by our mom.

The warm spring sun shines into the car, but it's not strong enough to hurt my eyes. I don't want to close them again anyway. Every time I do, I see her pale face. So pale she didn't look real. Her once rosy cheeks gone forever. It was like staring at a life-size porcelain doll.

I wish I hadn't gone to the funeral home to see her. My last image of her will be her lifeless body.

When I go back to school, I'll be fine. I'll swim and study until it doesn't hurt anymore.

Or I'll want that to work, but I know it's going to take more than a couple of distractions to make the pain disappear.

We turn down our road and my toes curl in my tennis shoes.

I swallow a lump that leaves my throat bone-dry.

Dad slows, pulling into our drive and parking out front. Our house feels like it's in the middle of nowhere, but there are about ten houses nearby and it's a five-minute drive into town. I love the quiet and the peace of my hometown, but I feel like it's going to drive me crazy. Right now I need loud and fast-paced. I need distractions and lots of them.

Iris gets out of the car first, her butt-length, silky blond hair blowing in the warm breeze. She's home with me and Dad forever now.

Our mom died after falling off a bridge while out running two weeks ago. She was by a farm and the land was uneven and hilly. It had been raining and there was mud on the ground. The rail on the steep side of the short bridge was low, there more for guidance than safety, and she slipped off. The bridge wasn't very high, apparently, but she hit her head and died instantly. That's what the police told us.

Mom ran to keep fit and healthy so she could be around for me and Iris longer, but it ended up killing her.

Her death is still impossible to process. I haven't lived with my mom or Iris for six years, since she and Dad divorced, but her permanent absence weighs heavy in my stomach like lead.

When I was ten and our parents sat me and Iris down to explain they were separating, I had been relieved. It had been coming for a long time, and I was sick of hearing arguments while I pretended to sleep upstairs. The atmosphere was cold at best, our parents barely speaking but smiling as if I couldn't see through the crap mask.

Iris and I have never had a conversation about it, but the separation was a surprise to her. She shouted and then she cried while I sat still, silently planning how I would tell them I wanted to live with Dad. It wasn't an easy choice for anyone, but we had to make one. Dad and I had always been close; we share a lot in common, from movies and music to hobbies and food. He's the one to give us clear guidelines, without which I would crumble. Mom was laid back, sometimes too much, and I would never get anything done.

Besides, Mom always wanted to live in the city, and I never liked how densely it's populated.

Mom and Iris moved out; then they moved away to the city. I have spent school holidays flitting between houses, sometimes missing out on time with my twin thanks to conflicting schedules. She would be with Dad while I was with Mom.

None of our family members, friends, or even neighbors could understand it. You don't separate twins. I get it—we're supposed to be able to communicate without speaking and literally feel each other's pain. But Iris and I have never been like that. We're too different.

We're not close, so although she's my sister, it feels more like a distant cousin is moving in.

She still has her bedroom here, which she and Dad redecorated last year when she visited for the summer. But she's brought a *lot* of stuff with her from Mom's. The trunk is full of her things.

I watch her walk to the front door as Dad cuts the engine. She has a key to the house, of course, so she lets herself in.

Dad scratches the dark stubble on his chin. He usually shaves every morning. "Are you okay, Ivy? You've barely said a word the entire time we've been on the road."

"I'm fine," I reply, my voice low and gravelly.

Fine, the modern *I'm not okay* definition of the word, is what I mean here. Everything has changed in the blink of an eye. Two weeks is all it has taken to turn my world upside down. And what about Iris? She was closer to Mom than anyone. What right do I have to fall apart when she has lost even more than me?

"You can talk about it. Whenever you want."

"I know, Dad. Thanks."

His eyes slide to the house. "Let's go inside."

I take a long breath and stare at the front door.

I don't want to go inside. When I go back in there, our new normal starts. I'm not ready to let go of the old just yet. Until I walk through that door, my twin isn't living with us again because our mom has died.

That's all total rubbish, obviously. Not walking through that door changes nothing, but I can pretend. I need longer.

"Ivy?" Dad prompts, watching me in the mirror with caution in his blue eyes, almost afraid to ask me if everything is okay again in case I crumble.

"Can I go to Ty's first? I won't be long."

His brow creases. "We *just* got home. . . ."

"I'll be back soon. I need a little time. It will give you an opportunity to check in with Iris too. She's going to need you a lot, sometimes without me."

He opens his door. "One hour."

I get out, my heart lighter knowing I have an extra sixty minutes, which I can stretch to seventy before he'll call. "Thanks, Dad."

Shutting the car door, I look back at the house.

What?

The hairs on my arms rise. Iris is watching me from the second-floor window.

But she's not in her bedroom.

She's in mine.

2

Tyler lives down the road, so I get there in under a minute and knock on the door.

He opens up and his leaf-green eyes widen. "Ivy." Reaching out, he tugs me into the tightest hug. His arms wrap around my back, and I sink into him. "Hey," he whispers. "You okay?"

"Not really," I mutter against his Ramones T-shirt.

"Come on." His arms loosen but he doesn't let go completely, his fingers sliding between mine as he leads me inside. "When did you get home?"

"A couple of minutes ago. I haven't been in the house yet."

He eyes me curiously as we walk up to his bedroom, his head turning back every second step. Even though his parents are at work, he leaves the bedroom door open. Rule one. If we break it, we'll never be allowed to spend time together without a chaperone.

Neither of us will break it.

I let go of his hand and collapse onto his bed. His pillow is so soft, and it smells like him. It's comforting and everything I need right now.

The bed dips beside me as Ty sits down. Running his hand through his surfer style chestnut hair, he asks, "Do you want to talk?"

I press against the ache in my chest. "I don't know what to say."

"I'm not your dad or sister, Ivy. I'm not looking for comforting words. You don't need to pretend you're okay for me. Tell me how you feel."

I roll from my side to my back so I can see him. "I feel lost, and I feel stupid for being such a wreck."

"Babe, your mom died. Why do you feel stupid?"

Shrugging, I shake my head and swallow so I don't cry. "I don't know. I'm supposed to be more together. Don't I have a reputation for having a cold heart?"

"No, that means you don't cry when whatever boy band breaks up, not that you're made of stone and don't cry for your mom."

I love that he doesn't know the names of any relevant boy bands.

Iris has always been the emotional one. I'm the logical one. Unless something *really* affects my life, I'm not going to cry over it. What I rock at doing, though, is stressing and overthinking.

"Iris hasn't cried once that I know of," I tell him. "And all

I've done is cry. It's like we've reversed roles." Dad and I arrived at their house eleven days ago, the day Mom died. Iris was like a robot. She got up, showered, dressed, and ate. She tidied and watched TV. Iris continued her routine as usual, but it was all in silence as if Dad and I weren't there. She only started talking properly again this morning.

"Everyone handles grief differently."

I look up at his ceiling. Everyone deals with all sorts of things differently; I just didn't realize that Iris and I would walk through this totally out of character. We may look the same, besides her hair being about five inches longer, but we're nothing alike. Now we're swapping parts of our personality?

Sighing, I stare straight into his eyes and whisper, "I don't know how to help her. I barely know her anymore."

"You can't fix it. You only have to be there for her. There's nothing anyone can do to accelerate the grief process; you have to let it happen."

I don't like that at all. I like my control. If there's a problem, I find a solution. I don't handle it well when there's nothing I can do.

He chuckles. "You'll learn how to do that, I promise."

Sighing, I blink rapidly as tears sting the backs of my eyes. "My mom is gone."

"I know, and I'm so sorry."

Get it together.

"Mom asked me to visit for the weekend last month," I tell him.

"Ivy, don't do this."

"I told her I couldn't because I was spending the weekend at the pool to prepare for a swim meet I missed because she died."

"Ivy," he groans. "You had stuff to do, and it's not like that's never happened before."

I sigh into the sinking feeling in my gut. "Logically, I understand that."

"There's no way you could have known what would happen, babe."

I'm not all that good at forgiving myself. Everyone else, sure, but not myself.

Ty shakes his head. "You can't live up to the standards you hold yourself to. No one's perfect."

All right, I'll give him that. But I constantly strive for perfect. The perfect grades, fastest swimmer, solid circle of friends, real relationships. I'm setting myself up to fail, I get that, and I would stop if I could.

"It feels like Iris is only back to visit. We haven't lived together in *six years*."

His fingertips brush my blond hair. "You'll all adjust, I promise."

We will but we shouldn't have to. Mom was too young to die. Iris and I are too young to be without her. "I want things to go back to the way they were."

"You don't want Iris there?" he asks softly.

"No, that's not it. Of course I want her with us. I wish she didn't have to be, you know? So much has changed, and I'm not ready for any of it. Mom is supposed to be here. Who is going to take me prom dress shopping? She was going to scream when I graduate and totally embarrass me. Who will cry first when I try on wedding dresses or when I have a baby? There is so much that she's going to miss. I don't know how to do it all without her."

I have Dad, but all those things won't be the same without Mom.

"Ivy," he says, brushing his fingers across my face and down my cheek. "She will be there for all of that and more."

Yeah, only she won't. Not in the way I need.

"Iris was in my room," I say, changing the subject before I lose the control I've only just regained after yesterday.

"Okay . . ."

"She was watching me from my room when I left to come here."

"Did you tell her you were going out?"

"No."

"Maybe she was curious."

I bite my bottom lip. Maybe, but what was she doing in my room in the first place? Hers is right next to mine, so she could see me outside from her window too.

"Hmm," I reply, not entirely sure where I'm going with this. I've been in her room, so it's not a big deal. "Yeah, maybe. It just seems weird."

Ty lies down beside me. "It's not weird for her to want to be close to you. There's a lot of change for her, and she's the one who's had to move, leaving behind all of her friends."

I wince at his words. "Yeah, I know."

Iris has lost so much, and if being around me and my stuff helps her even a little bit, then it's fine with me. Oh God, and I'm here. She was in my room probably wanting to be close to me, and I left.

I left her!

My heart sinks to my stomach. "I should go."

His hand freezes on my jaw. "Already?"

"I have an hour, but . . ." I've already been a terrible sister, no need to continue that.

He nods. "You need to be home with your dad and Iris."

"Thanks for understanding, Ty."

Well, this was brief, but worth it. We get off the bed and walk downstairs past the line of pictures showing Ty growing up. The last one is of us both, arms around each other smiling at the school Christmas dance.

Ty put things into perspective for me. I've been cooped up in a bubble of me, Dad, Iris, and Mom's side of the family— I haven't gotten enough distance to give myself any clarity.

I follow him out of the house, chewing my lip as I go. I've been so focused on me and how I feel that I haven't really thought about Iris. Maybe we will grow closer, and that can be the one good thing to come out of this tragedy.

"Call me if you need anything," he says, holding on to the edge of the front door.

I lean in and give him a quick kiss. "I will. Thanks." Then I turn and run along the sidewalk all the way back to my house.

My feet hit the asphalt so hard it sends sparks of pain along my shins, but I don't slow down. I pass our neighbors' houses in a blur, their pruned hedges and rosebushes flashing by. Sucking in air that burns, I reach out and almost slam right into the front door. Bowing my head, I grip the door handle, my lungs scream-ing for the oxygen I've deprived them of during my sprint.

"Dad? Iris?" I call as I walk into the house.

"In the kitchen," Dad replies.

I swing left and find Dad sitting alone at the table.

"Where's Iris?" I ask, breathless.

"Upstairs. She didn't want to talk."

Oh. It was selfish of me to run off the second we pulled up. "I'm going to check on her."

Dad nods. "And I'll start dinner. What do you want?"

I shrug. This past eleven days have been nutrient free. We've grabbed whatever food we could manage, usually sandwiches and takeout. I feel hungry, but when food is placed in front of me, I can barely stomach a bite.

"Anything," I reply, heading upstairs.

Iris must feel so lost. I don't know if she's had much contact with her friends, but I do know I haven't seen her on her phone at all. She needs them now, probably more than she needs me and Dad.

I climb the stairs, tying my long wavy hair in a knot on top of my head, and knock on her door. "Iris, it's me. Can I come in?"

"Sure," she replies.

Okay, I was expecting some resistance.

I open the door and offer a small smile as I head into the room. She's sitting on the edge of her bed, doing nothing. Her long hair fans around her body like a cloak.

"Dumb question, but . . . how do you feel?" I ask.

She shrugs one shoulder. "I'm not sure there's a word for it."

Her eyes are sunken, ringed with dark circles that make her look a lot older than she is. I don't think she's sleeping well either.

We have the same shade of dark blond hair and the same pale blue eyes.

"Well, do you need anything?" Besides the obvious.

"I'm good."

Raising my eyebrows, I move deeper into her room. "Are you?"

She meets my gaze. "Are *you*?"

"No, I'm not." I wring my hands. "We can talk . . . if you want?"

We don't talk, not about real, deep stuff, anyway. She has her friends for that, and I have mine. It's actually kind of sad how we've missed out on that close twin bond. It's the only thing I regret about staying with Dad when Iris moved away with Mom.

She tilts her head. "Can we talk?"

"Well, I know that's not usually our thing, but it can be. I mean, I'm willing . . . and we are twins."

"We shared a womb, share a birthday and DNA, but I've never felt like a twin. We never talk."

Okay, ouch. We used to talk when we were little. I remember being five and sneaking into each other's room at night. We didn't share because we were too different—her room candy pink and mine ocean blue. But it didn't matter after dark; we would make a den out of blankets, grab our flashlights, and talk about random fairy-tale things our imaginations would conjure.

Iris was going to marry a British prince and eventually become queen, and I was going to travel the world in an old Mustang like the one our grandad used to own.

Somewhere over time and our parents' separation, our silly dreams died, and we stopped sharing any new ones.

"Do you want to talk, Iris?"

Her haunted eyes look right through me. "I want so much more than that."

STAY UP ALL NIGHT WITH THESE UNPUTDOWNABLE READS!

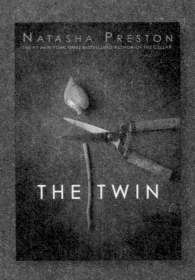

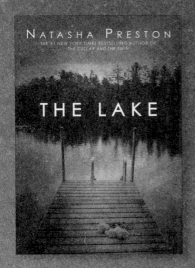